BlooDeath
The Best Vampire Stories
1800⁄1849

[A]n absolute "must-have" for any aficionado of vampire literature, highly recommended. **Midwest Book Review**

Special thanks to Thérèse (Renia) Romer who translated from original French a particularly difficult poem in "The Vampire of the Carpathian Mountains."

EDITED AND INTRODUCED
BY
Andrew Barger

Third Edition
Printed in the United States or the United Kingdom
ISBN: 978-1-933747-35-4

Fonts: Arial, Bookman Old Style and Lucida Blackletter

For Sage

Fiction by Andrew Barger

The Divine Dantes: Squirt Guns in Hades (Book #1)

The Divine Dantes: Paella in Purgatory (Book #2)

The Divine Dantes: Cruising in Paradise (Book #3)

Mailboxes–Mansions–Memphistopheles

Coffee with Poe: A Novel of Edgar Allan Poe's Life

Edited by Andrew Barger

Phantasmal: The Best Ghost Stories 1800-1849

6a66le: The Best Horror Short Stories 1800-1849

Shifters: The Best Werewolf Short Stories 1800-1849

Mesaerion: The Best Science Fiction Stories 1800-1849

Edgar Allan Poe: Annotated Entire Stories and Poems

Leo Tolstoy's 20 Greatest Short Stories Annotated

Orion: An Epic English Poem

Website

AndrewBarger.com

Blog

AndrewBarger.blogspot.com

CONTENTS

With Teeth

As one might expect from the stories in this anthology, teeth were used prominently in the nascent development of the vampirism mythos. And due to the human-monster theme, vampire stories developed more quickly and became more robust from both story and character development than other genres during the period in question, such as werewolf and ghost stories; so much so that they triumphed over most novels in this respect. Yet many claim that short stories are a lesser art form than the novel.

Does time bolster art and transform it into something more robust? Certainly as the aging of a Bordeaux brings out complexities of character unknown in newer wines, so too does the novel offer a bouquet of characters that are impossible to foster in the limited pages of a short story. Characters like certain wines take time to develop, and in this aspect deference must be given to the novel in whatever modern form it may take.

Where critics of short fiction often err, however, is assuming that more pages equate to greater literary art. It's been claimed Earnest Hemmingway said that the phrase "Baby carriage for sale – slightly used" is the best thing he ever wrote.

The literary world is marred with dead trees and terrible, fat novels. Does length equal creativity and originality? Do pages equal greatness? Does size matter in fiction? Edgar Allan Poe, the same author who formed the foundation of the modern short story, claimed that it does not. He preferred a complete tale that could be consumed in one sitting without interruption of the reader's concentration.

And it was the same Edgar Allan Poe who likely did not pen a vampire story from research in the edits of *Edgar Allan Poe Annotated and Illustrated Entire Stories and Poems* and *Coffee with Poe: A Novel of Edgar Allan Poe's Life*. If a reader has to stretch their imagination to determine if a character is a vampire, then it is likely *not* a vampire.

Teeth play a telling role (as does the presence of blood) in many vampire tales. Because of this a number of anthologist have placed Poe's "Ligeia" in their collections in the hopes that if the tale is put in a substantial number of vampire anthologies it will be transmogrified into a vampire story. This is certainly a misinterpretation of a story where the supposed vampire never comes in contact with another vampire. When Ligeia dies and is subsequently brought back to life through Rowena's body, the unnamed protagonist touches her and she moves away, again displaying no lust for blood. Before her death, Rowena is given a cup of reddish liquid that could easily be wine or a potion concocted by the protagonist. There is no evidence that anyone's blood was spilt. The only other hint of vampirism comes when Rowena's lips part on her deathbed to display a line of "pearly teeth."

Yes, it would be nice for this fifty year period, this cradle of all vampire short stories in the English language, to include a vampire tale by Edgar Allan Poe. But the sad answer is that Poe never penned a vampire story. Poe's only reference to vampires were in his poems. "Tamerlane" references a vampire-bat and "To Helen" calls out vampire-winged panels. Articles about the vampire motif in "The Fall of the House of Usher" have been disorganized and unconvincing. Essays about a volitional vampire in "Morella" have . . . well . . . sucked. The ponderous dissertations that seek to attribute the protagonist's lust for teeth to a vampire fixation in "Berenice" have felt chompy. Vampires do not lust for teeth, rather blood. A Poe story listed in the Table of Contents for an anthology boosts sales. Nevertheless, in the case of vampire anthologies, Poe's inclusion is misdirected.

Unlike the pure horror story genre in *6a66le: The Best Horror Short Stories 1800-1849*, where Edgar Allan Poe and Nathaniel Hawthorne penned five of the dozen tales selected, a third of the sci-fi tales in *Mesaerion: The Best Science Fiction Stories 1800-1849*, and the ghost story genre where Poe, Hawthorne and Irving collectively penned forty percent of tales in *Phantasmal: The Best Ghost Stories 1800-1849*, American writers (apart from one) are sadly lacking from authorship of the vampire stories for this period as they are for the werewolf genre. The top purveyors in these genres all hail from Europe apart from a few limited exceptions.

This makes sense given the rise of vampire legends throughout Europe, especially countries touching the Carpathian and Harz Mountains. In the April 1819 issue of the *New Monthly Magazine* "The Vampyre; A Tale." was published as the first vampire short story originating in the English language. The ruminations of a plot for the story were constructed by Lord Byron; yet it was fleshed out and ultimately written by John Polidori, his physician, on a literary dare. Lord Byron, in turn, got the idea from tradition and folktales. The state of the vampire legend before this story was best laid out in an article published in *The Monthly Review* of May 1819:

"The superstition, on which the tale is founded, universally prevailed less than a century ago, throughout Hungary, Moravia, Silesia, and Poland; and the legends to which it gave rise were not only believed, but were made the subject of learned disputations by the divines and physicians of the times. In Dr. Henry More's *Philosophical Works*, and in Calmet's *Dissertation on Apparitions*, may be found many interesting particulars relating to this fancy; and in the latter is an ample account of its origin and progress.

It was reported that men, who had been dead for some time, rose out of their graves and sucked the blood of their neighbours, principally the young and beautiful: that these objects of their attack became pale and livid, and frequently died; while the vampyres themselves, on their graves being opened, were found as fresh as if they were alive, and their veins full of good and florid blood, which also issued from the nose, mouth, and ears, and even through the very pores of the skin. The only mode of arresting the pranks of these tormentors was by driving a stake through the heart of the vampyre; a practice frequently adopted, and during the performance of which, we are told, he uttered a horrid groan. The body was then burned, and the ashes thrown into the grave."

In John Polidori's foreword to "The Vampyre" we learn that much of the vampire legend bubbled up through poetry and European legend as did many of the tales found in *Shifters: The Best Werewolf Short Stories 1800-1849*. Yet not all of them. In 1679 "The Blood-Drinking Corpse" was published from a posthumous collection by Pu Songling (1640-1715) titled *Strange Stories from a Chinese Studio*. He was an educator whose hobby, apparently, was to write down popular Chinese folktales. When he died he had collected nearly 500 of them. One of the first English translations was not until 1913 and it can be presumed that none of the authors in this collection read the original in Chinese.

In response to "The Vampyre" was the quick publication of "The Black Vampyre, a Legend of St. Domingo" by Robert Sands. And from there the vampire mythos fluttered off in the English language, darting from one short story to the next until, in 1847, the novel *Varney the Vampire, or the Feast of Blood* was serialized in a London Penny Dreadful.

From folktales to poetry to short stories to novels, the vampire mythos has developed into the robust, character-driven genre we have today—and it has done so *with teeth*.

These are, perhaps, the best vampire short stories published in the first half of the nineteenth century in the English language. Enjoy!

Andrew Barger
June 29, 2011

JOHN POLIDORI
(1795-1821)

Introduction
The Vampyre; A Tale.

Before you is the oldest known vampire short story originally published in the English language. One would expect it to be subpar and stumbling as it finds its way through the darkness of the upstart genre. That, however, is not the case. It has a storied and contentious past. It emerged from one of the most publicized literary challenges in recorded history and forever holds a controversy that extends far off the page to the personal lives of Lord Byron, John Polidori (a young physician travelling with Lord Byron), Percy Blythe Shelley, Mary Shelley (Mary Wollstonecraft Godwin at the time) and Claire Clairmont, stepsister of Mary who was pregnant with Lord Byron's baby.

In June 1816, while gathered at Villa Diodati, a Lake Geneva mansion Lord Byron was renting, these five literary figures began reading ghost stories. A challenge was laid down to see who could write the best supernatural story of them all. Mary Shelley began writing what would eventually become *Frankenstein; or, The Modern Prometheus.* Percy Shelley wrote five ghost stories. Lord Byron started a *[Fragment of a Vampire Novel].* John Polidori adapted Byron's outline to eventually write "The Vampyre; A Tale."

Three years later, in the April 1, 1819 issue of the *New Monthly Magazine,* "The Vampyre" was published with the Introduction explaining more of the doings at Villa Diodati:

"Mr. Percy Blythe Shelly, a gentleman well known for extravagance of doctrine, and for his daring, in their profession, even to sign himself with the title of Aflwj in the Album at Chamouny, having taken a house below, in which he resided with Miss M. W. Godwin and Miss Clermont, [sic] (the daughters of the celebrated Mr. Godwin) they were frequently visitors at Diodati, and were often seen upon the lake with his Lordship . . . . It appears that one evening Lord B., Mr. P. B. Shelly [sic], the two ladies and the gentleman before alluded to, after having perused a German work, which was entitled *Phantasmagoriana,* began relating ghost stories; when his lordship having recited the beginning of "Christabel," then unpublished, the whole took so strong a hold of Mr. Shelly's [sic] mind, that he suddenly started up and ran out of the room.

"The physician and Lord Byron followed, and discovered him leaning against a mantle-piece, with cold drops of perspiration trickling down his face. After having given him something to refresh him, upon enquiring into the cause of his alarm, they found that his wild imagination having pictured to him the bosom of one of the ladies with eyes (which was reported of a lady in the neighbourhood where he lived) he was obliged to leave the room in order to destroy the impression. It was afterwards proposed, in the course of conversation, that each of the company present should write a tale depending upon some supernatural agency, which was undertaken by Lord B., the physician, and Miss M. W. Godwin."

In its publication on April 1, 1819, the story was attributed to Lord Byron by the editor of the *New Monthly Magazine.* Polidori immediately set the editor straight in the succeeding May 1st issue.

"MR. EDITOR,

As the person referred to in the Letter from Geneva, prefixed to the Tale of the Vampyre, in your last Number, I beg leave to state, that your correspondent has been mistaken in attributing that tale, in *its present form,* to Lord Byron. The fact is, that though *the groundwork* is certainly Lord Byron's, its development is mine, produced at the request of a lady, who denied the possibility of any thing being drawn from the materials which Lord Byron had said he intended to have employed in the formation of his Ghost story.

I am, &c. JOHN W. POLIDORI."

Yet the controversy surrounding "The Vampyre" does not stop at its initial authorship. Before Lord Byron arrived in Geneva with his twenty-year-old physician John Polidori, a controversy was brewing over the first novel by Lady Carolyn Lamb. In 1816, after being jilted by Lord Byron who had been her lover for a number of years while both were married to other people, she published the autobiographical novel *Glenarvon* in three volumes. The novel was a commercial success with the public anxious to discover the unfavorable light in which Lord Byron was portrayed, and his not so private affair with Lady Lamb. That same year, shortly after the challenge at Lake Geneva and while the *Glenarvon* controversy was still brewing, Lord Byron fired Polidori in an abrupt manner that left Polidori without a substantial paying client or a place to live rent-free.

To get back at Lord Byron, Polidori made him the vampire of the horror story he was developing. He even named him Lord Ruthven, using the same name as a character in *Glenarvon*, linking the story and novel forever. Polidori went so far as to include the "common adulteress" Lady Mercer in "The Vampyre" as a portrayal of Lady Carolyn Lamb. The protagonist, Aubrey, represents Polidori who "gradually learnt that Lord Ruthven's affairs were embarrassed." Aubrey "is surprised to receive from him a proposal to join him" on a tour of Europe where Lord Ruthven (and ultimately Lord Byron) is portrayed as a womanizing gambler.

H. P. Lovecraft, in his 1927 *Supernatural Horror in Literature*, observed that in the story "we behold a suave villain of the true Gothic or Byronic type, and encounter some excellent passages of stark fright, including a terrible nocturnal experience in a shunned Grecian wood."

Before you is the first vampire short story originally published in the English language and it forms the cornerstone of modern vampiric literature. It is held in high esteem today, nearly 200 years after its original printing, despite the controversy surrounding its authorship and the antiquated European way of spelling certain words.

The Vampyre
(1819)

THE SUPERSTITION UPON which this tale is founded is very general in the East. Among the Arabians it appears to be common; it did not, however, extend itself to the Greeks until after the establishment of Christianity; and it has only assumed its present form since the division of the Latin and Greek churches; at which time, the idea becoming prevalent, that a Latin body could not corrupt if buried in their territory, it gradually increased, and formed the subject of many wonderful stories, still extant, of the dead rising from their graves, and feeding upon the blood of the young and beautiful. In the West it spread, with some slight variation, all over Hungary, Poland, Austria, and Lorraine, where the belief existed, that vampyres nightly imbibed a certain portion of the blood of their victims, who became emaciated, lost their strength, and speedily died of consumptions; whilst these human blood-suckers fattened — and their veins became distended to such a state of repletion, as to cause the blood to flow from all the passages of their bodies, and even from the very pores of their skins.

In the *London Journal*, of March, 1732, is a curious, and, of course, *credible* account of a particular case of vampyrism, which is stated to have occurred at Madreyga, in Hungary. It appears, that upon an examination of the commander-in-chief and magistrates of the place, they positively and unanimously affirmed, that, about five years before, a certain Heyduke, named Arnold Paul, had been heard to say, that, at Cassovia, on the frontiers of the Turkish Servia, he had been tormented by a vampyre, but had found a way to rid himself of the evil, by eating some of the earth out of the vampyre's grave, and rubbing himself with his blood. This precaution, however, did not prevent him from becoming a vampire (The universal belief is, that a person sucked by a vampire becomes a vampire himself, and sucks in his turn, /-Chief bailiff.) himself; for, about twenty or thirty days after his death and burial, many persons complained of having been tormented by him, and a deposition was made, that four persons had been deprived of life by his attacks. To prevent further mischief, the inhabitants having consulted their Hadagni,[1] took up the body, and found it (as is supposed to be usual in cases of vampyrism) fresh, and entirely free from corruption, and emitting at the mouth, nose, and ears, pure and florid blood. Proof having been thus obtained, they resorted to the accustomed remedy. A stake was driven entirely through the heart and body of Arnold Paul, at which he is reported to have cried out as dreadfully as if he had been alive. This done, they cut off his head, burned his body, and threw the ashes into his grave. The same measures were adopted with the corses of those persons who had previously died from vampyrism, lest they should, in their turn, become agents upon others who survived them.

This monstrous rodomontade[2] is here related, because it seems better adapted to illustrate the subject of the present observations than any other instance which could be adduced. In many parts of Greece it is considered as a sort of punishment after death, for some heinous crime committed whilst in existence, that the deceased is not only doomed to vampyrism, but compelled to confine his infernal visitations solely to those beings he loved most while upon earth—those to whom he was bound by ties of kindred and affection.—A supposition alluded to in the "Giaour."[3]

> But first on earth, as Vampyre sent,
> Thy corse shall from its tomb be rent;
> Then ghastly haunt the native place,
> And suck the blood of all thy race;
> There from thy *daughter, sister, wife,*
> At midnight drain the stream of life;
> *Yet loathe the banquet which perforce*
> Must feed thy livid living corse.
>
> Thy victims, ere they yet expire,
> Shall know the demon for their sire;
> As cursing thee, thou cursing them,
> Thy flowers are withered on the stem.
> But one that for *thy crime* must fall,
> The youngest, best beloved of all,
> Shall bless thee with *A father's* name—
> That word shall wrap thy heart in flames!

---

[1] Chief bailiff
[2] Blustery or exaggerated statements
[3] Poem by Lord George Gordon Byron (1788-1824) first published in 1813

Yet thou must end thy task and mark
Her cheek's last tinge—her eye's last spark,
And the last glassy glance must view
Which freezes o'er its lifeless blue;
Then with unhallowed hand shall tear
The tresses of her yellow hair,
Of which, in life a lock when shorn
Affection's fondest pledge was worn—
But now is borne away by thee
Memorial of thine agony!

Yet with thine own best blood shall drip;
Thy gnashing tooth, and haggard lip;
Then stalking to thy sullen grave,
Go—and with Gouls and Afrits rave,
Till these in horror shrink away
From spectre more accursed than they.

Mr. Southey has also introduced in his wild but beautiful poem of "Thalaba,"[4] the vampyre corse of the Arabian maid Oneiza, who is represented as having returned from the grave for the purpose of tormenting him she best loved whilst in existence. But this cannot be supposed to have resulted from the sinfulness of her life, she being pourtrayed throughout the whole of the tale as a complete type of purity and innocence. The veracious Tournefort[5] gives a long account in his travels of several astonishing cases of vampyrism, to which he pretends to have been an eyewitness; and Calmet,[6] in his great work upon this subject, besides a variety of anecdotes, and traditionary narratives illustrative of its effects, has put forth some learned dissertations, tending to prove it to be a classical, as well as barbarian error.

Many curious and interesting notices on this singularly horrible superstition might be added; though the present may suffice for the limits of a note, necessarily devoted to explanation, and which may now be concluded by merely

---

[4] "Thalaba the Destroyer" is an epic poem published in 1801 by Robert Southey (1774-1843)

[5] Joseph Pitton de Tournefort (1656-1708), French botanist and explorer

[6] Dom Augustin Calmet (1672-1757), Biblical scholar and French Benedictine who published in 1746 a treatise on the supernatural titled: *Dissertations sur les Apparitions des Anges, des Demons et des Esprits, et sur les Revenants et Vampires de Hongrie, de Boheme, de Moravie, et de Silesie*

marking, that though the term Vampyre is the one in most general acceptation, there are several others synonymous with it, made use of in various parts of the world: as Vroucolocha, Vardoulacha, Goul, Broucoloka, &c.

THE VAMPYRE.

IT HAPPENED THAT in the midst of the dissipations attendant upon a London winter, there appeared at the various parties of the leaders of the *ton*[7] a nobleman, more remarkable for his singularities, than his rank. He gazed upon the mirth around him, as if he could not participate therein. Apparently, the light laughter of the fair only attracted his attention, that he might by a look quell it, and throw fear into those breasts where thoughtlessness reigned. Those who felt this sensation of awe, could not explain whence it arose: some attributed it to the dead grey eye,[8] which, fixing upon the object's face, did not seem to penetrate, and at one glance to pierce through to the inward workings of the heart; but fell upon the cheek with a leaden ray that weighed upon the skin it could not pass.

His peculiarities caused him to be invited to every house; all wished to see him, and those who had been accustomed to violent excitement, and now felt the weight of *ennui,*[9] were pleased at having something in their presence capable of engaging their attention. In spite of the deadly hue of his face, which never gained a warmer tint, either from the blush of modesty, or from the strong emotion of passion, though its form and outline were beautiful, many of the female hunters after notoriety attempted to win his attentions, and gain, at least, some marks of what they might term affection: Lady Mercer, who had been the mockery of every monster shewn in drawing-rooms since her marriage, threw herself in his way, and did all but put on the dress of a mountebank, to attract his notice: — though in vain: — when she stood before him, though his eyes were apparently fixed upon her's, still it seemed as if they were unperceived;—even her unappalled impudence was baffled, and she left the field.

But though the common adultress could not influence even the guidance of his eyes, it was not that the female sex was

[7] High society
[8] Lord Byron had striking dark grey eyes
[9] Boredom

indifferent to him: yet such was the apparent caution with which he spoke to the virtuous wife and innocent daughter, that few knew he ever addressed himself to females. He had, however, the reputation of a winning tongue; and whether it was that it even overcame the dread of his singular character, or that they were moved by his apparent hatred of vice, he was as often among those females who form the boast of their sex from their domestic virtues, as among those who sully it by their vices.

About the same time, there came to London a young gentleman of the name of Aubrey: he was an orphan left with an only sister in the possession of great wealth, by parents who died while he was yet in childhood. Left also to himself by guardians, who thought it their duty merely to take care of his fortune, while they relinquished the more important charge of his mind to the care of mercenary subalterns, he cultivated more his imagination than his judgment. He had, hence, that high romantic feeling of honour and candour, which daily ruins so many milliners' apprentices. He believed all to sympathise with virtue, and thought that vice was thrown in by Providence merely for the picturesque effect of the scene, as we see in romances: he thought that the misery of a cottage merely consisted in the vesting of clothes, which were as warm, but which were better adapted to the painter's eye by their irregular folds and various coloured patches.

He thought, in fine, that the dreams of poets were the realities of life. He was handsome, frank, and rich: for these reasons, upon his entering into the gay circles, many mothers surrounded him, striving which should describe with least truth their languishing or romping favourites: the daughters at the same time, by their brightening countenances when he approached, and by their sparkling eyes, when he opened his lips, soon led him into false notions of his talents and his merit. Attached as he was to the romance of his solitary hours, he was startled at finding, that, except in the tallow and wax candles that flickered, not from the presence of a ghost, but from want of snuffing, there was no foundation in real life for any of that congeries of pleasing pictures and descriptions contained in those volumes, from which he had formed his study. Finding, however, some compensation in his gratified vanity, he was about to relinquish his dreams, when the extraordinary being we have above described, crossed him in his career.

He watched him; and the very impossibility of forming an idea of the character of a man entirely absorbed in himself, who gave few other signs of his observation of external objects, than the tacit assent to their existence, implied by the avoidance of their contact: allowing his imagination to picture every thing that flattered its propensity to extravagant ideas, he soon formed this object into the hero of a romance, and determined to observe the offspring of his fancy, rather than the person before him. He became acquainted with him, paid him attentions, and so far advanced upon his notice, that his presence was always recognised. He gradually learnt that Lord Ruthven's[10] affairs were embarrassed, and soon found, from the notes of preparation in Street, that he was about to travel.

Desirous of gaining some information respecting this singular character, who, till now, had only whetted his curiosity, he hinted to his guardians, that it was time for him to perform the tour, which for many generations has been thought necessary to enable the young to take some rapid steps in the career of vice towards putting themselves upon an equality with the aged, and not allowing them to appear as if fallen from the skies, whenever scandalous intrigues are mentioned as the subjects of pleasantry or of praise, according to the degree of skill shewn in carrying them on. They consented: and Aubrey immediately mentioning his intentions to Lord Ruthven, was surprised to receive from him a proposal to join him. Flattered by such a mark of esteem from him, who, apparently, had nothing in common with other men, he gladly accepted it, and in a few days they had passed the circling waters.

Hitherto, Aubrey had had no opportunity of studying Lord Ruthven's character, and now he found, that, though many more of his actions were exposed to his view, the results offered different conclusions from the apparent motives to his conduct. His companion was profuse in his liberality;—the idle, the vagabond, and the beggar, received from his hand more than enough to relieve their immediate wants. But Aubrey could not avoid remarking, that it was not upon the virtuous, reduced to indigence by the misfortunes attendant even upon virtue, that he bestowed his alms;—these were sent from the door with hardly suppressed sneers; but when the profligate came to ask something, not to relieve his wants, but to allow him to wallow in his lust, or to sink him still deeper in his iniquity, he was sent away with rich charity.

---

[10] Lord Byron's mother once leased their family home, called Newstead Abbey, to Edward Yelverton (19th Lord Grey de Ruthven) from 1803-1808

This was, however, attributed by him to the greater importunity of the vicious, which generally prevails over the retiring bashfulness of the virtuous indigent. There was one circumstance about the charity of his Lordship, which was still more impressed upon his mind: all those upon whom it was bestowed, inevitably found that there was a curse upon it, for they were all either led to the scaffold, or sunk to the lowest and the most abject misery.

At Brussels and other towns through which they passed, Aubrey was surprised at the apparent eagerness with which his companion sought for the centres of all fashionable vice; there he entered into all the spirit of the faro table:[11] he betted, and always gambled with success, except where the known sharper was his antagonist, and then he lost even more than he gained; but it was always with the same unchanging face, with which he generally watched the society around: it was not, however, so when he encountered the rash youthful novice, or the luckless father of a numerous family; then his very wish seemed fortune's law—this apparent abstractedness of mind was laid aside, and his eyes sparkled with more fire than that of the cat whilst dallying with the half-dead mouse.

In every town, he left the formerly affluent youth, torn from the circle he adorned, cursing, in the solitude of a dungeon, the fate that had drawn him within the reach of this fiend; whilst many a father sat frantic, amidst the speaking looks of mute hungry children, without a single farthing of his late immense wealth, wherewith to buy even sufficient to satisfy their present craving. Yet he took no money from the gambling table; but immediately lost, to the miner of many, the last gilder he had just snatched from the convulsive grasp of the innocent: this might but be the result of a certain degree of knowledge, which was not, however, capable of combating the cunning of the more experienced.

Aubrey often wished to represent this to his friend, and beg him to resign that charity and pleasure which proved the ruin of all, and did not tend to his own profit;—but he delayed it—for each day he hoped his friend would give him some opportunity of speaking frankly and openly to him; however, this never occurred. Lord Ruthven in his carriage, and amidst the various wild and rich scenes of nature, was always the same: his eye spoke less than his lip; and though Aubrey was near the object of his curiosity, he obtained no greater gratification from it than

---

[11] Faro is a French card game played on an oval table

the constant excitement of vainly wishing to break that mystery, which to his exalted imagination began to assume the appearance of something supernatural.

They soon arrived at Rome, and Aubrey for a time lost sight of his companion; he left him in daily attendance upon the morning circle of an Italian countess, whilst he went in search of the memorials of another almost deserted city. Whilst he was thus engaged, letters arrived from England, which he opened with eager impatience; the first was from his sister, breathing nothing but affection; the others were from his guardians, the latter astonished him; if it had before entered into his imagination that there was an evil power resident in his companion, these seemed to give him most sufficient reason for the belief. His guardians insisted upon his immediately leaving his friend, and urged, that his character was dreadfully vicious, for that the possession of irresistible powers of seduction, rendered his licentious habits more dangerous to society.

It had been discovered, that his contempt for the adulteress had not originated in hatred of her character; but that he had required, to enhance his gratification, that his victim, the partner of his guilt, should be hurled from the pinnacle of unsullied virtue, down to the lowest abyss of infamy and degradation: in fine, that all those females whom he had sought, apparently on account of their virtue, had, since his departure, thrown even the mask aside, and had not scrupled to expose the whole deformity of their vices to the public gaze.

Aubrey determined upon leaving one, whose character had not yet shown a single bright point on which to rest the eye. He resolved to invent some plausible pretext for abandoning him altogether, purposing, in the mean while, to watch him more closely, and to let no slight circumstances pass by unnoticed. He entered into the same circle, and soon perceived, that his Lordship was endeavouring to work upon the inexperience of the daughter of the lady whose house he chiefly frequented.

In Italy, it is seldom that an unmarried female is met with in society; he was therefore obliged to carry on his plans in secret; but Aubrey's eye followed him in all his windings, and soon discovered that an assignation had been appointed, which would most likely end in the ruin of an innocent, though thoughtless girl. Losing no time, he entered the apartment of Lord Ruthven, and abruptly asked him his intentions with respect to the lady, informing him at the same time that he was aware of his being about to meet her that very night.

Lord Ruthven answered, that his intentions were such as he supposed all would have upon such an occasion; and upon being pressed whether he intended to marry her, merely laughed. Aubrey retired; and, immediately writing a note, to say, that from that moment he must decline accompanying his Lordship in the remainder of their proposed tour, he ordered his servant to seek other apartments, and calling upon the mother of the lady, informed her of all he knew, not only with regard to her daughter, but also concerning the character of his Lordship. The assignation was prevented. Lord Ruthven next day merely sent his servant to notify his complete assent to a separation; but did not hint any suspicion of his plans having been foiled by Aubrey's interposition.

Having left Rome, Aubrey directed his steps towards Greece, and crossing the Peninsula, soon found himself at Athens. He then fixed his residence in the house of a Greek; and soon occupied himself in tracing the faded records of ancient glory upon monuments that apparently, ashamed of chronicling the deeds of freemen only before slaves, had hidden themselves beneath the sheltering soil or many coloured lichen.[12]

Under the same roof as himself, existed a being, so beautiful and delicate, that she might have formed the model for a painter, wishing to pourtray oil canvass the promised hope of the faithful in Mahomet's paradise,[13] save that her eyes spoke too much mind for any one to think she could belong to those who had no souls. As she danced upon the plain, or tripped along the mountain's side, one would have thought the gazelle a poor type of her beauties; for who would have exchanged her eye, apparently the eye of animated nature, for that sleepy luxurious look of the animal suited but to the taste of an epicure. The light step of Ianthe[14] often accompanied Aubrey in his search after antiquities, and often would the unconscious girl, engaged in the pursuit of a Kashmere butterfly, show the whole beauty of her form, floating as it were upon the wind, to the eager gaze of him, who forgot the letters he had just

---

[12] Low-growing, common plant

[13] The Koran states that the faithful will be waited on by beautiful maidens in Mohammed's paradise

[14] Means violet flower and is the name to whom Lord Byron dedicated his four part poem "Childe Harolde's Pilgrimage," who was actually Lady Charlotte Harley (1801-1880) and 11 years old at the time the first part was published, while Lord Byron was 24 years old

decyphered upon an almost effaced tablet, in the contemplation of her sylph-like[15] figure.

Often would her tresses falling, as she flitted around, exhibit in the sun's ray such delicately brilliant and swiftly fading hues, as might well excuse the forgetfulness of the antiquary, who let escape from his mind the very object he had before thought of vital importance to the proper interpretation of a passage in Pausanias. But why attempt to describe charms which all feel, but none can appreciate!—It was innocence, youth, and beauty, unaffected by crowded drawing-rooms and stifling balls. Whilst he drew those remains of which he wished to preserve a memorial for his future hours, she would stand by, and watch the magic effects of his pencil, in tracing the scenes of her native place; she would then describe to him the circling dance upon the open plain, would paint to him in all the glowing colours of youthful memory, the marriage pomp she remembered viewing in her infancy; and then, turning to subjects that had evidently made a greater impression upon her mind, would tell him all the supernatural tales of her nurse.

Her earnestness and apparent belief of what she narrated, excited the interest even of Aubrey; and often as she told him the tale of the living vampyre, who had passed years amidst his friends, and dearest ties, forced every year, by feeding upon the life of a lovely female to prolong his existence for the ensuing months, his blood would run cold, whilst he attempted to laugh her out of such idle and horrible fantasies; but Ianthe cited to him the names of old men, who had at last detected one living among themselves, after several of their near relatives and children had been found marked with the stamp of the fiend's appetite; and when she found him so incredulous, she begged of him to believe her, for it had been, remarked, that those who had dared to question their existence, always had some proof given, which obliged them, with grief and heartbreaking, to confess it was true.

She detailed to him the traditional appearance of these monsters, and his horror was increased, by hearing a pretty accurate description of Lord Ruthven; he, however, still persisted in persuading her, that there could be no truth in her fears, though at the same time he wondered at the many coincidences which had all tended to excite a belief in the supernatural power of Lord Ruthven.

---

[15] Slim and graceful, spirit-like

Aubrey began to attach himself more and more to Ianthe; her innocence, so contrasted with all the affected virtues of the women among whom he had sought for his vision of romance, won his heart; and while he ridiculed the idea of a young man of English habits, marrying an uneducated Greek girl, still he found himself more and more attached to the almost fairy form before him. He would tear himself at times from her, and, forming a plan for some antiquarian research, he would depart, determined not to return until his object was attained; but he always found it impossible to fix his attention upon the ruins around him, whilst in his mind he retained an image that seemed alone the rightful possessor of his thoughts. Ianthe was unconscious of his love, and was ever the same frank infantile being he had first known. She always seemed to part from him with reluctance; but it was because she had no longer any one with whom she could visit her favourite haunts, whilst her guardian was occupied in sketching or uncovering some fragment which had yet escaped the destructive hand of time.

She had appealed to her parents on the subject of Vampyres, and they both, with several present, affirmed their existence, pale with horror at the very name. Soon after, Aubrey determined to proceed upon one of his excursions, which was to detain him for a few hours; when they heard the name of the place, they all at once begged of him not to return at night, as he must necessarily pass through a wood, where no Greek would ever remain, after the day had closed, upon any consideration. They described it as the resort of the vampyres in their nocturnal orgies, and denounced the most heavy evils as impending upon him who dared to cross their path. Aubrey made light of their representations, and tried to laugh them out of the idea; but when he saw them shudder at his daring thus to mock a superior, infernal power, the very name of which apparently made their blood freeze, he was silent.

Next morning Aubrey set off upon his excursion unattended; he was surprised to observe the melancholy face of his host, and was concerned to find that his words, mocking the belief of those horrible fiends, had inspired them with such terror. When he was about to depart, Ianthe came to the side of his horse, and earnestly begged of him to return, ere night allowed the power of these beings to be put in action;—he promised. He was, however, so occupied in his research, that he did not perceive that day-light would soon end, and that in the horizon there was one of those specks which, in the warmer climates, so rapidly gather into a tremendous mass, and pour all their rage upon the devoted country. —He at last, however, mounted his horse, determined to make up by speed for his delay: but it was too late. Twilight, in these southern climates, is almost unknown; immediately the sun sets, night begins: and ere he had advanced far, the power of the storm was above—its echoing thunders had scarcely an interval of rest—its thick heavy rain forced its way through the canopying foliage, whilst the blue forked lightning seemed to fall and radiate at his very feet.

Suddenly his horse took fright, and he was carried with dreadful rapidity through the entangled forest. The animal at last, through fatigue, stopped, and he found, by the glare of lightning, that he was in the neighbourhood of a hovel that hardly lifted itself up from the masses of dead leaves and brushwood which surrounded it. Dismounting, he approached, hoping to find some one to guide him to the town, or at least trusting to obtain shelter from the pelting of the storm. As he approached, the thunders, for a moment silent, allowed him to hear the dreadful shrieks of a woman mingling with the stifled, exultant mockery of a laugh, continued in one almost unbroken sound;—he was startled: but, roused by the thunder which again rolled over his head, he, with a sudden effort, forced open the door of the hut. He found himself in utter darkness: the sound, however, guided him.

He was apparently unperceived; for, though he called, still the sounds continued, and no notice was taken of him. He found himself in contact with some one, whom he immediately seized; when a voice cried, "Again baffled!" to which a loud laugh succeeded; and he felt himself grappled by one whose strength seemed superhuman: determined to sell his life as dearly as he could, he struggled; but it was in vain: he was lifted from his feet and hurled with enormous force against the ground;—his enemy threw himself upon him, and kneeling upon his breast, had placed his hands upon his throat — when the glare of many torches penetrating through the hole that gave light in the day, disturbed him;—he instantly rose, and, leaving his prey, rushed through the door, and in a moment the crashing of the branches, as he broke through the wood, was no longer heard. The storm was now still; and Aubrey, incapable of moving, was soon heard by those without.

They entered; the light of their torches fell upon the mud walls, and the thatch loaded on every individual straw with heavy flakes of soot. At the desire of Aubrey they searched for her who had attracted him by her cries; he was again left in darkness; but what was his horror, when the light of the torches once more burst upon him, to perceive the airy form of his fair conductress brought in a lifeless corse.

He shut his eyes, hoping that it was but a vision arising from his disturbed imagination; but he again saw the same form, when he unclosed them, stretched by his side. There was no colour upon her cheek, not even upon her lip; yet there was a stillness about her face that seemed almost as attaching as the life that once dwelt there:— upon her neck and breast was blood, and upon her throat were the marks of teeth having opened the vein:—to this the men pointed, crying, simultaneously struck with horror, "A Vampyre! A Vampyre!"

A litter was quickly formed, and Aubrey was laid by the side of her who had lately been to him the object of so many bright and fairy visions, now fallen with the flower of life that had died within her. He knew not what his thoughts were—his mind was benumbed and seemed to shun reflection, and take refuge in vacancy—he held almost unconsciously in his hand a naked dagger of a particular construction, which had been found in the hut. They were soon met by different parties who had been engaged in the search of her whom a mother had missed. Their lamentable cries, as they approached the city, forewarned the parents of some dreadful catastrophe.—To describe their grief would be impossible; but when they ascertained the cause of their child's death, they looked at Aubrey, and pointed to the corse. They were inconsolable; both died broken-hearted.

Aubrey being put to bed was seized with a most violent fever, and was often delirious; in these intervals he would call upon Lord Ruthven and upon Ianthe—by some unaccountable combination he seemed to beg of his former companion to spare the being he loved. At other times he would imprecate maledictions upon his head, and curse him as her destroyer. Lord Ruthven chanced at this time to arrive at Athens, and, from whatever motive, upon hearing of the state of Aubrey, immediately placed himself in the same house, and became his constant attendant. When the latter recovered from his delirium, he was horrified and startled at the sight of him whose image he had now combined with that of a Vampyre; but Lord Ruthven, by his kind words, implying almost repentance for the fault that had caused their separation, and still more by the attention, anxiety, and care which he showed, soon reconciled him to his presence.

His lordship seemed quite changed; he no longer appeared that apathetic being who had so astonished Aubrey; but as soon as his convalescence began to be rapid, he again gradually

retired into the same state of mind, and Aubrey perceived no
difference from the former man, except that at times he was
surprised to meet his gaze fixed intently upon him, with a smile
of malicious exultation playing upon his lips: he knew not why,
but this smile haunted him. During the last stage of the
invalid's recovery, Lord Ruthven was apparently engaged in
watching the tideless waves raised by the cooling breeze, or in
marking the progress of those orbs, circling, like our world, the
moveless sun;—indeed, he appeared to wish to avoid the eyes of
all.

Aubrey's mind, by this shock, was much weakened, and that
elasticity of spirit which had once so distinguished him now
seemed to have fled for ever. He was now as much a lover of
solitude and silence as Lord Ruthven; but much as he wished
for solitude, his mind could not find it in the neighbourhood of
Athens; if he sought it amidst the ruins he had formerly
frequented, Ianthe's form stood by his side—if he sought it in
the woods, her light step would appear wandering amidst the
underwood, in quest of the modest violet; then suddenly turning
round, would show, to his wild imagination, her pale face and
wounded throat, with a meek smile upon her lips.

He determined to fly scenes, every feature of which created
such bitter associations in his mind. He proposed to Lord
Ruthven, to whom he held himself bound by the tender care he
had taken of him during his illness, that they should visit those
parts of Greece neither had yet seen. They travelled in every
direction, and sought every spot to which a recollection could be
attached: but though they thus hastened from place to place,
yet they seemed not to heed what they gazed upon. They heard
much of robbers, but they gradually began to slight these
reports, which they imagined were only the invention of
individuals, whose interest it was to excite the generosity of
those whom they defended from pretended dangers. In
consequence of thus neglecting the advice of the inhabitants, on
one occasion they travelled with only a few guards, more to
serve as guides than as a defence.

Upon entering, however, a narrow defile, at the bottom of
which was the bed of a torrent, with large; masses of rock
brought down from the neighbouring precipices, they had
reason to repent their negligence; for scarcely were the whole of
the party engaged in the narrow pass, when they were startled
by the whistling of bullets close to their heads, and by the
echoed report of several guns.

In an instant their guards had left them, and, placing themselves behind rocks, had begun to fire in the direction whence the report came. Lord Ruthven and Aubrey, imitating their example, retired for a moment behind the sheltering turn of the defile: but ashamed of being thus detained by a foe, who with insulting shouts bade them advance, and being exposed to unresisting slaughter, if any of the robbers should climb above and take them in the rear, they determined at once to rush forward in search of the enemy. Hardly had they lost the shelter of the rock, when Lord Ruthven received a shot in the shoulder, which brought him to the ground. Aubrey hastened to his assistance; and, no longer heeding the contest or his own peril, was soon surprised by seeing the robbers' faces around him—his guards having, upon Lord Ruthven's being wounded, immediately thrown up their arms and surrendered.

By promises of great reward, Aubrey soon induced them to convey his wounded friend to a neighbouring cabin; and having agreed upon a ransom, he was no more disturbed by their presence—they being content merely to guard the entrance till their comrade should return with the promised sum, for which he had an order. Lord Ruthven's strength rapidly decreased; in two days mortification ensued, and death seemed advancing with hasty steps.

His conduct and appearance had not changed; he seemed as unconscious of pain as he had been of the objects about him: but towards the close of the last evening, his mind became apparently uneasy, and his eye often fixed upon Aubrey, who was induced to offer his assistance with more than usual earnestness "Assist me! you may save me—you may do more than that—I mean not my life, I heed the death of my existence as little as that of the passing day; but you may save my honour, your friend's honour."—"How! tell me how? I would do any thing," replied Aubrey.—"I need but little—my life ebbs apace—I cannot explain the whole—but if you would conceal all you know of me, my honour were free from stain in the world's mouth—and if my death were unknown for some time in England—I—I—but life."—"It shall not be known."—"Swear!" cried the dying man, raising himself with exultant violence, "Swear by all your soul reveres, by all your nature fears, swear that for a year and a day you will not impart your knowledge of my crimes or death to any living being in any way, whatever may happen, or whatever you may see."—His eyes seemed bursting from their sockets: "I swear!" said Aubrey; he sunk laughing upon his pillow, and breathed no more.

Aubrey retired to rest, but did not sleep; the many circumstances attending his acquaintance with this man rose upon his mind, and he knew not why; when he remembered his oath a cold shivering came over him, as if from the presentiment of something horrible awaiting him. Rising early in the morning, he was about to enter the hovel in which he had left the corpse, when a robber met him, and informed him that it was no longer there, having been conveyed by himself and comrades, upon his retiring, to the pinnacle of a neighbouring mount, according to a promise they had given his lordship, that it should be exposed to the first cold ray of the moon that rose after his death.

Aubrey astonished, and taking several of the men, determined to go and bury it upon the spot where it lay. But, when he had mounted to the summit he found no trace of either the corpse or the clothes, though the robbers swore they pointed out the identical rock on which they had laid the body. For a time his mind was bewildered in conjectures, but he at last returned, convinced that they had buried the corpse for the sake of the clothes.

Weary of a country in which he had met with such terrible misfortunes, and in which all apparently conspired to heighten that superstitious melancholy that had seized upon his mind, he resolved to leave it, and soon arrived at Smyrna. While waiting for a vessel to convey him to Otranto, or to Naples, he occupied himself in arranging those effects he had with him belonging to Lord Ruthven. Amongst other things there was a case containing several weapons of offence, more or less adapted to ensure the death of the victim. There were several daggers and ataghans.[16]

Whilst turning them over, and examining their curious forms, what was his surprise at finding a sheath apparently ornamented in the same style as the dagger discovered in the fatal hut—he shuddered—hastening to gain further proof, he found the weapon, and his horror may be imagined when he discovered that it fitted, though peculiarly shaped, the sheath he held in his hand. His eyes seemed to need no further certainty—they seemed gazing to be bound to the dagger; yet still he wished to disbelieve; but the particular form, the same varying tints upon the haft and sheath were alike in splendour on both, and left no room for doubt; there were also drops of blood on each.

---

[16] Turkish saber with a curved blade

He left Smyrna, and on his way home, at Rome, his first inquiries were concerning the lady he had attempted to snatch from Lord Ruthven's seductive arts. Her parents were in distress, their fortune ruined, and she had not been heard of since the departure of his lordship. Aubrey's mind became almost broken under so many repeated horrors; he was afraid that this lady had fallen a victim to the destroyer of Ianthe.

He became morose and silent; and his only occupation consisted in urging the speed of the postilions,[17] as if he were going to save the life of some one he held dear. He arrived at Calais; a breeze, which seemed obedient to his will, soon wafted him to the English shores; and he hastened to the mansion of his fathers, and there, for a moment, appeared to lose, in the embraces and caresses of his sister, all memory of the past. If she before, by her infantine caresses, had gained his affection, now that the woman began to appear, she was still more attaching as a companion.

Miss Aubrey had not that winning grace which gains the gaze and applause of the drawing-room assemblies. There was none of that light brilliancy which only exists in the heated atmosphere of a crowded apartment. Her blue eye was never lit up by the levity of the mind beneath. There was a melancholy charm about it which did not seem to arise from misfortune, but from some feeling within, that appeared to indicate a soul conscious of a brighter realm. Her step was not that light footing, which strays where'er a butterfly or a colour may attract—it was sedate and pensive. When alone, her face was never brightened by the smile of joy; but when her brother breathed to her his affection, and would in her presence forget those griefs she knew destroyed his rest, who would have exchanged her smile for that of the voluptuary!

It seemed as if those eyes,—that face were then playing in the light of their own native sphere. She was yet only eighteen, and had not been presented to the world, it having been thought by her guardians more fit that her presentation should be delayed until her brother's return from the continent, when he might be her protector. It was now, therefore, resolved that the next drawing-room, which was fast approaching, should be the epoch of her entry into the "busy scene."

Aubrey would rather have remained in the mansion of his fathers, and fed upon the melancholy which overpowered him. He could not feel interest about the frivolities of fashionable

---

[17] Carriage drivers

strangers, when his mind had been so torn by the events he had witnessed; but he determined to sacrifice his own comfort to the protection of his sister. They soon arrived in town, and prepared for the next day, which had been announced as a drawing-room.

The crowd was excessive—a drawing-room had not been held for a long time, and all who were anxious to bask in the smile of royalty, hastened thither. Aubrey was there with his sister. While he was standing in a corner by himself, heedless of all around him, engaged in the remembrance that the first time he had seen Lord Ruthven was in that very place—he felt himself suddenly seized by the arm, and a voice he recognized too well, sounded in his ear—"Remember your oath."

He had hardly courage to turn, fearful of seeing a spectre that would blast him, when he perceived, at a little distance, the same figure which had attracted his notice on this spot upon his first entry into society.

He gazed till his limbs almost refusing to bear their weight, he was obliged to take the arm of a friend, and forcing a passage through the crowd, he threw himself into his carriage, and was driven home. He paced the room with hurried steps, and fixed his hands upon his head, as if he were afraid his thoughts were bursting from his brain. Lord Ruthven again before him—circumstances started up in dreadful array—the dagger—his oath.— He roused himself, he could not believe it possible—the dead rise again!—He thought his imagination had conjured up the image his mind was resting upon. It was impossible that it could be real—he determined, therefore, to go again into society; for though he attempted to ask concerning Lord Ruthven, the name hung upon his lips, and he could not succeed in gaining information. He went a few nights after with his sister to the assembly of a near relation. Leaving her under the protection of a matron, he retired into a recess, and there gave himself up to his. own devouring thoughts.

Perceiving, at last, that many were leaving, he roused himself, and entering another room, found his sister surrounded by several, apparently in earnest conversation; he attempted to pass and get near her, when one, whom he requested to move, turned round, and revealed to him those features he most abhorred. He sprang forward, seized his sister's arm, and, with hurried step, forced her towards the street: at the door he found himself impeded by the crowd of servants who were waiting for their lords; and while he was engaged in passing them, he again heard that voice whisper close to him—"Remember your oath!"—

He did not dare to turn, but, hurrying his sister, soon reached home.

Aubrey became almost distracted. If before his mind had been absorbed by one subject, how much more completely was it engrossed, now that the certainty of the monster's living again pressed upon his thoughts. His sister's attentions were now unheeded, and it was in vain that she intreated him to explain to her what had caused his abrupt conduct. He only uttered a few words, and those terrified her. The more he thought, the more he was bewildered.

His oath startled him;—was he then to allow this monster to roam, bearing ruin upon his breath, amidst all he held dear, and not avert its progress! His very sister might have been touched by him. But even if he were to break his oath, and disclose his suspicions, who would believe him! He thought of employing his own hand to free the world from such a wretch; but death, he remembered, had been already mocked. For days he remained in this state; shut up in his room, he saw no one, and eat only when his sister came, who, with eyes streaming with tears, besought him, for her sake, to support nature. At last, no longer capable of bearing stillness and solitude, he left his house, roamed from street to street, anxious to fly that image which haunted him. His dress became neglected, and he wandered, as often exposed to the noon-day sun as to the midnight damps.

He was no longer to be recognized; at first he returned with the evening to the house; but at last he laid him down to rest wherever fatigue overtook him. His sister, anxious for his safety, employed people to follow him; but they were soon distanced by him who fled from a pursuer swifter than any—from thought. His conduct, however, suddenly changed.

Struck with the idea that he left by his absence the whole of his friends, with a fiend amongst them, of whose presence they were unconscious, he determined to enter again into society, and watch him closely, anxious to forewarn, in spite of his oath, all whom Lord Ruthven approached with intimacy. But when he entered into a room, his haggard and suspicious looks were so striking, his inward shudderings so visible, that his sister was at last obliged to beg of him to abstain from seeking, for her sake, a society which affected him so strongly. When, however, remonstrance proved unavailing, the guardians thought proper to interpose, and, fearing that his mind was becoming alienated, they thought it high time to resume again that trust which had been before imposed upon them by Aubrey's parents.

Desirous of saving him from the injuries and sufferings he had daily encountered in his wanderings, and of preventing him from exposing to the general eye those marks of what they considered folly, they engaged a physician to reside in the house, and take constant care of him. He hardly appeared to notice it, so completely was his mind absorbed by one terrible subject. His incoherence became at last so great, that he was confined to his chamber.

There he would often lie for days, incapable of being roused. He had become emaciated, his eyes had attained a glassy lustre;—the only sign of affection and recollection remaining displayed itself upon the entry of his sister; then he would sometimes start, and, seizing her hands, with looks that severely afflicted her, he would desire her not to touch him. "Oh, do not touch him—if your love for me is aught, do not go near him!"

When, however, she inquired to whom he referred, his only answer was, "True! true!" and again he sank into a state, whence not even she could rouse him. This lasted many months: gradually, however, as the year was passing, his incoherences became less frequent, and his mind threw off a portion of its gloom, whilst his guardians observed, that several times in the day he would count upon his fingers a definite number, and then smile.

The time had nearly elapsed, when, upon the last day of the year, one of his guardians entering his room, began to converse with his physician upon the melancholy circumstance of Aubrey's; being in so awful a situation, when his sister was going next day to be married. Instantly Aubrey's attention was attracted; he asked anxiously to whom. Glad of this mark of returning intellect, of which they feared he had been deprived, they mentioned the name of the Earl of Marsden. Thinking this was a young Earl whom he had met with in society, Aubrey seemed pleased, and astonished them still more by his expressing his intention to be present at the nuptials, and desiring to see his sister.

They answered not, but in a few minutes his sister was with him. He was apparently again capable of being affected by the influence of her lovely smile; for he pressed her to his breast, and kissed her cheek, wet with tears, flowing at the thought of her brother's being once more alive to the feelings of affection. He began to speak with all his wonted warmth, and to congratulate her upon her marriage with a person so distinguished for rank and every accomplishment; when he suddenly perceived a locket upon her breast; opening it, what was his surprise at beholding the features of the monster who had so long influenced his life.

He seized the portrait in a paroxysm of rage, and trampled it under foot. Upon her asking him why he thus destroyed the resemblance of her future husband, he looked as if he did not understand her—then seizing her hands, and gazing on her with a frantic expression of countenance, he bade her swear that she would never wed this monster, for he— But he could not advance— it seemed as if that voice again bade him remember his oath—he turned suddenly round, thinking Lord Ruthven was near him but saw no one. In the meantime the guardians and physician, who had heard the whole, and thought this was but a return of his disorder, entered, and forcing him from Miss Aubrey, desired her to leave him. He fell upon his knees to them, he implored, he begged of them to delay but for one day. They, attributing this to the insanity they imagined had taken possession of his mind, endeavoured to pacify him, and retired.

Lord Ruthven had called the morning after the drawing-room, and had been refused with every one else. When he heard of Aubrey's ill health, he readily understood himself to be the cause of it; but when he learned that he was deemed insane, his exultation and pleasure could hardly be concealed from those among whom he had gained this information. He hastened to the house of his former companion, and, by constant attendance, and the pretence of great affection for the brother and interest in his fate, he gradually won the ear of Miss Aubrey.

Who could resist his power? His tongue had dangers and toils to recount—could speak of himself as of an individual having no sympathy with any being on the crowded earth, save with her to whom he addressed himself;—could tell how, since he knew her, his existence had begun to seem worthy of preservation, if it were merely that he might listen to her soothing accents;—in fine, he knew so well how to use the serpent's art, or such was the will of fate, that he gained her affections. The title of the elder branch falling at length to him, he obtained an important embassy, which served as an excuse for hastening the marriage, (in spite of her brother's deranged state,) which was to take place the very day before his departure for the continent.

Aubrey, when he was left by the physician and his guardians, attempted to bribe the servants, but in vain. He asked for pen and paper; it was given him; he wrote a letter to his sister, conjuring her, as she valued her own happiness, her own honour, and the honour of those now in the grave, who once held her in their arms as their hope and the hope of their house, to delay but for a few hours that marriage, on which he denounced the most heavy curses. The servants promised they would deliver it; but giving it to the physician, he thought it better not to harass any more the mind of Miss Aubrey by, what he considered, the ravings of a maniac.

Night passed on without rest to the busy inmates of the house; and Aubrey heard, with a horror that may more easily be conceived than described, the notes of busy preparation. Morning came, and the sound of carriages broke upon his ear. Aubrey grew almost frantic. The curiosity of the servants at last overcame their vigilance, they gradually stole away, leaving him in the custody of an helpless old woman. He seized the opportunity, with one bound was out of the room, and in a moment found himself in the apartment where all were nearly assembled.

Lord Ruthven was the first to perceive him: he immediately approached, and, taking his arm by force, hurried him from the room, speechless with rage. When on the staircase, Lord Ruthven whispered in his ear— "Remember your oath, and know, if not my bride to day, your sister is dishonoured. Women are frail!"

So saying, he pushed him towards his attendants, who, roused by the old woman, had come in search of him. Aubrey could no longer support himself; his rage not finding vent, had broken a blood-vessel, and he was conveyed to bed. This was not mentioned to his sister, who was not present when he entered, as the physician was afraid of agitating her. The marriage was solemnized, and the bride and bridegroom left London.

Aubrey's weakness increased; the effusion of blood produced symptoms of the near approach of death. He desired his sister's guardians might be called, and when the midnight hour had struck, he related composedly what the reader has perused—he died immediately after.

The guardians hastened to protect Miss Aubrey; but when they arrived, it was too late. Lord Ruthven had disappeared, and Aubrey's sister had glutted the thirst of a VAMPYRE!

**Ernst Raupach
(1784-1852)**

Introduction
Wake Not the Dead

Johann Ludwig Tieck. For many years this story was attributed to this purveyor of the German Romantic School. The English version of "Wake Not the Dead" first appeared in Vol. I of a tri-volume anthology of German stories in 1823. It was titled *Popular Tales and Romances of the Northern Nations* and offered in London by the popular seller of German books: Johann Heinrich Bohte. The story is also called "The Bride of the Grave," which is derived from the 1826 publication *Legends of Terror and Tales of the Wonderful and Wild* that listed the full title as "Wake Not the Dead or The Bride of the Grave, a German Romance."

In the 1823 anthology, no direct authorship was given to Tieck. His name appeared in a list of German authors and it happens to match with the order of the stories as laid out in the table of contents. There is no other evidence he wrote the story, including the fact that it wasn't contained in the collected works of Tieck.

It has since been learned that German dramatist, preacher

and university professor—Ernst Benjamin Salomo Raupach—penned the story. His German title is literally translated "Let the Dead Rest."

The machinations of Raupach's vampire are unique. The vampire does not leave a mark on its victim and sucks blood from the victim's heart area after putting them to sleep with its breath. Unfortunately, the story employs the awkward (and frustrating) use of Old English words as originally translated. This tactic was used a number of times in the first half of the nineteenth century when monsters were resurrected from ancient legend and brought to life in the short story. This was most apparent in a number of short werewolf tales collected in *Shifters: The Best Werewolf Short Stories 1800-1849* such as "The Man-Wolf" by Leitch Ritchie and "The Wehr-wolf: A Legend of the Limousin" by Richard Thomson.

Regardless, this story is firmly planted in this collection of the best vampire stories for the fifty year period in review and it presents the first female vampire story published in the English language.

Wake Not the Dead
(1822)

Wake not the Dead:—they bring but gloomy night
And cheerless desolation into day;
For in the grave who mouldering lay,
No more can feel the influence of light,
Or yield them to the sun's prolific might;
Let them repose within their house of cloy—
Corruption, vainly wilt thou e'er essay
To quicken:—it sends forth a pest'lent blight;
And neither fiery sun, nor bathing dew,
Nor breath of spring the dead can e'er renew.
That which from life is pluck'd, becomes the foe
Of life, and whoso wakes it waketh woe.
Seek not the dead to waken from that sleep
In which from mortal eye they lie enshrouded deep.

"WILT THOU FOR *ever* sleep? wilt thou never more awake, my beloved? but henceforth repose for ever from thy short pilgrimage on earth? O yet once again return! and bring back with thee the vivifying dawn of hope to one whose existence hath, since thy departure, been obscured by the dunnest shades. What! dumb? for ever dumb? Thy friend lamenteth, and thou heedest him not? He sheds bitter, scalding tears, and thou reposest unregarding his affliction? He is in despair, and thou no longer openest thy arms to him as an asylum from his grief? Say then, doth the pall shroud become thee better than the bridal veil? Is the chamber of the grave a warmer bed than the couch of love? Is the spectre death more welcome to thy arms than thy enamoured consort? O return, my beloved, return once again to this anxious, disconsolate bosom."

Such were the lamentations which Walter poured forth for his Brunhilda, the partner of his youthful, passionate love: thus did he bewail over her grave at the midnight hour, what time the spirit that presides in the troublous atmosphere, sends his legions of monsters through mid-air; so that their shadows, as they flit beneath the moon and across the earth, dart as wild, agitating thoughts that chase each other o'er the sinner's bosom:—thus did he lament under the tall linden trees by her grave, while his head reclined on the cold stone.

Walter was a powerful lord in Burgundy, who, in his earliest youth, had been smitten with the charms of the fair Brunhilda, a beauty far surpassing in loveliness all her rivals; for her tresses, dark as the raven face of night, streaming over her shoulders, set off to the utmost advantage the beaming lustre of her slender form, and the rich dye of a cheek whose tint was deep and brilliant as that of the western heaven: her eyes did not resemble those burning orbs[1] whose pale glow gem the vault of night, and whose immeasurable distance fills the soul with deep thoughts of eternity, but rather as the sober beams which cheer this nether world, and which, while they enlighten, kindle the sons of earth to joy and love.

Brunhilda became the wife of Walter, and both equally enamoured and devoted, they abandoned themselves to the enjoyment of a passion that rendered them reckless of aught besides, while it lulled them in a fascinating dream.

Their sole apprehension was less aught should awaken them from a delirium which they prayed might continue for ever. Yet how vain is the wish that would arrest the decrees of destiny! as well might it seek to divert the circling planets from their eternal course. Short was the duration of this phrenzied passion; not that it gradually decayed and subsided into apathy, but death snatched away his blooming victim, and left Walter to a widowed couch. Impetuous, however, as was his first burst of grief, he was not inconsolable, for ere long another bride became the partner of the youth.

Swanhilda also was beautiful; although nature had formed her charms on a very different model from those of Brunhilda. Her golden locks waved bright as the beams of morn: only when excited by some emotion of her soul did a rosy hue tinge the lily paleness of her cheek: her limbs were proportioned in the nicest symmetry, yet did they not possess that luxuriant fullness of animal life: her eye beamed eloquently, but it was with the milder radiance of a star tranquillizing to tenderness rather than exciting to warmth.

Thus formed, it was not possible that she should steep him in his former delirium, although she rendered happy his waking hours: tranquil and serious, yet cheerful, studying in all things her husband's pleasure, she restored order and comfort in his family, where her presence shed a general influence all around.

---

[1] Eyes

Her mild benevolence tended to restrain the fiery, impetuous disposition of Walter: while at the same time her prudence recalled him in some degree from his vain, turbulent wishes, and his aspirings after unattainable enjoyments, to the duties and pleasures of actual life.

Swanhilda bore her husband two children, a son and a daughter; the latter was mild and patient as her mother, well contented with her solitary sports, and even in these recreations displayed the serious turn of her character. The boy possessed his father's fiery, restless disposition, tempered, however, with the solidity of his mother. Attached by his offspring more tenderly towards their mother, Walter now lived for several years very happily: his thoughts would frequently, indeed, recur to Brunhilda, but without their former violence, merely as we dwell upon the memory of a friend of our earlier days, borne from us on the rapid current of time to a region where we know that he is happy.

But clouds dissolve into air, flowers fade, the sand of the hour-glass runs imperceptibly away, and even so, do human feelings dissolve, fade, and pass away, and with them too, human happiness. Walter's inconstant breast again sighed for the extatic dreams of those days which he had spent with his equally romantic, enamoured Brunhilda: again did she present herself to his ardent fancy in all the glow of her bridal charms, and he began to draw a parallel between the past and the present; nor did imagination, as it is wont, fail to array the former in her brightest hues, while it proportionably obscured the latter; so that lie pictured to himself, the one much more rich in enjoyment, and the other, much less so than they really were.

This change in her husband did not escape Swanhilda; whereupon, redoubling her attentions towards him, and her cares towards their children, she expected, by this means, to reunite the knot that was slackened; yet the more she endeavoured to regain his affections, the colder did he grow,— the more intolerable did her caresses seem, and the more continually did the image of Brunhilda haunt his thoughts. The children, whose endearments were now become indispensable to him, alone stood between the parents as genii[2] eager to effect a reconciliation; and, beloved by them both, formed a uniting link between them. Yet, as evil can be plucked from the heart of man, only ere its root has yet struck deep, its fangs being

---

[2] In Roman mythology the genii was the guiding spirit

afterwards too firm to be eradicated; so was Walter's diseased fancy too far affected to have its disorder stopped, for, in a short time it completely tyrannized over him. Frequently of a night, instead of retiring to his consort's chamber, he repaired to Brunhilda's grave, where he murmured forth his discontent, saying: "Wilt thou sleep for ever?"

One night as he was thus reclining on the turf, indulging in his wonted sorrow, a sorcerer from the neigbouring mountains, entered into this field of death for the purpose of gathering, for his mystic spells, such herbs as grow only from the earth wherein the dead repose, and which, as if the last production of mortality, are gifted with a powerful and supernatural influence. The sorcerer perceived the mourner, and approached the spot where he was lying.

"Wherefore, fond wretch, dost thou grieve thus, for what is now a hideous mass of mortality—mere bones, and nerves, and veins? Nations have fallen unlamented; even worlds themselves, long ere this globe of ours was created, have mouldered into nothing; nor hath any one wept over them: why then should thou indulge this vain affliction for a child of the dust—a being as frail as thyself, and like thee the creature but of a moment?"

Walter raised himself up:—"Let yon worlds that shine in the firmament" replied he, "lament for each other as they perish. It is true, that I who am myself clay, lament for my fellow-clay: yet is this clay impregnated with a fire,—with an essence, that none of the elements of creation possess—with love: and this divine passion, I felt for her who now sleepeth beneath this sod."

"Will thy complaints awaken her: or could they do so, would she not soon upbraid thee for having disturbed that repose in which she now is hushed?"

"A vaunt, cold-hearted being: thou knowest not what is love. Oh! that my tears could wash away the earthy covering that conceals her from these eyes;—that my groan of anguish could rouse her from her slumber of death!—No, she would not again seek her earthy couch."

"Insensate that thou art, and couldst thou endure to gaze without shuddering on one disgorged from the jaws of the grave? Art thou too thyself the same from whom she parted; or hath time passed o'er thy brow and left no traces there? Would not thy love rather be converted into hate and disgust?"

"Say rather that the stars would leave yon firmament, that the sun will henceforth refuse to shed his beams through the heavens. O that she stood once more before me;—that once again she reposed on this bosom!—how quickly should we then forget that death or time had ever stepped between us."

"Delusion! mere delusion of the brain, from heated blood, like to that which arises from the fumes of wine. It is not my wish to tempt thee;—to restore to thee thy dead; else wouldst thou soon feel that I have spoken sooth."

"How! restore her to me," exclaimed Walter casting himself at the sorcerer's feet, "Oh! if thou art indeed able to effect that, grant it to my earnest supplication; if one throb of human feeling vibrates in thy bosom, let my tears prevail with thee: restore me my beloved; so shalt thou hereafter bless the deed, and see that it was a good work,"

"A good work! a blessed deed!"—returned the sorcerer with a smile of scorn; "for me there exists nor good, nor evil; since my will is always the same, Ye alone know evil, who will that which ye would not. It is indeed in my power to restore her to thee: yet, bethink thee well, whether it will prove thy weal. Consider too, how deep the abyss between life and death; across this, my power can build a bridge, but it can never fill up the frightful chasm."

Walter would have spoken, and have sought to prevail on this powerful being by fresh entreaties, but the latter prevented him, saying: "Peace! bethink thee well! and return hither to me to-morrow at midnight. Yet once more do I warn thee, 'wake not the dead.'"

Having uttered these words, the mysterious being disappeared. Intoxicated with fresh hope, Walter found no sleep on his couch; for fancy, prodigal of her richest stores, expanded before him the glittering web of futurity; and his eye, moistened with the dew of rapture, glanced from one vision of happiness to another. During the next day he wandered through the woods, lest wonted objects by recalling the memory of later and less happier times, might disturb the blissful idea, that he should again behold her—again fold her in his arms, gaze on her beaming brow by day, repose on her bosom at night: and, as this sole idea filled his imagination, how was it possible that the least doubt should arise; or that the warning of the mysterious old man should recur to his thoughts.

No sooner did the midnight hour approach, than he hastened towards the grave-field where the sorcerer was already standing by that of Bruuhilda.

"Hast thou maturely considered?" enquired he.

"Oh! restore to me the object of my ardent passion," exclaimed Walter with impetuous eagerness. "Delay not thy generous action, lest I die even this night, consumed with disappointed desire; and behold her face no more."

"Well then, answered the old man," return hither again to-morrow at the same hour. But once more do I give thee this friendly warning, 'wake not the dead.'"

In all the despair of impatience, Walter would have prostrated himself at his feet, and supplicated him to fulfill at once a desire now increased to agony; but the sorcerer had already disappeared. Pouring forth his lamentations more wildly and impetuously than ever, he lay upon the grave of his adored one, until the grey dawn streaked the east. During the day, which seemed to him longer than any he bad ever experienced, he wandered to and fro, restless and impatient, seemingly without any object, and deeply buried in his own reflections, in quiet as the murderer who meditates his first deed of blood: and the stars of evening found him once more at the appointed spot. At midnight the sorcerer was there also.

"Hast thou yet maturely deliberated?" enquired he, "as on the preceding night?"

"On what should I deliberate?" returned Walter impatiently. "I need not to deliberate: what I demand of thee, is that which thou hast promised me—that which will prove my bliss. Or dost thou but mock me? if so, hence from my sight, lest I be tempted to lay my hand on thee."

"Once more do I warn thee," answered the old man with undisturbed composure, 'wake not the dead'—let her rest."

"Aye, but not in the cold grave: she shall rather rest on this bosom which burns with eagerness to clasp her."

"Reflect, thou may'st not quit her until death, even though aversion and horror should seize thy heart. There would then remain only one horrible means."

"Dotard!" cried Walter, interrupting him, "how may I hate that which I love with such intensity of passion? how should I abhor that for which my every drop of blood is boiling?"

"Then be it even as thou wishest," answered the sorcerer; "step back."

The old man now drew a circle round the grave, all the while muttering words of enchantment. Immediately the storm began to howl among the tops of the trees; owls flapped their wings, and uttered their low voice of omen; the stars hid their mild, beaming aspect, that they might not behold so unholy and impious a spectacle; the stone then rolled from the grave with a hollow sound, leaving a free passage for the inhabitant of that dreadful tenement.

The sorcerer scattered into the yawning earth, roots and herbs of most magic power, and of most penetrating odour, so that the worms crawling forth from the earth congregated together, and raised themselves in a fiery column over the grave: while rushing wind burst from the earth, scattering the mould before it, until at length the coffin lay uncovered.

The moon-beams fell on it, and the lid burst open with a tremendous sound. Upon this the sorcerer poured upon it some blood from out of a human skull, exclaiming at the same time:— "Drink, sleeper, of this warm stream, that thy heart may again beat within thy bosom."

And, after a short pause, shedding on her some other mystic liquid, he cried aloud with the voice of one inspired: "Yes, thy heart beats once more with the flood of life: thine eye is again opened to sight. Arise, therefore, from thy tomb."

As an island suddenly springs forth from the dark waves of the ocean, raised upwards from the deep by the force of subterraneous fires, so did Brunhilda start from her earthy couch, borne forward by some invisible power. Taking her by the hand, the sorcerer lead her towards Walter, who stood at some little distance, rooted to the ground with amazement.

"Receive again," said he, "the object of thy passionate sighs: mayest thou never more require my aid; should that however happen, so wilt thou find me, during the full of the moon, upon the mountains in that spot and where the three roads meet."

Instantly did Walter recognize in the form that stood before him, her whom he so ardently loved; and a sudden glow shot through his frame at finding her thus restored to him: yet the night-frost had chilled his limbs and palsied his tongue. For a while he gazed upon her without either motion or speech, and during this pause, all was again become hushed and serene; and the stars shone brightly in the clear heavens.

"Walter!" exclaimed the figure; and at once the well-known sound, thrilling to his heart, broke the spell by which he was bound.

"Is it reality? is it truth?" cried he, "or a cheating delusion?"

"No, it is no imposture: I am really living:—conduct me quickly to thy castle in the mountains."

Walter looked around: the old man had disappeared, but he perceived close by his side, a coal-black steed of fiery eye, ready equipped to conduct him thence; and on his back lay all proper attire for Brunhilda, who lost no time in arraying herself.

This being done, she cried: "Haste, let us away ere the dawn breaks, for my eye is yet too weak to endure the light of day."

Fully recovered from his stupor, Walter leaped into his saddle, and catching up, with a mingled feeling of delight and awe, the beloved being thus mysteriously restored from the power of the grave, he spurred on across the wild, towards the mountains, as furiously as if pursued by the shadows of the dead, hastening to recover from him their sister.

The castle to which Walter conducted his Brunhilda, was situated on a rock between other rocks rising up above it. Here they arrived, unseen by any, save one aged domestic, on whom Walter imposed secrecy by the severest threats.

"Here will we tarry," said Brunhilda, "until I can endure the light, and until thou canst look upon me without trembling: as if struck with a cold chill."

They accordingly continued to make that place their abode: yet no one knew that Brunhilda existed, save only that aged attendant, who provided their meals. During seven entire days, they had no light except that of tapers; during the next seven, the light was admitted through the lofty casements only while the rising or setting-sun faintly illumined the mountain-tops, the vallies being still enveloped in shade.

Seldom did Walter quit Brunhilda's side: a nameless spell seemed to attach him to her; even the shudder which he felt in her presence, and which would not permit him to touch her, was not unmixed with pleasure, like that thrilling, aweful emotion felt when strains of sacred music float under the vault of some temple; he rather sought, therefore, than avoided this feeling.

Often too as he had indulged in calling to mind the beauties of Brunhilda, she had never appeared so fair, so fascinating, so admirable when depicted by his imagination, as when now beheld in reality. Never till now had her voice sounded with such tones of sweetness; never before did her language possess such eloquence as it now did, when she conversed with him on the subject of the past.

And this was the magic fairyland towards which her words constantly conducted him. Ever did she dwell upon the days of their first love, those hours of delight which they had participated together when the one derived all enjoyment from the other: and so rapturous, so enchanting, so full of life did she recall to his imagination that blissful season, that he even doubted whether he had ever experienced with her so much felicity, or had been so truly happy.

And, while she thus vividly pourtrayed their hours of past delight, she delineated in still more glowing, more enchanting colours, those hours of approaching bliss which now awaited them, richer in enjoyment than any preceding ones. In this manner did she charm her attentive auditor with enrapturing hopes for the future, and lull him in dreams of more than mortal extacy; so that while he listened to her syren strain, he entirely forgot how little blissful was the latter period of their union, when he had often sighed at her imperiousness, and at her harshness both to himself and all his household. Yet even had he recalled this to mind would it have disturbed him in his present delirious trance?

Had she not now left behind in the grave all the frailty of mortality? Was she not cheerful as the morning hour in spring—affectionate and mild as the last beams of an autumnal sun? Was not her whole being refined and purified by that long sleep in which neither passion nor sin had approached her even in dreams? How different now was the subject of her discourse!

Only when speaking of her affection for him, did she betray any thing of earthly feeling: at other times, she uniformly dwelt, upon themes relating to the invisible and future world; when in descanting and declaring the mysteries of eternity, a stream of prophetic eloquence would burst from her lips.

In this manner had twice seven days elapsed, and, for the first time, Walter beheld the being now dearer to him than ever, in the full light of day. Every trace of the grave had disappeared from her countenance: a roseate tinge[3] like the ruddy streaks of dawn again beamed on her pallid cheek; the faint, mouldering taint of the grave was changed into a delightful violet scent; the only sign of earth that never disappeared.

He no longer felt either apprehension or awe, as he gazed upon her in the sunny light of day: it was not until *now,* that he seemed to have recovered her completely; and, glowing with all his former passion towards her, he would have pressed her to his bosom, but she gently repulsed him, saying: "Not yet: spare your caresses until the moon has again filled her horn."

Spite of his impatience, Walter was obliged to await the lapse of another period of seven days; but, on the night when the moon was arrived at the full, he hastened to Brunhilda, whom he found more lovely than she had ever appeared before. Fearing no obstacles to his transports, he embraced her with all the fervour of a deeply enamoured and successful lover. Brunhilda, however, still refused to yield to his passion.

---

[3] Rosy color

"What!" exclaimed she, "is it fitting that I who have been purified by death from the frailty of mortality, should become thy concubine, while a mere daughter of the earth bears the title of thy wife: never shall it be. No, it must be within the walls of thy palace, within that chamber where I once reigned as queen, that thou obtained the end of thy wishes,—and of mine also," added she, imprinting a glowing kiss on his lips, and immediately disappeared.

Heated with passion, and determined to sacrifice every thing to the accomplishment of his desires, Walter hastily quitted the apartment, and shortly after the castle itself. He travelled over mountain and cross heath, with the rapidity of a storm, so that the turf was flung up by his horse's hoofs; nor once stopped until he arrived home.

Here, however, neither the affectionate caresses of Swanhilda, or those of his children could touch his heart, or induce him to restrain his furious desires. Alas! is the impetuous torrent to be checked in its devastating course by the beauteous flowers over which it rushes, when they exclaim: "Destroyer, commiserate our helpless innocence and beauty, nor lay us waste?"—the stream sweeps over them unregarding, and a single moment annihilates the pride of a whole summer.

Shortly afterwards, did Walter begin to hint to Swanhilda, that they were ill-suited to each other;—that he was anxious to taste that wild, tumultuous life, so well according with the spirit of his sex, while she, on the contrary, was satisfied with the monotous circle of household enjoyments:—that he was eager for whatever promised novelty, while she felt most attached to what was familiarized to her by habit; and lastly, that her cold disposition, bordering upon indifference, but ill assorted with his ardent temperament: it was therefore more prudent that they should seek apart from each other, that happiness which they could not find together.

A sigh, and a brief acquiescence in his wishes was all the reply that Swanhilda made: and, on the following morning upon his presenting her with a paper of separation, informing her that she was at liberty to return home to her father, she received it most submissively: yet, ere she departed, she gave him the following warning: "Too well do I conjecture to whom I am indebted for this our separation. Often have I seen thee at Brunhilda's grave, and beheld thee there even on that night when the face of the heavens was suddenly enveloped in a veil of clouds. Hast thou rashly dared to tear aside the awful veil that separates the mortality that dreams, from that which dreameth not, O! then woe to thee, thou wretched man, for thou hast attached to thyself that which will prove thy destruction."

She ceased: nor did Walter attempt any reply, for the similar admonition uttered by the sorcerer flashed upon his mind, all obscured as it was by passion, just as the lightning glares momentarily through the gloom of night without dispersing the obscurity.

Swanhilda then departed, in order to pronounce to her children, a bitter farewell, for they, according to the custom of his nation, belonged to the father; and, having bathed them in her tears, and consecrated them with the holy water of maternal love, she quitted her husband's residence, and departed to the home of her fathers.

Thus was the kind and benevolent Swanhilda, driven in exile from those halls, where she had presided with such grace;— from halls which were now newly decorated to receive another mistress. The day at length arrived, on which Walter, for the second time, conducted Brunhilda home, as a newly-made bride. And he caused it to be reported among his domestics, that his new consort had gained his affections by her extraordinary likeness to Brunhilda, their former mistress.

How ineffably happy did he deem himself, as he conducted his beloved once more into the chamber which had often witnessed their former joys, and which was now newly gilded and adorned in a most costly style: among the other decorations were figures of angels scattering roses, which served to support the purple draperies, whose ample folds o'er shadowed the nuptial couch. With what impatience did he await the hour that was to put him in possession of those beauties, for which he had already paid so high a price, but, whose enjoyment was to cost him most dearly yet?

Unfortunate Walter! revelling in bliss, thou beholdest not the abyss that yawns beneath thy feet, intoxicated with the luscious perfume of the flower thou hast plucked, thou little deemest how deadly is the venom with which it is fraught, although, for a short season, its potent fragrance bestows new energy on all thy feelings.

Happy however, as Walter now was, his household were far from being equally so. The strange resemblance between their new lady and the deceased Brunhilda, filled them with a secret dismay,—an undefinable horror; for there was not a single difference of feature, of tone of voice, or of gesture. To add to these mysterious circumstances, her female attendants discovered a particular mark on her back, exactly like one which

Brunhilda had. A report was now soon circulated, that their lady was no other than Brunhilda herself, who had been recalled to life by the power of necromancy.[4]

How truly horrible was the idea of living under the same roof with one who had been an inhabitant of the tomb, and of being obliged to attend upon her, and acknowledge her as mistress! There was also in Brunhilda, much to increase this aversion, and favour their superstition: no ornaments of gold ever decked her person; all that others were wont to, wear of this metal, she had formed of silver: no richly coloured, and sparkling' jewels glittered upon her; pearls alone, lent, their pale lustre to adorn her bosom.

Most carefully did she always avoid the cheerful light of the sun, and was wont to spend, the brightest days in the most retired and gloomy apartments: only during the twilight of the commencing, or declining day did she ever walk abroad, but her favourite hour was, when the phantom light of the moon bestowed on all objects a shadowy appearance, and a sombre hue; always too at the crowing of the cock, an involuntary shudder was observed to seize her limbs.

Imperious as before her death, she quickly imposed her iron yoke on every one around her, while, she seemed even far more terrible than ever, since a dread of some supernatural power, attached to her, appalled all who approached her. A malignant withering glance seemed to shoot from her eye on the unhappy object of her wrath, as if it would annihilate its victim. In short, those halls which, in the time of Swanhilda were the residence of cheerfulness and mirth, now resembled an extensive desert tomb.

With fear imprinted on their pale countenances, the domestics glided through the apartments of the castle; and, in this abode of terror, the crowing of the cock caused the living to tremble, as if they were the spirits of the departed; for the sound always reminded them of their mysterious mistress.

There was no one but who shuddered at meeting her in a lonely place, in the dusk of evening, or by the light of the moon, a circumstance that was deemed to be ominous of some evil: so great was the apprehension of her female attendants, that they pined in continual disquietude, and, by degrees, all quitted her. In the course of time even others of the domestics fled, for an insupportable horror had seized them.

---

[4] Wizardry

The art of the sorcerer had indeed bestowed upon Brunhilda an artificial life, and due nourishment had continued to support the restored body; yet, this body was not able of itself to keep up the genial glow of vitality, and to nourish the flame whence springs all the affections and passions, whether of love or hate; for death had for ever destroyed and withered it: all that Brunhilda now possessed was a chilled existence, colder than that of the snake.

It was nevertheless necessary that she should love, and return with equal ardour the warm caresses of her spell-enthralled husband, to whose passion alone she was indebted for her renewed existence. It was necessary that a magic draught should animate the dull current in her veins, and awaken her to the glow of life and the flame of love—a potion of abomination—one not even to be named without a curse—human blood, imbibed whilst yet warm, from the veins of youth.

This was the hellish drink for which she thirsted: possessing no sympathy with the purer feelings of humanity; deriving no enjoyment from aught that interests in life, and occupies its varied hours; her existence was a mere blank, unless when in the arms of her paramour[5] husband, and therefore was it that *she* craved incessantly after the horrible draught. It was even with the utmost effort that she could forbear sucking even the blood of Walter himself, as he reclined beside her.

Whenever she beheld some innocent child, whose lovely face denoted the exuberance of infantine health and vigour, she would entice it by soothing words and fond caresses into her most secret apartment, where, lulling it to sleep in her arms, she would suck from its bosom the warm, purple tide of life. Nor were youths of either sex safe from her horrid attack: having first breathed upon her unhappy victim, who never failed immediately to sink into a lengthened sleep, she would then in a similar manner drain his veins of the vital juice.

Thus children, youths, and maidens quickly faded away, as flowers gnawn by the cankering Worm: the fullness of their limbs disappeared; a sallow hue succeeded to the rosy freshness of their cheeks, the liquid lustre of the eye was deadened, even as the sparkling stream when arrested by the touch of frost; and their locks became thin and grey, as if already ravaged by the storm of life. Parents beheld with horror this desolating pestilence devouring their offspring; nor could simple or charm, potion or amulet avail aught against it. The grave swallowed up

---

[5] Illicit partner

one after the other; or did the miserable victim survive, he became cadaverous and wrinkled even in the very morn of existence.

Parents observed with horror, this devastating pestilence snatch away their offspring—a pestilence which, nor herb however potent, nor charm, nor holy taper, nor exorcism could avert. They either beheld their children sink one after the other into the grave, or their youthful forms withered by the unholy, vampire embrace of Brunhilda assume the decrepitude of sudden age.

At length strange surmises and reports began to prevail; it was whispered that Brunhilda herself was the cause of all these horrors; although no one could pretend to tell in what manner she destroyed her victims, since no marks of violence were discernable.

Yet when young children confessed that she had frequently lulled them asleep in her arms, and elder ones said that a sudden slumber had come upon them whenever she began to converse with them, suspicion became converted into certainty, and those whose offspring had hitherto escaped unharmed, quitted their hearths and home—all their little possessions—the dwellings of their fathers and the inheritance of their children, in order to rescue from so horrible a fate those who were dearer to their simple affections than aught else the world could give.

Thus did the castle daily assume a more desolate appearance; daily did its environs become more deserted: none but a few aged decrepid old women and grey-headed menials were to be seen remaining of the once numerous retinue.[6] Such will, in the latter days of the earth, be the last generation of mortals, when child-bearing shall have ceased, when youth shall no more be seen, nor any arise to replace those who shall await their fate in silence.

Walter alone noticed not, or heeded not, the desolation around him; he apprehended not death, lapped as he was in a glowing Elysium[7] of love far more happy than formerly did he *now* seem in the possession of Brunhilda. All those caprices and frowns which had been wont to over cloud their former union had now entirely disappeared. She even seemed to dote on him with a warmth of passion that she had never exhibited even during the happy season of bridal love; for the flame of that

---

[6] Group of assistants
[7] Perfect happiness

youthful blood, of which she drained the veins of others, rioted in her own.

At night, as soon as he closed his eyes, she would breathe on him till he sank into delicious dreams, from which be awoke only to experience more rapturous enjoyments. By day she would continually discourse with him on the bliss experienced by happy spirits beyond the grave, assuring them that, as his affection had recalled her from the tomb, they were now irrevocably united.

Thus fascinated by a continual spell, it was not possible that he should perceive what was taking place around him. Brunhilda, however, foresaw with savage grief that the source of her youthful ardour was daily decreasing, for, in a short time, there remained nothing gifted with youth, save Walter and his children, and these latter she resolved should be her next victims.

On her first return to the castle, she had felt an aversion towards the offspring of another, and therefore abandoned them entirely to the attendants appointed by Swanhilda. Now, however, she began to pay considerable attention to them, and caused them to be frequently admitted into her presence. The aged nurses were filled with dread at perceiving these marks of regard from her towards their young charges, yet dared they not to oppose the will of their terrible and imperious mistress.

Soon did Brunhilda gain the affection of the children, who were too unsuspecting of all guile to apprehend any danger from her; on the contrary, her caresses won them completely to her. Instead of ever checking their mirthful gambols,[8] she would rather instruct them in new sports; often too did she recite to them tales of such strange and wild interest as to exceed all the stories of their nurses. Were they wearied either with play or with listening to her narratives, she would take them on her knees and lull them to slumber.

Then did visions of the most surpassing magnificence attend their dreams: they would fancy themselves in some garden, where flowers of every hue rose in rows one above the other, from the humble violet to the tall sun-flower, forming a party-coloured broidery of every hue, sloping upwards towards the golden clouds, where little angels, whose wings sparkled with azure and gold, descended to bring them delicious cakes, or splendid jewels; or sung to them soothing melodious hymns. So delightful did these dreams in short time become to the

---

[8] Playfulness

children, that they longed for nothing so eagerly as to slumber on Brunhilda's lap, for never did they else enjoy such visions of heavenly forms. Thus were they most anxious for that which was to prove their destruction:—yet do we not all aspire after that which conducts us to the grave—after the enjoyment of life?

These innocents stretched out their arms to approaching death, because it assumed the mask of pleasure; for, while they were lapped in these exstatic slumbers, Brunhilda sucked the life-stream from their bosoms. On waking, indeed, they felt themselves faint and exhausted, yet did no pain, nor any mark betray the cause. Shortly, however, did their strength entirely fail, even as the summer brook is gradually dried up: their sports became less and less noisy; their loud, frolicksome laughter was converted into a faint smile; the full tones of their voices died away into a mere whisper.

Their attendants were filled with horror and despair; too well did they conjecture the dreadful truth, yet dared not to impart their suspicions to Walter, who was so devotedly attached to his horrible partner. Death had already smote his prey: the children were but the mere shadows of their former selves, and even this shadow quickly disappeared.

The anguished father deeply bemoaned their loss, for, notwithstanding his apparent neglect, he was strongly attached to them, nor until he had experienced their loss, was he aware that his love was so great.

His affliction could not fail to excite the displeasure of Brunhilda: "Why dost thou lament so fondly," said she, "for these little ones? What satisfaction could such unformed beings yield to thee, unless thou wert still attached to their mother? Thy heart then is still hers! Or dost thou now regret her and them, because thou art satiated with my fondness, and weary of my endearments? Had these young ones grown up, would they not have attached thee, thy spirit and thy affections more closely to this earth of clay—to this dust, and have alienated thee from that sphere to which I, who have already passed the grave, endeavour to raise thee? Say is thy spirit so lumpish, or thy love so weak, or thy faith so hollow, that the hope of being mine for ever is unable to touch thee?"

Thus did Brunhilda express her indignation at her consort's grief, and forbade him her presence. The fear of offending her beyond forgiveness, and his anxiety to appease her soon dried up his tears; and he again abandoned himself to his fatal passion, until approaching destruction, at length awakened him from his delusion.

Neither maiden, nor youth, was any longer to be seen, either within the dreary walls of the castle, or the adjoining territory:— all had disappeared; for those whom the grave had not swallowed up, had fled from the region of death. Who, therefore, now remained to quench the horrible thirst of the female vampire, save Walter himself? and his death she dared to contemplate unmoved; for that divine sentiment that unites two beings in one joy and one sorrow was unknown to her bosom. Was he in his tomb, so was she free to search out other victims, and glut herself with destruction, until she herself should, at the last day, be consumed with the earth itself: such is the fatal law, to which the dead are subject, when awoke by the arts of necromancy from the sleep of the grave.

She now began to fix her blood-thirsty lips on Walter's breast, when cast into a profound sleep by the odour of her violet breath, he reclined beside her quite unconscious of his impending fate: yet soon did his vital powers begin to decay; and many a grey hair peeped through his raven locks. With his strength, his passion also declined; and he now frequently left her in order to pass the whole day in the sports of the chase, hoping thereby, to regain his wonted vigour.

As he was reposing one day in a wood beneath the shade of an oak, he perceived, on the summit of a tree, a bird of strange appearance, and quite unknown to him; but, before he could take aim at it with his bow, it flew away into the clouds; at the same time, letting fall a rose-coloured root which dropped at Walter's feet, who immediately took it up, and, although he was well acquainted with almost every plant, he could not remember to have seen any at all resembling this.

Its delightfully odoriferous scent induced him to try its flavour, but ten times more bitter than wormwood,[9] it was even as gall in his mouth; upon which, impatient of the disappointment, he flung it away with violence. Had he, however, been aware of its miraculous quality, and that it acted as a counter-charm against the opiate perfume of Brunhilda's breath, he would have blessed it spite of its bitterness: thus do mortals often blindly cast away in displeasure, the unsavoury remedy that would otherwise work their weal.[10]

When Walter returned home in the evening, and laid him down to repose as usual by Brunhilda's side, the magic power of her breath produced no effect upon him; and, for the first time

---

[9] Bitter herb once thought to be an hallucinogenic
[10] Well-being

during many months did he close his eyes in a natural slumber. Yet hardly had he fallen asleep, ere a pungent, smarting pain disturbed him from his dreams; and, opening his eyes, he discerned, by the gloomy rays of a lamp, that glimmered in the apartment, what for some moments transfixed him quite aghast, for it was Brunhilda, drawing with her lips, the warm blood from his bosom. The wild cry of horror which at length escaped him, terrified Brunhilda, whose mouth was besmeared with the warm blood.

"Monster!" exclaimed he, springing from the couch, "is it thus that you love me?"

"Aye, even as the dead love," replied she, with a malignant coldness.

"Creature of blood," continued Walter, "the delusion which has so long blinded me is at an end: thou art the fiend who hast destroyed my children—who hast murdered the offspring of my vassals."

Raising herself upwards, and, at the same time, casting on him a glance that froze him to the spot with dread, she replied: "It is not I who have murdered them:— I was obliged to pamper myself with warm youthful blood, in order that I might satisfy thy furious desires—thou art the murderer!"—These dreadful words summoned, before Walter's terrified conscience, the threatening shades of all those who had thus perished; while despair choked his voice.

"Why," continued she, in a tone that increased his horror, "why dost thou make mouths at me like a puppet? Thou who hadst the courage to love the dead—to take into thy bed, one who had been sleeping in the grave, the bed-fellow of the worm—who hast clasped in thy lustful arms, the corruption of the tomb—dost thou, unhallowed as thou art, now raise this hideous cry for the sacrifice of a few lives?—They are but leaves swept from their branches by a storm.—Come, chase these idiot fancies, and taste the bliss thou hast so dearly purchased."

So saying, she extended her arms towards him; but this motion served only to increase his terror and exclaiming: "Accursed Being,"—he rushed out of the apartment.

All the horrors of a guilty, upbraiding conscience became his companions, now that he was awakened from the delirium of his unholy pleasures. Frequently did he curse his own obstinate blindness, for having given no heed to the hints and admonitions of his children's nurses, but treating them as vile calumnies.[11] But his sorrow was now too late, for, although repentance may gain pardon for the sinner, it cannot alter the immutable decrees of fate—it cannot recall the murdered from the tomb.

No sooner did the first break of dawn appear, than he set out for his lonely castle in the mountains, determined no longer to abide under the same roof with so terrific a being; yet vain was his flight, for, on waking the following morning, he perceived himself in Brunhilda's arms, and quite entangled in her long raven tresses, which seemed to involve him, and bind him in the fetters of his fate; the powerful fascination of her breath held him still more captivated, so that, forgetting all that had passed, he returned her caresses, until awakening as if from a dream he recoiled in unmixed horror from her embrace.

During the day he wandered through the solitary wilds of the mountains, as a culprit seeking an asylum from his pursuers; and, at night, retired to the shelter of a cave; fearing less to couch himself within such a dreary place, than to expose himself to the horror of again meeting Brunhilda; but, alas! it was in vain that he endeavoured to flee her. Again, when he awoke, he found her the partner of his miserable bed.

Nay, had he sought the centre of the earth as his hiding place; had he even imbedded himself beneath rocks, or formed his chamber in the recesses of the ocean, still had he found her his constant companion; for, by calling her again into existence, he had rendered himself inseparably hers; so fatal were the links that united them.

Struggling with the madness that was beginning to seize him, and brooding incessantly on the ghastly visions that presented themselves to his horror stricken-mind, he lay motionless in the gloomiest recesses of the woods, even from the rise of sun till the shades of eve.

But, no sooner was the light of day extinguished in the west, and the woods buried in impenetrable darkness, than the apprehension of resigning himself to sleep drove him forth among the open mountains. The storm played wildly with the fantastic clouds, and with the rattling leaves, as they were caught up into the air, as if some dread spirit was sporting with these images of transitoriness and decay: it roared among the summits of the oaks as if uttering a voice of fury, while its hollow sound rebounding among the distant hills, seemed as the moans of a departing sinner, or as the faint cry of some wretch

---

[11] False statements

expiring under the murderer's hand: the owl too, uttered its ghastly crys if forboding the wreck of nature.

Walter's hair flew disorderly in the wind, like black snakes wreathing around his temples and shoulders; while each sense was awake to catch fresh horror. In the clouds he seemed to behold the forms of the murdered; in the howling wind to hear their laments and groans; in the chilling blast itself he felt the dire kiss of Brunhilda; in the cry of the screeching bird he heard her voice; in the mouldering leaves he scented the charnel-bed[12] out of which he had awakened her.

"Murderer of thy own offspring," exclaimed he in a voice making night, and the conflict of the element still more hideous, "paramour of a blood-thirsty vampire, reveller with the corruption of the tomb!" while in his despair he rent the wild locks from his head.

Just then the full moon darted from beneath the bursting clouds; and this sight recalled to his remembrance the advice of the sorcerer, when *he* trembled at the first apparition of Brunhilda rising from her sleep of death;—namely, to seek him, at the season of the full moon, in the mountains, where three roads met. Scarcely had this gleam of hope broke in on his bewildered mind than he flew to the appointed spot.

On his arrival, Walter found the old man seated there upon a stone, as calmly as though it had been a bright sunny day, and completely regardless of the uproar around. "Art thou come then?" exclaimed he to the breathless wretch, who, flinging himself at his feet, cried in a tone of anguish: "Oh save me— succour me—rescue me from the monster that scattereth death and desolation around her."

"I am acquainted with all," returned the sorcerer; "thou now perceivest how wholesome was the advice—'WAKE NOT THE DEAD.'"

"And wherefore a mere mysterious warning? why didst thou not rather disclose to me, at once, all the horrors that awaited my sacrilegious profanation of the grave?"

"Wert thou able to listen to any other voice than that of thy impetuous passions? Did not thy eager impatience shut my mouth at the very moment I would have cautioned thee?"

"True, true:—thy reproof is just: but what does it avail now;—I need the promptest aid."

---

[12] Unholy bed

"Well," replied the old man, "there remains even yet a means of rescuing thyself, but it is fraught with horror, and demands all thy resolution."

"Utter it then, utter it; for what can be more appalling, more hideous than the misery I now endure?"

"Know then," continued the sorcerer, "that only on the night of the new moon, does she sleep the sleep of mortals; and then all the supernatural power which she inherits from the grave totally fails her. 'Tis then that thou must murder her."

"How! murder her!" echoed Walter.

"Aye," returned the old man calmly, "pierce her bosom with a sharpened dagger, which I will furnish thee with; at the same time renounce her memory for ever, swearing never to think of her intentionally, and that, if thou dost involuntarily, thou wilt repeat the curse."

"Most horrible! yet what can be more horrible than she herself is?—I'll do it."

"Keep then this resolution until the next new moon."

"What, must I wait until then?" cried Walter, "alas ere then, either her savage thirst for blood will have forced me into the night of the tomb, or horror will have driven me into the night of madness."

"Nay," replied the sorcerer, "that I can prevent;" and, so saying, he conducted him to a cavern further among the mountains. "Abide here twice seven days," said he; "so long can I protect thee against her deadly caresses. Here wilt thou *find* all due provision for thy wants; but take heed that nothing tempt thee to quit this place. Farewell, when the moon renews itself, then do I repair hither again."

So saying, the sorcerer drew a magic circle around the cave, and then immediately disappeared.

Twice seven days did Walter continue in this solitude, where his companions were his own terrifying thoughts, and his bitter repentance. The present was all desolate and dread; the future presented the image of a horrible deed, which he must perforce commit; while the past was empoisoned by the memory of his guilt.

Did he think on his former happy union with Brunhilda, her horrible image presented itself to his imagination with her lips defiled with dropping blood: or, did he call to mind the peaceful days he had passed with Swanhilda, he beheld her sorrowful spirit, with the shadows of her murdered children. Such were the horrors that attended him by day: those of night were still more dreadful, for then he beheld Brunhilda herself, who, wandering round the magic circle which she could not pass, called upon his name, till the cavern re-echoed the horrible sound.

"Walter, my beloved," cried she, wherefore dost thou avoid me? art thou not mine? for ever mine—mine here, and mine hereafter? And dost thou seek to murder me?—ah! Commit not a deed which hurls us both to perdition—thyself as well as me." In this manner did the horrible visitant torment him each night, and, even when she departed, robbed him of all repose.

The night of the new moon at length arrived, dark as the deed it was doomed to bring forth. The sorcerer entered the cavern; "Come," said he to Walter, "let us depart hence, the hour is now arrived:" and he forthwith conducted him in silence from the grave, to a coal-black steed, the sight of which recalled to Walter's remembrance the fatal night.

He then related to the old man Brunhilda's nocturnal visits, and anxiously enquired whether her apprehensions of eternal perdition would be fulfilled or not.

"Mortal eye," exclaimed the sorcerer, "may not pierce the dark secrets of another world, or penetrate the deep abyss that separates earth from heaven."

Walter hesitated to mount the steed.

"Be resolute," exclaimed his companion, "but this once is it granted to thee to make the trial, and, should thou fail now, nought can rescue thee from her power."

"What can be more horrible than she herself?—I am determined:" and he leaped on the horse, the sorcerer mounting also behind him.

Carried with a rapidity equal to that of the storm that sweeps across the plain, they in brief space arrived at Walter's castle. All the doors flew open at the bidding of his companion, and they speedily reached Brunhilda's, chamber, and stood beside her couch.

Reclining in a tranquil slumber; she reposed in all her native loveliness, every trace of horror had disappeared from her countenance; she looked so pure, meek and innocent that all the sweet hours of their endearments rushed to Walter's memory, like interceding angels pleading in her behalf. His unnerved hand could not take the dagger which the sorcerer presented to him.

"The blow must be struck even now:" said the latter, "shouldst thou delay but an hour, she will lie at day-break on thy bosom, sucking the warm life-drops from thy heart."

"Horrible! most horrible!" faultered the trembling Walter, and turning away his face, he thrust the dagger into her bosom, exclaiming: "I curse thee for ever!"—and the cold blood gushed upon his hand.

Opening her eyes once more, she cast a look of ghastly horror on her husband, and, in a hollow dying accent said:— "Thou too art doomed to perdition."

"Lay now thy hand upon her corse," said the sorcerer, "and swear the oath."—Walter did as commanded, saying:—"Never will I think of her with love, never recall her to mind intentionally, and, should her image recur to my mind involuntarily, so will I exclaim to it: be thou accursed."

"Thou hast now done every thing," returned the sorcerer;— restore her therefore to the earth, from which thou so foolishly recalled her; and be sure to recollect thy oath: for, shouldst thou forget it but once, she would return, and thou wouldst be inevitably lost. *Adieu*: we see each other no more."

Having uttered these words he quitted the apartment, and Walter also fled from this abode of horror, having first given directions that the corse should be speedily interred.

Again did the terrific Brunhilda repose within her grave; but her image continually haunted Walter's imagination, so that his existence was one continued martyrdom,[13] in which he continually struggled, to dismiss from his recollection the hideous phantoms of the past; yet, the stronger his effort to banish them, so much the more frequently and the more vividly did they return; as the night-wanderer, who is enticed by a fire-wisp[14] into quagmire or bog, sinks the deeper into his damp grave the more he struggles to escape.

His imagination seemed incapable of admitting any other image than that of Brunhilda: now he fancied he beheld her expiring, the blood streaming from her beautiful bosom: at others he saw the lovely bride of his youth, who reproached him with having disturbed the slumbers of her tomb: and to both he was compelled to utter the dreadful words, "I curse thee for ever."

The terrible imprecation was constantly passing his lips; yet was he in incessant terror lest he should forget it, or dream of her without being able to repeat it, and then, on awaking, find himself in her arms. Else would he recall her expiring words,

---

[13] Self-sacrifice
[14] Firefly

and, appalled at their terrific import, imagine that the doom of
his perdition was irrecoverably passed.

Whence should he fly from himself? or how erase from his
brain these images and forms of horror in the din[15] of combat,
in the tumult of war and its incessant pour of victory to defeat;
from the cry of anguish to the exultation of victory—in these he
hoped to find at least the relief of distraction: but here too he
was disappointed.

The giant fang of apprehension now seized him who had
never before known fear: each drop of blood that sprayed upon
him seemed the cold blood that had gushed from Brunhilda's
wound; each dying wretch that fell beside him looked like her,
when expiring, she exclaimed: "Thou too art doomed to
perdition," so that the aspect of death seemed more full of dread
to him than aught beside, and this unconquerable terror
compelled him to abandon the battle-field.

At length, after many a weary and fruitless wandering he
returned to his castle. Here all was deserted and silent, as if the
sword, or a still more deadly pestilence had laid every thing
waste: for the few inhabitants that still remained, and even
those servants who had once shewn themselves the most
attached, now fled from him, as though he had been branded
with the mark of Cain.[16]

With horror he perceived that, by uniting himself as he had
done with the dead, he had cut himself off from the living, who
refused to hold any intercourse with him. Often, when he stood
on the battlements of his castle, and looked down upon desolate
fields, he compared their present solitude with the lively activity
they were wont to exhibit, under the strict but benevolent
discipline of Swanhilda. He now felt that she alone could
reconcile him to life, but durst he hope that one, whom he had
so deeply agrieved, could pardon him, and receive him again?

Impatience at length got the better of fear; he sought
Swanhilda, and, with the deepest contrition, acknowledged his
complicated guilt; embracing her knees he beseeched her to
pardon him, and to return to his desolate castle, in order that it
might again become the abode of contentment and peace.

The pale form which she beheld at her feet, the shadow of
the lately blooming youth, touched Swanhilda. "Thy folly," said
she gently, "though it has caused me much sorrow, has never

---

[15] Sound

[16] In the Biblical book of Genesis, Cain is given a mark by God so that others
would not do harm to him for murdering his brother Abel

excited my resentment or my anger. But say, where are my children? To this dreadful interrogation the agonized father could for a while frame no reply: at length he was obliged to confess the dreadful truth.

"Then we are asundered for ever," returned Swanhilda; nor could all his tears or supplications prevail upon her to revoke the sentence she had given.

Stripped of his last earthly hope, bereft of his last consolation, and thereby rendered as poor as mortal can possibly be on this side of the grave, Walter returned homewards; when, as he was riding through the forest in the neighbourhood of his castle, absorbed in his gloomy meditations, the sudden sound of a horn roused him from his reverie.

Shortly after he saw appear a female figure clad in black, and mounted on a steed of the same colour: her attire was like that of a huntress, but, instead of a falcon she bore a raven on her hand; and she was attended by a gay troop of cavaliers and dames. The first salutations being passed, he found that she was proceeding the same road as himself; and, when she found that Walter's castle was close at hand, she requested that he would lodge her for that night, the evening being far advanced.

Most willingly did he comply with this request, since the appearance of the beautiful stranger had struck him greatly; so wonderfully did she resemble Swanhilda, except that her locks were brown, and her eye dark and full of fire. With a sumptuous banquet did he entertain his guests, whose mirth and songs enlivened the lately silent halls.

Three days did this revelry continue, and so exhilarating did it prove to Walter, that he seemed to have forgotten his sorrows and his fears; nor could he prevail upon himself to dismiss his visitors, dreading lest, on their departure, the castle would seem a hundred times more desolate than before, and his grief be proportionably increased.

At his earnest request, the stranger consented to stay seven days, and again another seven days. Without being requested, she took upon herself the superintendance of the household, which she regulated as discreetly and cheerfully as Swanhilda had been wont to do, so that the castle, which had so lately been the abode of melancholy and horror, became the residence of pleasure and festivity, and Walter's grief disappeared altogether in the midst of so much gaiety.

Daily did his attachment to the fair unknown increase; he even made her his confidante; and, one evening as they were walking together apart from any of her train, he related to her his melancholy and frightful history.

"My dear friend," returned she, as soon as he had finished his tale, "it ill beseems a man of thy discretion to afflict thyself, on account of all this. Thou hast awakened the dead from the sleep of the grave, and afterwards found,—what might have been anticipated, that the dead possess no sympathy with life.

"What then? thou wilt not commit this error a second time. Thou hast however murdered the being whom thou hadst thus recalled again into existence—but it was only in appearance, for thou couldst not deprive that of life, which properly had none. Thou hast too, lost a wife and two children: but, at your years, such a loss is most easily repaired. There are beauties who will gladly share your couch, and make you again a father.

"But you dread the reckoning of hereafter:—go, open the graves and ask the sleepers there whether that hereafter disturbs them."

In such manner would she frequently exhort and cheer Walter, and, so successful were her efforts, that, in a short time, his melancholy entirely disappeared. He now ventured to declare to the unknown the passion with which she had inspired him, nor did she refuse him her hand. Within seven days afterwards the nuptials were celebrated with the utmost magnificence: with the first dawn of day commenced the labours of those who were busied in preparing the festival; and, if the walls of the castle had often echoed before to the sounds of mirth and revelry, the very foundations now seemed to rock from the wild tumultuous uproar of unrestrained riot.

The wine streamed in abundance; the goblets circled incessantly: intemperance reached its utmost bounds, while shouts of laughter, almost resembling madness, burst from the numerous train belonging to the unknown. At length Walter, heated with wine and love, conducted his bride into the nuptial chamber: but, oh horror! scarcely had he clasped her in his arms, ere she transformed herself into a monstrous serpent, which, entwining him in its horrid folds, crushed him to death.

Flames crackled on every side of the apartment; in a few minutes after, the whole castle was enveloped in a blaze that consumed it entirely: while, as the walls fell in with a horrid crash, a voice exclaimed aloud—WAKE NOT THE DEAD.

ALEXANDER DUMAS
(1802-1870)

Introduction
The Vampire of the Carpathian Mountains

In this book's first edition, an English translation of this story was used that was printed in a 1849 volume of the *New Monthly Magazine* (the same magazine that published Polidori's "The Vampyre" in 1819). In that version "The Vampire of the Carpathian Mountains" ends rather abruptly and fails to contain a poem included in the original French version. I am sure that would be unacceptable to Alexander Dumas as it is for someone who strives to create the best anthologies possible. Here the complete original, translated as close as I could get it into the English language.

Also called "The Pale Lady," this story was published serially by Alexander Dumas in *Le Constitutionnel* during 1849 and was later included in his collection *Les Mille et un Fantômes* (One Thousand and One Ghosts). "The Vampire of the Carpathian Mountains" is the only vampire short story ever written by Alexander Dumas and it is still one of the best vampire stories for the first half of the nineteenth century. It is written in the first person singular voice of a young female whose virginity plays an important role in the story.

At first blush it would appear that it is also the first vampire story to take its setting in the haunted Carpathian Mountains. But the 1823 tri-volume anthology of German stories translated into English (*Popular Tales and Romances of the Northern Nations*), which includes "Wake Not the Dead" also contains "The Sorcerers," which starts on page 123 of Vol I. Although it is not a tale of vampirism, it is set in the Carpathian Mountains and makes passing reference to the white people who live there and feed off blood.

But the story at hand still presents a number of firsts in vampire lore. Dumas gives us a vampire with flaming eyes and one that can open a locked door as if the latches do not exist.

The Vampire of the Carpathian Mountains (1849)

I'M POLISH, BORN in Sandomierz, that is to say, in a country where legends become articles of faith. We believe in our family traditions as much, perhaps more, than the Gospel. Not one of our castles is without its ghost, not one of our cottages is without a familiar spirit. Among the rich as among the poor, in the castle as in the cottage, we recognize these principles as both an enemy and a friend. Sometimes, they are at odds with each other. So when there are mysterious noises in the hallways, terrible roars in the old towers, frightening tremors in the walls, from the cottage as well as the castle, gentlemen and farmers alike run to their churchs to seek the blessed cross or holy relics to ward off the demons that torment us.

But there are also two more principles that are the most terrible and fiercest, most implacable, which are still present today: tyranny and freedom.

The year 1825 witnessed a terrible war between Russia and Poland in which you'd think all the blood of a people is used up, as we sometimes experience in the case of family line dying out.

My father and two brothers were raised to despise the new Tzar. They had left our village to fight under the flag of Polish independence that seemed to always be struck down only to rise again.

One day I learned that my younger brother was killed. The next day I was told my other brother was wounded and near death. Finally, after a day during which I listened with terror to the sounds of cannons and guns and musketry that kept getting nearer and nearer, I saw my father return with 100 horsemen, which was all that remained of the 3000 men that used to be under his command.

He had shut us all up in our castle, intending to be buried under its ruins. My father, who feared nothing in life, trembled at the thought of my capture. But I could see that my father even now feared life itself because if he fell into the hands of his enemies it would mean slavery, dishonor, and shame for me.

My father chose 10 from among the 100 men who remained with him and called forth the steward and gave him all the gold and all the jewels that we had. Remembering that in the second uprising of Poland, my mother, then almost a child, had found a refuge in the Sahasten Monastery located in the middle of the Carpathian Mountains, he ordered the steward to take me there. He hoped the monastery would be no less hospitable to his daughter than it had been to his wife.

Despite the love my father had for me, it was not a long farewell. In all likelihood, the Russians were near the castle. There was no time to lose. In haste I dressed in a riding habit, which I used to wear while accompanying my brothers hunting. I saddled the horse at the stable. My father slipped his own guns, masterpieces of the Tula factory, into my holster. He embraced me and gave the order to start on our journey.

During the night and the next day, we traversed a distance of twenty leagues, or almost seventy miles, along the edges of one of those unnamed rivers that flow into the Vistula. This first stage of our trip put us out of reach of the Russians. Then, through the last rays of sunshine, we saw the snowy peaks of the Carpathian Mountains.

Towards the end of the next day, we reached the base of the mountains, and finally, on the morning of the third day, we began to ascend its rugged passes.

Our Carpathian Mountains do not resemble the mountains of your civilized West. All in nature that is strange and magnificent presents itself to the eye in its fullest majesty. The mountain peaks, which are frequently lost in the stormy skies, are always snow covered and contain immense pine forests. The lakes in the mountains are like a polished mirror, unfurrowed by any boat. Never has a fisherman's net disturbed their deep waters, which are sky blue. The human voice will be heard only occasionally, and the cries of wild animals will astonish and far surpass any scary tale about such cries that man has heard.

For many miles we travelled through the dark vaults of the woods, seeing and hearing unexpected wonders revealed to us at every step and that alternated in our minds from astonishment to admiration. There was danger everywhere, and consisted of a thousand different hazards, but there was no time to be afraid. Sometimes the steps of our horses were impinged by the melting of ice, which, crashing from rock to rock, suddenly invaded the narrow path we followed. It was a path marked by the passage of the beast and the hunter who pursued it. Sometimes the trees were compromised by the loose soil and fell with a tremendous crash as though an earthquake, or a tornado that you were about to be caught up into the middle of; while in the dark clouds lightning writhed like a fiery serpent.

After the alpine peaks, after the primeval forests, we entered the upper regions of the mountains. Where you once had boundless woods, now you had endless steppes. Where you once felt you were in a sea with its waves and storms, you now were presented with arid savannas and rocky outcroppings where the view melded together on a boundless horizon. At this point in the journey it was no longer terror that seized us, but rather sadness, a broad and deep melancholy from which nothing can distract because the whole aspect of the landscape, as far as your eye could see, was always the same. When we ascended, we were confronted with twenty more similar rocky outcroppings and searched in vain for a way out. We were lost and isolated in the wilderness and felt alone in nature. Our melancholy became desolation. Walking seemed to have become futile because it would lead to nothing. For hours we did not experience village or castle or cottage. There was no trace of human habitation across the bleak landscape.

We came across a small, reedless lake void of surrounding bushes, sleeping at the bottom of a ravine, as if another Dead Sea. It blocked the road with its green waters. On our approach a waterfowl gave off a prolonged and discordant shout. We had to take a detour and climbed the hill that was before us, which then led down into another valley, causing us to climb another hill to get back out. This monotony lasted across the chain of mountains, as if never ending.

But the monotony did end once we made a bend to the south, where there appeared a grandiose landscape. We had never seen a mountain look more picturesque or more richly appointed with its plumed forests and inlaid streams. With shade and water, life was surely flourishing. Many streams were snaking the side of the mountain. Finally, through the last rays of the sun and a band of white birds, there appeared village houses that seemed to have been grouped to secure against a night attack. The new signs of life brought danger, not danger as we had experience in the first band of mountains that we crossed where there were bears and wolves to be feared, but hordes of Moldavian brigands that were ready to fight.

Regardless, we approached. Ten days' journey had passed without incident or accident. We could already see the summit of Mount Pion, which protrudes like the tallest head in this family of mountain giants, on the southern side of which is located the Sahasten Monastery. Three more days and we had finally arrived.

It was the end of July. The day was hot. It was with much pleasure when four o'clock came and we began to enjoy the first chills of evening. We passed the ruined towers of Niantzo and descended to a plain that we began to see through the opening of the mountains. Our eyes led us to follow the course of Bistriza, its shoreline dotted with red affrines and bluebells with large white flowers. We carefully made our way down a precipice, which was carved toward the river, through which there flowed a shallow torrent of water. Our horses barely had enough space to walk two abreast.

Our guide led us on his horse, singing a monotone song. I listened to his words with a singular interest. The singer was also a poet. As for the melody, it was like those the mountain men sing. It was enough to make one wild in all its sadness and its dark simplicity.

> In the Stavila marshes
> Where so much warrior blood has been spilled
> See this slain human form?
> He is not an Illyrian hero but a fierce bandit
> Who, betrayed gentle Marie
> And slew, misled, razed by fire.
>
> A bullet crossed the robber's heart
> A yatagan sticks in his throat.
> But for three days, mysteriously,
> Under the lone pine tree,
> His warm blood has watered the earth
> Blackening the Origan's pale features.
>
> His blue eyes no longer will shine
> All flee him, a curse upon those
> Who come near him in the fen.
> He's a vampire! The wild woolf shuns the evil remains,
> The unclean vulture has flown away.[1]

---

[1] Poem by Prosper Mérimée (1803-1870) in his collection *La Guzla*

Suddenly the detonation of a gun was heard. A bullet whistled through the air. The song stopped and the guide was shot to death. He rolled to the bottom of the precipice while his horse quivered in place, extending his head in an intelligent way toward the bottom of the abyss where his master lay.

At the same time, a great shout went up, and we saw a formation of thirty bandits on the flanks of the mountain. We were completely surrounded.

Everyone grabbed their guns. Although taken by surprise, those who accompanied me were old soldiers and accustomed to gunfire. They did not let themselves be intimidated and returned fire against the bandits. As for me, I seized a gun and feeling the disadvantage of my position, shouted: "Forward!" and spurred my horse, who sped off in the direction of the plain.

But we had to deal with the mountain, leaping from rock to rock, as though demons of the abyss jumping fire, and always keeping our side to the position the bandits had taken.

Moreover, the bandits' attack was well planned. In a place where the road widened, where the mountain was flat, a young man was waiting for us along with a dozen bandits on horseback. They put their horses to a gallop and blocked our escape from the front. Still other bandits continued to roll around to the left flank. Our retreat had been cut off. We were surrounded on all sides.

The situation was dire. Yet I was accustomed to war scenes from my early childhood. I took it all in without losing any detail.

The bandits were dressed in sheepskins and wore round hats crowned with huge flowers, like Hungarians. At the waist each wore a curved sword and a pair of holstered pistols. In the hands of the footmen were long Turkish guns. After shooting them in the air they waved them, shouting wildly as they encircled us.

Their leader was a young man of twenty-two. He had a pale complexion, large black eyes and curly hair that fell to his shoulders. He wore a Moldavian habit. Around his waist was a fur-trimmed belt with a sash of gold-colored silk. A curved sword shone in his hand. There were four pistols in his belt. During the battle, he shouted inarticulate words that seemed not to belong to any human language, yet his men obeyed his shouts. In doing so the bandits on foot kept firing with their long Turkish muskets and then would throw themselves on the ground while reloading to avoid the discharges of our soldiers. With deft precision they managed to shoot those who were still standing and finish off the wounded. In doing so they changed the combat to a slaughter.

I saw the bandits kill, one after the other, two thirds of my defenders. The four that remained, huddled around me, shaking. They weren't about to ask any favors from the bandit leader that they knew they were certain not to get. The remaining men were thinking of only one thing, to end their lives if it meant saving me.

Then the young chief uttered a cry more expressive than any other, extending the tip of his sword to us. Undoubtedly this order was to shoot us all at once. One of the bandits lowered his weapon in the same way. I realized that our last hour had come. I raised my eyes and hands to heaven with a last prayer, and waited for death.

In that moment I saw a young man above us. He stopped on top of a large rock that overlooked the entire scene. He stood there like a statue on a pedestal. Extending one hand toward the battlefield, he uttered the word: "Enough."

Toward that voice all eyes rose, each seemed to obey the new master. Except when one bandit put his rifle back to his shoulder, it accidentally fired.

One of our men cried out, the round had broken his left arm.

The bandit who shot him turned to the man who had been wounded and was now lying in pain on the ground. Lightning shone above our heads and frightened the horse of the bandit, which reared back and in coming down blugeoned the head of the wounded solider on the ground.

So many different emotions ran through me that I fainted away.

When I came to, I was lying on the grass, my head resting on the lap of the man who had rescued us. I saw his pallid hand, covered with rings, around my waist. While standing in front of me, arms folded, his sword under one of them, stood the young Moldavian leader who had led the attack against us.

"Kostaki," said the one who supported me, in excellent French and in a tone of authority, "you will at once take your men and leave the care of this young woman to me."

"My brother, my brother," answered the one to whom these words were addressed and who seemed to have difficulty restraining himself, "my brother, do not try my patience. I leave you the castle and you leave me the forest. In the castle you are the master, but here I am all-powerful. Here, a mere word should force you to obey me."

"Kostaki, I am the eldest. I am the master everywhere; in the forest as in the castle, there as here. Oh! In my veins run the blood of the Brankovans,[2] just like you—royal blood. We are used to being in command."

"Then you, Gregoriska, order your servants and I will order my soldiers."

"Your soldiers are brigands,[3] Kostaki ... brigands I will hang from the battlements of the castle if they do not obey me now!"

"Well! Try and order them then and see if they obey."

Whoever was behind me took my head off his knee and gently placed it on a stone. I followed his gaze anxiously. I could see the same young man who had fallen, so to speak, out of the sky in the middle of the fray.

Gregoriska was a young man of twenty-four years, tall, with big blue eyes in which he conveyed a resolution and singular firmness. His long blond hair, an indicator of the Slavic race, fell on his shoulders like that of the Archangel Michael, framing his fresh young cheeks, his lips were identified by a contemptuous smile, like a double row of pearls. His look was of an eagle crossed with lightning. He was dressed in a sort of black velvet tunic. A little cap like that of Raphael,[4] decorated with an eagle feather, covered his head. He wore tights and embroidered boots. Around his waist was a belt that carried a hunting knife. Over his shoulder was slung a small double-barreled rifle, identical to the ones the bandits were able to use with such accuracy.

He stretched out his hand and it seemed to command his brother. He spoke a few words in the Moldavian language. These words seemed to make a deep impression on the bandits.

So, in the same language, the young chief spoke in turn, and I guessed that his words were mingled with threats and imprecations. But during this long speech, Gregoriska, the elder of the two brothers did not answer a word.

The bandits bowed.

He gestured and the bandits lined up behind us.

Gregoriska, resuming the French language said, "This woman will not go to the cave, but to the castle."

---

[2] The Brancovan family was considered a heroic and noble family throughout Romania and the Carpathian Mountains

[3] Gangs that rob people passing through wooded areas

[4] Perhaps reference to famous portrait of Raffaello Sanzio da Urbino (1483-1520), Renaissance painter, which shows him wearing a dark, flat cap

"I find her beautiful and I won her by conquest. I want her." And saying these words, Kostaki took me up in his arms.

"Stop! This woman will be conducted to the castle and given to the care of my mother. I will not leave until I am assured of this," said my protector.

"My horse!" cried Kostaki in the Moldavian language.

Ten bandits hastened to obey their master and brought the horse he wanted.

Gregoriska looked around, grabbed the bridle of a horse without a rider, and jumped on its back without touching the stirrups.

Kostaki did the same, landing almost as lightly into the saddle as did his brother. He pulled me up and ordered me to hold on. He commanded the horse into a gallop.

Gregoriska's horse seemed to have received the same impulse. Soon the two horses were side-by-side.

It was a curious thing to see these two riders flying side-by-side, dark, silent. They rode without seeming to look. The desperate race carried us through the woods, over rocks and along dangerous precipices. When I turned my head back I could see the beautiful eyes of Gregoriska fixed on mine. At other times, when Kostaki glanced back at me, I saw nothing but his dark eyes that devoured me. I lowered my eyelids in vain. Through my veil I could still see that stabbing look that penetrated to the bottom of my heart and pierced it. Then a strange hallucination took hold of me. I felt as though I were the woman carried by the horse and specter rider in the ballad Lenore penned by Bürger. Then suddenly the horse stopped. The terror was so acute that I feared to open my eyes. I was convinced I was going to see around us broken crosses and opened tombs.

What I saw was little happier. It was the inner courtyard of a Moldavian castle, built in the fourteenth century.

Kostaki let me slide down his arms onto the ground and immediately dismounted near me.

On seeing the young brothers and me—the stranger—the servants ran to us. Although they showed affection to both Kostaki and Gregoriska. It was clear that the deepest respects were for Gregoriska. He truly was the master of the castle, as he had said.

Gregoriska gave two women an order in Moldavian and motioned for me to follow them with his hand.

There was so much care reflected in his eyes that I did not hesitate to follow the servants. I was taken inside and up a curving staircase, where, in niches along the wall, stood larger than life statues of three ancient Brankovan men. Five minutes later, I was in a large square room that was sparsely appointed. It contained a couch covered in a sheet of green baize[5] that obviously served as a seat during the day and a bed at night. Scattered about were five or six large oak chairs, a wide chest, and in one corner of the room a large and beautiful canopy that had once covered the last row of stalls or pews in a church.

As for curtains on the windows, or ones to surround the makeshift bed, there were none.

I had not been long in the room when my luggage trunks were brought to me that must have been carried to the castle by the bandits. The women servants offered me their services, but I kindly declined. When they left I began unpacking my trunks into the closet. When I swung open the doors I was surprised to find lavish and exprensive dresses that were in line with those of my captors. I simply could not consider wearing such fine garments. After I had unpacked, I heard a gentle knock at my door.

"Come in," I said in French, as it is the closest I know to the Polish language or Moldavian.

Gregoriska entered.

"Ah! madam, I am glad that you speak French."

"And I, sir," I replied, "am pleased to speak the language, as it allowed me a chance to enjoy your generous kindness. This is the language in which you defended me against the designs of your brother and it is in this language that I offer you the expression of my sincere gratitude."

"Thank you, madam. It is quite natural that I intercede when I come upon a woman in such a position as I found you. I was hunting in the mountains when I heard the shots. I realized that it was an armed robbery, and I walked on fire, as they say in military terms. I arrived in time, thank God, but will you tell me, madam, by what chance a woman of your distinction had ventured into our mountains?"

"I am Polish, sir," I replied, "my two brothers were killed in the war against Russia. When I fled my home on horseback I left my father who was ready to defend against the enemy. He has probably joined my brothers in eternity. On fleeing the massacre, I was to seek refuge in the monastery of Sahastru, where my mother in her youth, and in similar circumstances, found a safe haven.

---

[5] Wool material with felt-like texture

"If you are an enemy of the Russians, so much the better," said the young man, "as you will be a powerful ally to the castle. We need every bit of strength to fight against them. Because I now know who you are, madam, know that you are in the royal house of the Brankovans.

I bowed.

"My mother is the last princess of the Brankovans and the last descendant of the illustrious leader that killed Demetrius Cantimir,[6] one of those wretched courtiers of Peter the Great. My mother married my father, Serban Voivode, who was a prince but from a less illustrious race. My father was raised in Vienna where he was able to enjoy the benefits of high society. Growing up, he resolved to make me a European. We travelled in France, Italy, Spain and Germany.

"My mother, however, harbors much guilt. And what I am about to relay to you is for our salvation. For this to happen it is necessary that you know us well. Very soon you will appreciate the causes of this revelation. Please let me continue.

"When my father was off on one of his many European trips with me, my mother had had an illicit relationship with the chief of the partisans,[7] as we call them in the mountains," said Gregoriska smiling. "These were the common, mixed breed men who attacked you. As I said, my mother had the relationship with Count Giordaki Koproli—half Greek, half Moldavian. He boldly wrote to my father, telling him everything and asked him to divorce my mother. How could she, a Brankovan, remain the wife of a man who was from day to day becoming more alien to his country. Alas! my father did not need to consent to this strange request. My father suddenly died from an aneurysm of which he had suffered for a long time. It was I who received the letter.

"I had nothing to do but give well wishes for the happiness of my mother. So I sent a letter back to the count telling him she was now a widow. In the same letter I requested permission to continue my travels, which was granted. My future was before me in France and Germany, not before a man who likely hated me and that I could not love, that is to say, the new husband of my mother.

---

[6] Twice the ruler of Moldavia, Demetrius Cantimir (1673-1723) and served as advisor to Peter the Great (1672-1725) ruler of the Russian empire
[7] Guerilla fighters

"To my amazement, only a short time thereafter, I heard that Count Giordaki Koproli had been murdered by Cossacks[8] loyal to my recently deceased father. I hurried back to my mother in this castle to be with her at such a time. Although we had never been very close, I was her son. When I arrived I found a young man that I first took to be a foreigner, but soon realized was my half brother. It was Kostaki, the son of adultery, legitimized only by the second marriage of my mother. Kostaki, the indomitable creature you saw, whose passions are his only law and who knows nothing sacred in this world except our mother. He obeys me only like a tamed tiger, but with a roar outside the castle he upholds with the vague hope of devouring me one day. Inside the castle, the power remains with that of the Brankovan family. I'm still the master. But outside these walls, after Kostaki has spent time in the countryside, he becomes the wild child of the woods and mountains that wants to do everything under his own iron will. Why did he have his men surrender today? I do not know, an old habit, perhaps, or a last remnant of respect to me. But I would not hazard that it will not happen a second time. Stay here. Do not leave this room, or take a step out of the castle. Within these walls I will defend you with my life; without, I cannot guarantee your safety."

"Am I unable, then, according to the wishes of my father, to continue my journey to the Sahastru Monastery?"

"If you must, I will go with you – but we must stay on the road. Even then the journey will be very dangerous."

"What should I do then?"

"Stay here for a time and enjoy your surroundings. Suppose you fall into another den of bandits? Your courage alone cannot save you. My mother, despite her preference for Kostaki, the son of her lover, is kind and generous. Moreover, she is a Brankovan, that is to say, a real princess. She will defend you from the brutal passions of Kostaki. Put yourself under her protection, you will love it. Besides," he looked at me with an indefinable expression, "who could lay eyes on you and not love you? Come now to the dinning room, where she is expecting us. Do not show embarrassment or mistrust; speak Polish. Nobody knows the language here. I will translate your words to my mother, and, rest assured, I will not put words in your mouth. Above all, not a word about what I have revealed to you. Do not doubt what you have heard. You still do not know the cunning and conniving of Kostaki."

---

[8] Skilled horsemen trained as fighters

I followed him into the stairway where the burning torches resembled iron hands coming out of the walls. It was obvious that it was for me that they had lit so many as I walked under their unusual illumination. Soon we arrived at the dining room. When Gregoriska opened the door, he uttered a word in Moldavian that I have since learned means: the stranger. A tall woman walked up to us. It was the princess.

She wore her gray hair in a braid. Atop it was a little cap of black marten, surmounted by a feather plume, evidence of her royal origin. She wore a kind of golden tunic cloth, which was jeweled, and made of a Turkish fabric trimmed with fur like that of the cap. She was holding an amber rosary.[9] She rolled it quickly between her fingers.

Beside her was Kostaki, dressed in the majestic and splendid clothing of a Magyar noble,[10] which seemed even stranger than the outfit of his mother. The suit coat was green velvet with wide sleeves falling below the knee. He wore red cashmere pants and Moroccan slippers embroidered with gold. His head was uncovered and his long black hair fell across his bare neck, and shown off the background of a white silk shirt that he wore under the suit coat.

He greeted me awkwardly, and uttered in Moldavian some words that remained unintelligible to me.

"You can speak French, my brother," said Gregoriska. "Madame is Polish, and she can make out the language."

So Kostaki pronounced, in French, some words that were almost as unintelligible to me as those he had spoken in Moldavian. But the mother, quickly extending her arms and saying a quick word, interrupted his speaking. It was obvious to me that she was to do the talking.

Then she began in Moldavian a welcome speech, in which, given her facial expressions, was easy way to understand. She showed me the table and offered me a seat next to her, but first gestured toward the whole castle, as if to say I was their welcomed guest. Then she crossed herself and began a prayer.

Each took their place at the table. Gregoriska sat next to me. Because I was a guest, I was given the place of honor at the table. Kostaki sat next to his mother.

Gregoriska wore a Hungarian coat like his brother, only it was red velvet. His pants were blue cashmere. A beautiful

---

[9] String of beads used for counting prayers
[10] Highbred group of people who lived primarily in Hungary and dressed flamboyantly

decoration hung from his neck. It was the nichan of the Sultan Mahmud.[11]

The rest of those in the castle supped at the same time, the positioning of the tables made clear whether they were friends or servants.

Supper was quiet. Not once did Kostaki speak to me. His brother, when he spoke, always talked to me in French. This was a language understood by the brothers. As for the princess, she did not understand French, but always spoke under a tone of elegance and gravity. Gregoriska was right, she was a real princess.

After supper, Gregoriska approached his mother. He explained in the Moldavian language that he needed to be alone, and further that I needed to rest after the emotions of the day. She made a sign of approval, held my hand, kissed my forehead as if I were her daughter, and wished me a good night in her castle.

Gregoriska had not lied. I longed for a moment of solitude. I thanked the princess, who took me to the door. There, I said goodnight to her two sons, and returned to my room guided by the same two women who had escorted me earlier in the day.

The sofa became a bed. This was the only change. I thanked the women. They were very respectful, which indicated that they had orders to obey me in all things.

I surveyed the huge room, with my light illuminating only the parts in which I wandered, without ever being able to enlighten all of it at once. The singular play of light established a struggle between the light of my candle and the moonlight passing by my curtainless window.

In addition to the door through which I entered and that overlooked the stairs, two other doors opened onto my room. But there were huge locks placed on them, which gave me reassurance.

I opened my window and looked out onto a precipice that could not be scaled. I understood now that Gregoriska had given me this room as a conscious choice.

Finally, returning to my sofa, I found on my bedside table a small folded note. I opened it and read in Polish:

---

[11] Diamond and emerald necklace worn by religious Arabs as in honor of Muhammad (570-632)

Sleep tight, you have nothing to fear as long as you remain in the castle.

/s/Gregoriska

I followed the advice that was given me. Fatigue outweighing my concerns, I went to bed and fell asleep. From that moment I was established in the castle, and, as from that moment began the drama that I'm going to tell you.

The next day Kostaki told me he loved me with all the nuances of his character. In his mind I would belong to him and no other. He said he would kill me rather than allow me to belong to any other man. Gregoriska, on the other hand, said nothing about his feelings for me, but paid me the utmost care and attention. All the resources of his brilliant education, all the memories of a youth spent in the noblest courts of Europe were used to please me. Alas! The very sound of his voice caressed my soul and mere glance of his eyes penetrated my heart.

After three months Kostaki had told me a hundred times that he loved me, and I hated him. Meanwhile, Gregoriska had not said a single word of affection to me, yet I felt that when that time came, I would be all his.

Kostaki had renounced his races throughout the mountains. He never left the castle. In his place he appointed a kind of lieutenant, who, from time to time came to receive his orders and then quickly disappeared.

Smerande, the princess, extended to me a deep friendship, but the way she expressed it often frightened me. She visibly protected Kostaki, and seemed to be more jealous of Gregoriska than Kostaki was himself. But as she understood neither Polish nor French, and I did not understand Moldavian, she could not comprehend the urgent requests Kostaki was always speaking for my affections. She had, however, learned to say three words in French, which she kept telling me whenever her lips rested on my forehead – "Kostaki love Hedwig."

One day I learned that the four men who had survived the battle with me were leaving for Poland. They gave me their word that one of them would, within three months, give me news of my father. One of them appeared, in fact, one morning. Our castle was taken, burned and razed, and my father had been killed defending it.

I was now alone in the world.

Kostaki redoubled his efforts and Smerande her tenderness, but I hid behind the mourning for my father to fend them off. Kostaki insisted that I needed comforting, saying that the more I was isolated, the more I needed support. His mother insisted also.

Gregoriska told me that the persuasive power of the Moldavians is great when they seek to have people understand their feelings. He himself was a living example. It was impossible that he did not love me, and yet, if you had asked me what proof I had of this certainty, it would have been impossible for me say. No one in the castle had seen his hand touching mine, his eyes searching mine. Jealousy alone could empower Kostaki in this rivalry, as my love alone could empower me.

However, I admit, this power Gregoriska had over me, worried me. I certainly thought he loved me, but it was not enough. I needed to be convinced. When one evening, as I had just returned to my room, I heard a soft knock at the door. From the gentle rapping I guessed that it was a friend. I approached and asked who was there.

"Gregoriska," replied a voice in a tone that told me I was in danger.

"What do you want?" I asked, trembling.

"If you trust me," said Gregoriska, "if you believe me a man of honor, grant me my request."

"What is it?"

"Turn off the light, as if you were in bed, and in half an hour open your door."

"Come back in half an hour was my only answer." I turned off my light and waited. My heart beat violently as I realized that this was serious.

The half-hour passed, and I heard a knock even more slowly than the first time. While he was knocking I undid the bolts so he only had to open the door. Gregoriska entered. I pushed the door closed behind him, and engaged the locks. He remained silent and motionless, forcing me to stand there in awkward silence. Then, when he was assured that no pressing danger was threatening us, he took me in the middle of the vast room, and feeling me quiver such that I could not stand, he fetched me a chair.

I sat, or rather collapsed, on it. "Oh! my God!" I said, "what is the matter and why are you taking so many precautions?"

"Because my life, which would be nothing without you, may depend on the conversation we're about to have."

I took his hand, terrified.

He lifted it to his lips while looking at me, and asked forgiveness for such audacity.

I looked down.

"I love you," he told me in his melodious voice like a song. "Do you love me?"

"Yes," I replied.

"Would you be willing to be my wife?"

"Yes."

He passed his hand over his forehead, taking a deep sigh of relief.

"So you will not refuse to follow me?"

"I will follow you everywhere!"

"As you know," he continued, "we cannot be happy by fleeing."

"Oh yes," I cried, "running away would make me happy."

"Silence!" he said, wincing. "Silence!"

"You're right." And I approached him trembling.

"This is what I did," he told me, "this is what I have kept so long inside without confessing. I love you. That's what I wanted, once sure of your love, that nothing could oppose our union. I'm rich, Hedwig, immensely rich, but in the manner of the Moldavian lords: - rich in land, cattle, serfs.[12] Well! I have changed that. I have just sold to the Hango Monastery a substantial amount of land and cattle. They gave me three hundred thousand jewels, a hundred thousand gold francs and the rest in Vienna bills of exchange. Will this be enough?"

I took his hand. "Your love would have been enough for me, Gregoriska."

"Tomorrow I go to the Hango Monastery to make my final arrangements with those in charge. My horses will be ready at nine o'clock tomorrow. They will be hidden one hundred paces from the castle. After supper, just as you did today, extinguish the light in your room. I will join you gain. But tomorrow, instead of me leaving alone, you follow. We will head for the countryside. Outside we will find our horses. We will arrive the day after tomorrow. The journey is about thirty miles.

"I cannot wait for tomorrow!"

"Dear Hedwig!" Gregoriska pressed me against his heart - our lips met. Oh! he said he was a man of honor, but he knew well, if I did not belong to him in body yet, I belonged to his soul.

The night passed without my being able to sleep. I saw myself fleeing with Gregoriska, but suddenly Kostaki was chasing us and it turned into a terrible race that was frightening and death defying. From the back of the horse I hugged

---

[12] Indentured field servants

Gergoriska tighter and it at once turned into a sweet and lovely hug and I was no longer afraid.

Morning came. I went down to breakfast. It seemed to me there was something even darker than usual in how Kostaki greeted me at the table. His smile was threatening. As for Princess Smerande, she acted as she always did toward me. Afterwards Gregoriska ordered his horses to be readied. Kostaki did not seem to pay any attention.

About eleven o'clock Gregoriska greeted us and said that he would return for dinner but he did not know the exact time. So he politely asked his mother not to wait for him to eat. Then, turning to me, he asked me to accept his apology also.

The eye of his brother followed him until he left the room, and I saw spring from that very eye a flash of hatred. I shuddered.

The entire day I was in a horrible trance. I had not confided our plans to anyone, barely even in my prayers—if I dared to talk to God—yet it felt like everyone knew our plans. Each gaze that was fixed on me was as though it could see to the bottom of my heart.

Dinner was torture: dark and silent, Kostaki rarely spoke, and the two or three times he did, he would speak Moldavian to his mother. His voice startled me each time.

When I got up to go back to my room, Princess Smerande, as usual, kissed me. In doing so, she told me again the sentence in French that I hated: "Kostaki love Hedwig!"

The phrase haunted me as a threat. Once in my room it seemed a fatal voice whispered in my ear: "Kostaki love Hedwig!" But the love of Kostaki, Gregoriska had told me, was death.

About seven o'clock in the evening, as the day began to wane, I saw Kostaki across the yard from my window. He turned to look at me, but I drew back so he could not see me.

I became even more worried because the position of my window allowed me to track him at such a distance that I realized there was a possibility he was heading toward the stables. I locked my door and ran into the next room, where I could see from another window what he was doing. As I suspected, he went to the stables. There he saddled his favorite horse with his own hands and with the care of a man who attaches great importance to details. He wore the same costume in which he had appeared to me the first time. For a weapon he carried his sword.

Once his horse was saddled, he glanced again at the window of my room. Then, not seeing me, he sprang into the saddle and exited through the same stable door through which he entered. He galloped off in the direction of the Hango Monastery.

Then my heart sank, a fatal presentiment told me that Kostaki was going to meet his brother. I stood at the window as long as I could. I could distinguish the road, which at one mile from the castle, took a turn and got lost in the start of the forest. Night descended while I stood there and the road eventually faded altogether from my sight. Finally my concern, by its very excess, gave me my strength, and, as it was obviously in the room downstairs that I would hear the first news of either of the two brothers, I descended.

My first sight was of Pricess Smerande. Her face was still and she gave off no apprehension. She gave orders for the usual dinner and wished that the two brothers were in their usual places at the table.

I dared not ask anyone where they were. Moreover, who could I ask? Nobody in the castle, except Kostaki and Gregoriska, could speak my language.

All was quiet. At the slightest sound, I trembled.

Nine o'clock is when we usually sat down for dinner. It was half past eight. I followed the minute hand of the large clock as though it were a slowly walking traveler.

The traveler crossed the distance that separated the halfway point from the quarter point. The clock rang out at the quarter. The vibration sounded dark and sad - and then the traveler resumed its silent walk with regularity and slowness.

A few minutes before nine o'clock, I thought I heard the gallop of a horse in the yard. Princess Smerande heard it too, as she turned her head towards the window, but the night air was too thick for her to see.

Oh! if she had looked at me at that moment she would have guessed what was going on in my mind. We had only heard the trot of a single horse - and it was quite simple. I knew that only one had returned.

But which one?

Footsteps sounded in the hall. The steps were slow and weighed on my heart. The door opened. I saw, coming out from the darkness, a shadow. The shadow paused at the door. My heart stopped.

The shadow stepped forward, and, as he walked into the circle of light, I breathed. I recognized Gregoriska, but he was pale as death and I sensed that something terrible had happened.

"Is that you, Kostaki?" asked Princess Smerande.

"No, my mother," Gregoriska replied in a low voice.

"Ah! it is you," she said. "When should your mother expect him?"

"Mother," said Gregoriska, casting a glance at the clock, "it is only nine o'clock."

At the same time, the clock struck.

"That's true," said Princess Smerande. "Where is your brother?"

I thought to myself that it was the same question God issued Cain.

Gregoriska gave no reply.

"Nobody has seen Kostaki?" asked Princess Smerande.

The butler spoke up. "About seven o'clock," he said, "the count was at the stables. He saddled his horse himself and went on the road to Hango."

At this moment, my eyes met the eyes of Gregoriska. I do not know if it was real or a hallucination, but it seemed he had a drop of blood on his forehead. I slowly carried my finger to my own forehead, indicating where I thought I saw this spot. Gregoriska understood me, and he took his handkerchief and wiped the area.

"Yes, yes," murmured Princess Smerande, "he could meet a bear or a wolf. A mother is waiting for her child. Where have you left him, Gregoriska?"

"My mother," Gregoriska replied in a trembling voice, "I can assure you that my brother and I did not go out together."

"That's right!" Princess Smerande said. "Come to the table and close the doors. Those who are outside the castle will remain so."

The first two orders were carried out to the letter. Princess Smerande took her place, Gregoriska sat to her right, and me on the left. Then the servants went out to do the third, which is to say, close the castle gates.

At this moment we heard a loud noise in the yard, and a very scared valet rushed into the room saying, "Princess, the Count's horse just returned to the court alone, and is covered in blood."

"Oh!" gasped Princess Smerande who now stood pale and menacing, "this is how the horse of his father returned one night."

I glanced at Gregoriska: he was no longer pale. He was livid.

Indeed, the horse of Kostaki's father had come home one night covered with blood. An hour later, the servants had found and reported his body was covered in wounds.

Princess Smerande took a torch from the hands of one of the servants and dashed into the yard.

The horse was terrified. Three or four servants united their efforts to try and appease him. Princess Smerande approached the animal, looked at the blood that stained his saddle and saw an injury to the top of his forehead.

"Kostaki was killed face-to-face," she said, "in a duel with one enemy. Search for his body. Later we will seek his murderer."

As the horse was led into the stables, the servants rushed through the gates into the night. We saw their torches wander across the countryside and into the forest, as if fireflies flickering among the plains of Nice and Pisa on a beautiful summer evening.

Princess Smerande appeared convinced that the search would not take long. Standing at the door, not a tear flowed from the eyes of the desolate mother, and yet they appeared full of despair. Gregoriska stood behind her, and I behind Gregoriska. He normally would have offered me his arm, but he dared not.

After a quarter of an hour or so, we saw a torch reappear along the path, then two, then all of them. Only this time, instead of being scattered around the countryside, they were massed at a common center. We could soon see that the common center held a litter and a man was lying on it.

The funeral procession moved slowly, but it progressed. After ten minutes it was at the door. The living mother who was waiting for the dead son, said nothing. Instead she motioned that that the body should be taken inside. She followed them and we followed her. We soon reached the great hall in which the body was laid.

Making a gesture of supreme majesty, Princess Smerande approached the corpse. She knelt down before him, her parted hair making a veil over his face. She gazed long into his dry eyes. Then, opening his Moldavian outfit, spread the blood stained shirt.

The puncture wound was on the right side of the chest. It had to have been inflicted by a two-edged blade since the wound showed cutting on both sides. I remembered having seen the same day, the long hunting knife that served as the bayonet on Gregoriska's rifle. It also was a two-edged blade.

Princess Smerande asked for water, into which she dipper her handkerchief and then washed the wound. A fresh and pure blood came blushing it.

The event I saw happening before me was both sublime and terrible at the same time: the spacious room, smoky by resin torches; the barbaric faces, bright eyed with ferocity; the strange costumes, the mother who was calculating how long it had taken her son to die in view of the still warm blood; the silence, broken only by the sobs of those brigands of which Kostaki was the chief; I repeat, was both sublime and terrible to behold.

Princess Smerande finally put her lips to her son, then rising, threw back the long braids of her white hair. "Gregoriska!"

Gregoriska started. He shook his head in his weakened state. "My mother," he replied.

"Come here, my son, listen to me."

Gregoriska obeyed. He was trembling, but he obeyed.

As he approached the body, the blood began to flow more freely from the wound. Fortunately, Princess Smerande had looked to the side. In her mind it became apparent who was the murderer.

"Gregoriska, she said, "I know that you and Kostaki did not love each other. I know you have different blood by your fathers, but by your mother, you were both Brankovan. I know you are a man of the western cities, and Kostaki was a child of the eastern mountains, but by the womb that bore you both, you are brothers. Gregoriska, I want to know if you will bring my son's murderer to me or if I will cry alone?"

"Name me the murderer of my brother, madam, and I swear he will brought before you by one o'clock, or I will cease to live."

"Swear always Gregoriska, swear under penalty of my curse. Do you hear, my son? Swear that the murderer will die – that you will not leave one stone of this house unturned even if it his mother, his children, his brothers, his wife or girlfriend – that they will die by your hand. Swear, and by swearing call upon your head the wrath of heaven if you fail to carry out this sacred oath. If you fail to carry out this sacred oath, submit to the misery, the execration of your friends, and your mother's curse!"

Gregoriska stretched his hand over the corpse. "I swear that the murderer will die!"

Perhaps only the dead and I could understand the true meaning of this strange oath. At that moment I saw, or thought I saw, a terrible thing. The eyes of the corpse reopened. Its fixing gaze clung to me more than when he was alive, and I felt as if those eyes were palpable, hot irons burning circles into my heart. It was more than I could bear, and I fainted.

When I awoke, I was in my room, lying on my bed watching one of two women near me. I asked where was Princess Smerande and was told she was watching over the body of her son.

I asked where was Gregoriska. They told me he was at the monastery of Hango. How could our secret have been leaked? Was not Kostaki dead? The question of marriage was uncertain. How could I marry someone who killed his brother?

Three days and three nights passed in my room. I had strange dreams. In my sleep I always saw the eyes of the dead face. It was a horrible sight. On the third day was scheduled the burial of Kostaki. That morning the servants brought me a full outfit to wear, compliments of the princess. I dressed and went down.

The house seemed empty and everyone was in the chapel. I proceeded to the place of the funeral. At the moment I crossed the threshold, Princess Smerande, whom I had not seen for three days, met me there.

She seemed to be a statue of pain. With a slow, statuelike movement, she put her icy lips on my forehead. With a voice that seemed to come from the grave, she uttered the usual words: "Kostaki love you."

You can get an idea of the effect these words had on me. They were stated in the present tense loves you, instead of in the past tense, loved you. This announcement of love coming from beyond the grave terrified me. At the same time, a strange feeling came over me, as if I were indeed the woman who was dead, and not the bride-to-be who was alive. The coffin attracted me to it just as they say the snake attracts the bird. I tried to focus on the eyes of Gregoriska. He was pale and standing against a column, his eyes to heaven. I cannot tell if he saw me. He seemed rather to be attending a consistory of demons than a meeting of priests.

The monks of Hango surrounded the body in singing chants of the Greek rite, sometimes harmonious, often monotonous. I wanted them to pray for me, too, but nothing left my lips my mind was so upset.

When the body was removed, I wanted to follow, but my lack of strength would not let me. I felt my legs buckle under me and I leaned against the door.

Princess Smerande stood next to me and motioned to Gregoriska. He obeyed and came over. The princess then spoke to me in the Moldavian language.

"My mother ordered me to repeat word for word what she said," responded Gregoriska.

Princess Smerande then spoke again, and when she had finished:

"These are the words of my mother," he said: "You cry for my son, Hedwig, and therefore must have feelings for him, no? I thank you for your tears and your love like you're my daughter, as if Kostaki had been your husband. You now have a homeland, a mother, a family. Let's spread out among us the tears we owe to the dead. Farewell! I'll take my son to his final resting place. On my return, you will not see me until I have conquered my pain. Do not worry. I'll kill the pain, because I do not want it to kill me.'"

A whimper was my only response to these words translated by Gregoriska.

I went up to my room. The convoy departed. I saw it disappear around the corner of the road from my window. The monastery of Hango was only a mile from the castle, in a straight line, but the natural obstacles forced the road to deviate, and, following the road, it would take nearly two hours to return.

We were in the month of November. The days were short and cold. At five o'clock in the evening, it was quite dark. About seven o'clock, I saw torches. The funeral procession had returned. The body had been placed in the tomb of his father. All the words that laid him to rest had been said.

I told you what a strange feeling I had from the fatal event that evening. Perhaps it was because we were all dressed in mourning, especially since I had seen those eyes reopen that which death had closed. That night, overwhelmed by the emotions of the day, I was even more melancholy. I listened to the sound of the castle clock in my room. My sadness increased as the night drew on.

I heard the ringing of a quarter to nine. Then a strange feeling came over me. It was a chilling terror that ran through my body and froze me in place. An impenetrable sleep weighed down on me. My chest could barely move when I tried to breathe. My eyelids became heavy veils. I spread out my arms and involuntarily fell backwards on my bed.

But my senses could still make out an approach at my door. Then it opened. I saw and heard nothing. In a blink I felt a sharp pain in my neck.

After that I fell into a complete lethargy.

At midnight I awoke. My lamp was still burning. I tried to get up, but I was so weak that I had to try more than once. I felt the same pain in my neck that I had experienced in my sleep. I dragged myself, pressing against the wall, over to the mirror and looked.

A mere pinprick marked the artery of my neck. I thought a bug had bitten me in my slumber. As I was overwhelmed with fatigue, I lay down and fell asleep.

The next day I awoke at my usual time. I tried to get up as soon as my eyes were open, but I felt a weakness that I had not experienced but once in my life. It was the day after the first time I bled.

I approached my mirror, and was horrified by my white pallor.

The day was dark and gloomy. I felt a strange presence in the room, yet I had no desire to leave given my fatigue.

Night came. My women brought me a lit candle. They could tell I was not feeling well and offered to stay with me. I thanked them, but refused. They left.

At the exact time as the previous night I experienced the same symptoms. I wanted to get up and call for help, but I could not reach the door. I vaguely heard the bell of the clock sounding quarter to nine. The door opened, but I did not see anyone. I heard nothing, as before. Suddenly I fell on my bed.

As before, I felt a sharp pain in the same place on my neck. As before, I woke up at midnight, only I woke weaker and paler than before. The next day my horrible suspicion was verified.

I was determined to confront Princess Smerande but I was too weak. When my women servants came into my room, I uttered the name Gregoriska.

Gregoriska soon entered. I wanted to get up to greet him, but I fell on my chair.

He screamed when he saw me, and rushed towards me. I barely had the strength to extend my arms to him.

"Why did you come here?" I asked.

"Alas!" he said, "I came to say goodbye! I came to tell you that I am leaving to the monastery of Hango. This world is unbearable without your love and without you."

"My presence has not been with you, Gregoriska," I replied, "but my love has. Alas! I still love you, and my great sorrow is that now this love is almost a crime."

"So pray for me, Hedwig."

"Yes, only I cannot pray long," I added with a wan smile.

"What ails you, and why are you so pale?"

"God have mercy on me even if he should call me to him!"

Gregoriska approached me, took my hand, I did not have the strength to move. Staring at me he said, "This is not a natural pallor, Hedwig, where does it come from?"

"If I told you, Gregoriska, you'd think I'm crazy."

"No, no, tell me, Hedwig. I beg of you. We are here in a country like no other country, in a family like no other family. Say all, I beg you."

I told him about the strange hallucinations I started having right to the present hour: Kostaki had died, the terror, the numbness, the ice cold sensation, falling prostrate on my bed, the sound of footsteps that I thought I heard, then the door opening, then the sharp pain followed by pallor and weakness that was constantly increasing. I thought my story would seem to Gregoriska the beginning of madness, when, on the contrary, I saw that he was paying profound attention.

After I had finished speaking, he thought for a moment. "So," he asked, "you fall asleep every night at a quarter to nine?"

"Yes, I make some effort to resist sleep."

"You think you see your door open?"

"Yes, although I engage the lock."

"You then feel a sharp pain in the neck?"

"Yes, although my collar protects me."

"Will you allow me to see?"

I tilted my head to my shoulder.

He examined the scar. "Hedwig," he said after a moment, "do you trust me?"

"Do you need to ask?" I replied.

"Do you believe in my words?"

"As I believe in the Holy Gospels."

"Hedwig, on my word, I swear that you do not have a week to live, unless you do as I instruct."

"And if I consent?"

"If you agree, you will be saved . . . perhaps."

"Maybe?"

He paused.

"Whatever the consequences, Gregoriska," I replied, "I'll do what you command me to do."

"Listen," he said, "and do not be alarmed. In your country, as in Hungary, as in our Romania, there is a tradition."

I shivered as a particular tradition had come to my mind.

"Ah!" he said, "you know what I mean?"

"Yes," I replied, "I saw, in Poland, persons subject to this horrible fate."

"You are referring to vampires, no?"

"Yes, in my childhood, I have seen graves dug up in a village of my father. Forty people had died in two weeks and no one could guess the cause of death. Seventeen had the signs of vampirism. That is to say, we found them fresh in their graves, with ruddy complexions, as if they were still alive. The others were their victims."

"And what was done to deliver the village from this evil?"

"A stake was thrust through their hearts and then the bodies were burned."

"Yes, that is how it is usually conducted, but for us it is not enough. To deliver the specter, I first want to know if it is him, and, by Heaven, I will know. Yes, and if necessary, I will fight him."

"Oh! Gregoriska," I cried, frightened.

"I said, and I repeat, whatever it is. But it is necessary to carry out this terrible adventure and you must consent to all that I require of you."

"Yes."

"At seven go to the chapel. Go down alone. You must overcome your weakness, Hedwig, you must. Once there, I will meet you and we will receive the holy nuptials. Agree now, my beloved, it is necessary to defend yourself. I will then have the right to watch over you, before God and before men. We will then see what happens."

"Oh! Gregoriska," I cried, "if he is a vampire, he will kill you."

"Do not worry, my beloved Hedwig. Only agree."

"You know I'll do whatever you want, Gregoriska."

"See you tonight, then."

"Do what you must in preparation, and I will do my best, too."

He left. Fifteen minutes later, I saw a rider racing his steed on the road to the monastery. It was him!

Instantly I fell to my knees and prayed. We do not pray in my country without belief. I waited seven hours, offering to God and the saints the holocaust of my thoughts. I lifted myself when the clock struck seven. I was weak as though dying, pale as a corpse. I threw on a long black veil and went downstairs with much support of the walls. I made it to the chapel without meeting anyone.

Gregoriska was waiting with Father Bazile, superior of the monastery of Hango. Alongside him was a holy sword, a relic of an old crusader who overtook Constantinople, Villehardouin and Beaudoin de Flandre.[13]

"Hedwig," he said, striking his hand on his sword, "with God's help, we will break the spell that threatens your life. Here is a holy man who, after receiving my confession, will receive our oaths."

The ceremony began. Perhaps never were nuptials given in such a simple and solemn tone. No one attended. The priest himself put on our headdress. Both dressed in mourning, we walked around the altar under the flicker of a candle in Gregoriska's hand.

Then the priest who spoke the sacred words, added: "Go now, my children, and may God give you the strength and courage to fight against the enemy of man. You're armed with your innocence and justice by which you will defeat the demon. Come and be blessed."

We placed our hands on the holy book and left the chapel.

For the first time, I leaned on the arm of Gregoriska, and it seemed to me that in touching his arm, I touched his noble heart. Life was returning to my veins. I thought I was certain to prevail, since Gregoriska was with me. We went up to my room.

Eight thirty sounded.

"Hedwig," Gregoriska said, "we have no time to lose. Will you fall asleep again or do you wish to stay awake and see everything?"

"Being close to you, I fear nothing. I want to stay awake. I want to see everything."

Gregoriska drew from within his coat a small boxwood branch that had been blessed. It was still wet with holy water. He gave it to me. "Take this branch," he said. "Lie down on your bed, recite prayers to the Virgin, and wait without fear. God is with us. Please do not drop the branch. With it you will command the demon to hell itself. Do not call for me. Do not cry. Pray, hope and wait."

I lay down on the bed. I folded my hands on my chest, to which I pressed the blessed branch. As for Gregoriska, he hid behind the dais, of which I spoke, at one corner of my room.

I counted the minutes. Three quarters after the hour sounded.

The impact of the clock hammer vibrated again. I felt the same numbness, the same fear, the same freezing cold. I raised

---

[13] Perhaps Baldwin I of Constantinople (1172-1205), first emperor of Constantinople

the blessed branch to my lips, and the first sensation dissipated.

Then I distinctly heard the sound of the slow and measured footsteps that echoed down the stairs and approached the door. My door opened slowly, quietly, as if pushed by a supernatural force, and then ...

The voice paused as if stifled in the throat.

And then he continued with some effort. I saw Kostaki, pale as I had seen him on the litter, his long black hair scattered over his shoulders, dripping with blood. He wore his usual outfit, only it was open on his chest, and showed his bleeding wound.

Everything was dead except the eyes alone, those terrible eyes, they were alive.

Strange! Instead of feeling my horror redouble, I felt my courage grow. God wished me to stand my position and defend against hell. The first step the specter made towards my bed, I met his gaze boldly with leaden eyes.

The specter tried to move, but a power within me kept him in his place. He paused: "Oh!" he whispered, "she does not sleep, she knows everything." He spoke in Moldova, and yet I heard as if these words had been spoken in a language that I understood.

We stood opposite, glaring at each other. I saw no need to turn my head away. Gregoriska shot from the corner as though an angel of death. He was brandishing his sword. He made the sign of the cross with his left hand and walked slowly toward the specter. At the sight of his brother he drew his sword. A terrible laugh issued from Kostaki. Gregoriska swung. The sword grazed the arm of the specter.

Kostaki's face was filled with despair. "What do you want?" he said to his brother.

"On behalf of the living God," Gregoriska said, "I charge thee to answer me."

"Speak," the specter said through gritted teeth.

"Is it me that you've been waiting for?"

"No."

"Is it me who you believe attacked you while living?"

"No."

"Is it me who stabbed you?"

"No."

"In the eyes of God and man, I am not guilty of the crime of fratricide. You have not received a divine mission from God. Your mission comes from hell. You're arisen from the grave, not as a holy shadow, but as a cursed specter, and to your grave you will return."

"With her, yes!" exclaimed Kostaki, making a supreme effort to get hold of me.

"Only!" exclaimed turn Gregoriska, "this woman belongs to me. We have been joined in holy matrimony."

In uttering these words, the end of the blessed sword touched the open wound. Kostaki screamed as if a flaming sword had pierced his heart. His left hand covered his chest and he took a step back.

At the same time, Gregoriska stepped forward, eyes on the eyes of the dead, the sword on chest of his brother. They began a slow walk, terrible, solemn, something like the passage of Don Juan and the Commander. The specter began moving backwards beneath the sacred sword, under the irresistible will of the champion of God. Step-by-step, without a word, both livid. Gregoriska began pushing the living dead before him, forcing him to leave the castle, which had been his past home. The grave was his home forevermore.

Oh! it was horrible to witness, I swear.

Yet, driven by my invisible strength, without realizing what I was doing, I got up and I followed. We descended the staircase, lit only by the glowing eyes of Kostaki. We crossed the gallery and courtyard. And we passed the door of the castle in measured steps: the specter walking backwards, Gregoriska's arm outstretched, me following.

This fantastic spectacle lasted an hour. In forcing death to his grave, we did not follow the usual path. Gregoriska cut a straight line to Hango, paying no attention to former obstacles as they now ceased to exist. Under the feet of the brothers the ground flattened, streams dried up, trees fell out of the way, the rocks parted. The same miracle that had given me strength was happening for Gregoriska. Yet, it was not without foreboding. The sky was covered in a black veil. The moon and the stars were gone. All that could be plainly seen in the night were the flaming eyes of the vampire.

We finally arrived at the monastery of Hango. We passed through the Arbutus hedge,[14] which served as the cemetery fence. Just inside, I distinguished in the shadows Kostaki's tomb that had been placed beside that of his father. I did not know how, yet I recognized it.

That night I knew everything.

---

[14] Flowering, evergreen shrub

At the edge of the open pit, Gregoriska stopped.

"Kostaki," he said, "all is not over for you yet" - and his voice, as if from heaven, boomed, "You'll be forgiven if you repent, but you must promise to go to your grave - promise you'll never get out again - promise to finally dedicate yourself to God or would you rather be doomed to hell?"

"No!" Kostaki answered.

"Do you repent?" asked Gregoriska.

"No!"

"For the last time, Kostaki?"

"No!"

"Satan awaits your call for your help, as I call God to help me. We will see once again, who will win."

Kostaki grabbed the family sword that was buried with him. Two cries were heard at the same time; irons crossed while sparks flew. The fight lasted only one minute, yet it seemed a century.

Kostaki lifted his terrible sword one last time. Then he fell into the grave. I watched him sink into the freshly turned earth. One last cry (one not of this earth), went into the air.

I ran to my husband.

Gregoriska remained standing over the grave, but tottering.

I held him in my arms.

"Are you hurt?" I asked anxiously.

"No," he said, "but in such a duel, dear Hedwig, it is not the injury that kills, it's the struggle. I struggled with death. Now I belong to the dead."

"Friend, friend," I cried, "get away, get away from here, and life will come back to you."

"No," he said, "my Hedwig, do not waste time, take a little of this ground soaked in blood. Apply it to the bite on your neck. It is the only way to protect yourself in the future from this horrible vampirism."

Shivering, I obeyed. I stooped to pick up the bloody earth, and there I saw the corpse on the ground. The blessed sword was across his heart. A black and abundant blood flowed from the wound, as if he had only just died. I kneaded a little earth with the blood and applied the talisman to my injury.

"Now, my beloved Hedwig," Gregoriska said in a weak voice, "listen to my last instructions. Leave the country as soon as you can. Distance alone is security for you. Father Bazile today received my last wishes, and he will fulfill them. Hedwig! a kiss! the last one, the only one. Hedwig! I die."

And saying these words, Gregoriska fell near his brother.

In any other circumstances, amid the cemetery, near the open grave, with these two bodies lying next to each other, I would have been terrified. But, as I have already said, God had given me the power to not only be a witness to these events, but an actor.

To my great relief I saw the open door of the monastery and the monks, led by Father Bazile, marching toward me, two-by-two, carrying lighted torches and chanting prayers for the dead. In a vision Father Bazile had foreseen what happened and had rushed to the cemetery. He found me alive near the two dead brothers.

At this moment Kostaki issued a last, horrid convulsion.

Gregoriska, however, was calm and almost smiling in death. As desired, Gregoriska was later buried near his brother by Christian rituals.

Princess Smerande, learning of this misfortune, wanted to see me. She visited me at the monastery of Hango where she learned straight from my mouth all that happened on that terrible night. I told her in detail the fantastic story, but she listened to me as I had listened to Gregoriska, that is without astonishment, without fear.

"Hedwig," she replied after a moment's silence, "strange though it is what you have told me, you have not told the complete truth. The Brankovan race is cursed down to the third and fourth generations. The reason why is because many decades ago a Brankovan killed a priest. But the end of the curse came – because you are a virgin. If my son has left you a million, take it and enjoy it. After I expire, you will have the rest of my fortune. Now follow the advice of your deceased husband. Return as fast as you can to countries where God does not permit to occur these terrible wonders. I do not need another to mourn my son with me. Farewell. My future fate no longer belongs to me but to God." And having kissed me on the forehead as usual, she left and went to lock up the castle Brankovan.

Eight days later I left for France. As hoped by Gregoriska, my nights ceased to be frequented by the terrible specter. Even my health is restored, but I have kept the deathly pallor that comes to visit every creature that has received the kiss of a vampire.

JOSEPH SHERIDAN LE FANU
(1814-1873)

Introduction
Strange Event in the Life of Schalken the Painter

R*evenant,* French for "to return," is a term used loosely in supernatural circles for a being who has come back from the dead. All ghosts are gray and given this limiting definition, all ghosts are revenants. Yet the darkling man in this tale is a step beyond a mere revenant. There is a sheen of malice about his appearance and his unyielding personality. *Récupérer* ("to reclaim") is a more apt term for the specter of the "Strange Event in the Life of Schalken the Painter" who comes to reclaim his bride.

But let's step back and consider the origins of this Gothic story, which is the first historical fiction vampire story. In the seventeenth century Dutch painter Godfried Schalcken ("Schalken" in the story) became known for his gloomy paintings that often depicted his subjects drenched in candlelight. For a period he studied art under Gerrit Dou ("Gerhard Douw" in the story) who is considered one of the best Dutch painters of the candle effect. Rose Velderkaust was Dou's niece and "the only love of Godfrey Schalken."

Like Schalcken's paintings, "Strange Event in the Life of Schalken the Painter" is equally a story veiled in shadow and tremulous light. It bids the reader to ponder that which is not shown, that which is left unpainted and unsaid. We know little of what is going on in the background of Schalcken's paintings and little of what is happening behind the scenes in Fanu's vampire tale; so little, in fact, that many have mistook it for a ghost story or a play on the legend of the demon lover who comes to claim his bride. But if this is a demon lover when did Rose, the female protagonist, have relations with him prior to death? The subtle reference to the long hair that hides the neck of the vampire and a mouth that opens "in order to give egress to two long, discoloured fangs, which projected from the upper jaw, far below the lower lip" makes clear that this is squarely a vampire story.

In M.R. James's introduction to *Ghosts and Marvels* of 1927, he pointed out that "'Schalken' conforms more strictly to my own ideals. It is indeed one of the best of Le Fanu's good things."

Fanu shows, but does not tell, in this story of reclamation from the grave. Through the gloom he sheds light on the hopelessness of a nineteenth century woman trapped in an unwanted (and unholy) marriage to a vampiric *récupérer*.

Strange Event in the Life of Schalken the Painter (1839)

YOU WILL NO doubt be surprised, my dear friend, at the subject of the following narrative. What had I to do with Schalken,[1] or Schalken with me? He had returned to his native land, and was probably dead and buried, before I was born; I never visited Holland nor spoke with a native of that country. So much I believe you already know. I must, then, give you my authority, and state to you frankly the ground upon which rests the credibility of the strange story which I am, about to lay before you.

I was acquainted, in my early days, with a Captain Vandael, whose father had served King William[2] in the Low Countries,[3] and also in my own unhappy land during the Irish campaigns. I know not how it happened that I liked this man's society, spite of his politics and religion: but so it was; and it was by means of the free intercourse to which our intimacy gave rise that I became possessed of the curious tale which you are about to hear.

I had often been struck, while visiting Vandael, by a remarkable picture,[4] in which, though no connoisseur myself, I could not fail to discern some very strong peculiarities, particularly in the distribution of light and shade, as also a certain oddity in the design itself, which interested my curiosity. It represented the interior of what might be a chamber in some

---

[1] Godfried Schalcken (1643-1706) Dutch painter known for his gloomy paintings that often depicted people in candlelight

[2] King William III (1650-1702) of England

[3] Low-lying territory in delta of three rivers near Benelux countries, Western Germany and areas of Northern France

[4] Fictional painting by Godfried Schalcken, but work titled "Girl with a Candle" shows a grinning young lady

antique religious building—the foreground was occupied by a female figure, arrayed in a species of white robe, part of which is arranged so as to form a veil.

The dress, however, is not strictly that of any religious order. In its hand the figure bears a lamp, by whose light alone the form and face are illuminated; the features are marked by an arch smile, such as pretty women wear when engaged in successfully practising some roguish trick; in the background, and, excepting where the dim red light of an expiring fire serves to define the form, totally in the shade, stands the figure of a man equipped in the old fashion, with doublet and so forth, in an attitude of alarm, his hand being placed upon the hilt of his sword, which he appears to be in the act of drawing.

'There are some pictures,' said I to my friend, 'which impress one, I know not how, with a conviction that they represent not the mere ideal shapes and combinations which have floated through the imagination of the artist, but scenes, faces, and situations which have actually existed. When I look upon that picture, something assures me that I behold the representation of a reality.'

Vandael smiled, and, fixing his eyes upon the painting musingly, he said:

'Your fancy has not deceived you, my good friend, for that picture is the record, and I believe a faithful one, of a remarkable and mysterious occurrence. It was painted by Schalken, and contains, in the face of the female figure, which occupies the most prominent place in the design, an accurate portrait of Rose Velderkaust,[5] the niece of Gerard Douw,[6] the first and, I believe, the only love of Godfrey Schalken. My father knew the painter well, and from Schalken himself he learned the story of the mysterious drama, one scene of which the picture has embodied. This painting, which is accounted a fine specimen of Schalken's style, was bequeathed to my father by the artist's will, and, as you have observed, is a very striking and interesting production.'

I had only to request Vandael to tell the story of the painting in order to be gratified; and thus it is that I am enabled to submit to you a faithful recital of what I heard myself, leaving you to reject or to allow the evidence upon which the truth of the tradition depends, with this one assurance, that Schalken

---

[5] Rose Velderkaust
[6] Gerrit Dou (1613-1675) pupil of Rembrandt and teacher of Godfried Schalcken

was an honest, blunt Dutchman, and, I believe, wholly incapable of committing a flight of imagination; and further, that Vandael, from whom I heard the story, appeared firmly convinced of its truth.

There are few forms upon which the mantle of mystery and romance could seem to hang more ungracefully than upon that of the uncouth and clownish Schalken—the Dutch boor—the rude and dogged, but most cunning worker in oils, whose pieces delight the initiated of the present day almost as much as his manners disgusted the refined of his own; and yet this man, so rude, so dogged, so slovenly, I had almost said so savage, in mien[7] and manner, during his after successes, had been selected by the capricious[8] goddess, in his early life, to figure as the hero of a romance by no means devoid of interest or of mystery.

Who can tell how meet he may have been in his young days to play the part of the lover or of the hero—who can say that in early life he had been the same harsh, unlicked, and rugged boor that, in his maturer age, he proved—or how far the neglected rudeness which afterwards marked his air, and garb, and manners, may not have been the growth of that reckless apathy not unfrequently produced by bitter misfortunes and disappointments in early life?

These questions can never now be answered.

We must content ourselves, then, with a plain statement of facts, or what have been received and transmitted as such, leaving matters of speculation to those who like them.

When Schalken studied under the immortal Gerard Douw, he was a young man; and in spite of the phlegmatic[9] constitution and unexcitable manner which he shared, we believe, with his countrymen, he was not incapable of deep and vivid impressions, for it is an established fact that the young painter looked with considerable interest upon the beautiful niece of his wealthy master.

Rose Velderkaust was very young, having, at the period of which we speak, not yet attained her seventeenth year, and, if tradition speaks truth, possessed all the soft dimpling charms of the fail; light-haired Flemish maidens. Schalken had not studied long in the school of Gerard Douw, when he felt this interest deepening into something of a keener and intenser feeling than

---

[7] Appearance
[8] Whimsical
[9] Lackadaisical

was quite consistent with the tranquillity of his honest Dutch heart; and at the same time he perceived, or thought he perceived, flattering symptoms of a reciprocity of liking, and this was quite sufficient to determine whatever indecision he might have heretofore experienced, and to lead him to devote exclusively to her every hope and feeling of his heart. In short, he was as much in love as a Dutchman could be. He was not long in making his passion known to the pretty maiden herself, and his declaration was followed by a corresponding confession upon her part.

Schalken, however, was a poor man, and he possessed no counterbalancing advantages of birth or position to induce the old man to consent to a union which must involve his niece and ward in the strugglings and difficulties of a young and nearly friendless artist.

He was, therefore, to wait until time had furnished him with opportunity, and accident with success; and then, if his labours were found sufficiently lucrative, it was to be hoped that his proposals might at least be listened to by her jealous guardian. Months passed away, and, cheered by the smiles of the little Rose, Schalken's labours were redoubled, and with such effect and improvement as reasonably to promise the realisation of his hopes, and no contemptible eminence in his art, before many years should have elapsed.

The even course of this cheering prosperity was, however, destined to experience a sudden and formidable interruption, and that, too, in a manner so strange and mysterious as to baffle all investigation, and throw upon the events themselves a shadow of almost supernatural horror.

Schalken had one evening remained in the master's studio considerably longer than his more volatile companions, who had gladly availed themselves of the excuse which the dusk of evening afforded, to withdraw from their several tasks, in order to finish a day of labour in the jollity and conviviality of the tavern.

But Schalken worked for improvement, or rather for love. Besides, he was now engaged merely in sketching a design, an operation which, unlike that of colouring, might be continued as long as there was light sufficient to distinguish between canvas and charcoal. He had not then, nor, indeed, until long after, discovered the peculiar powers of his pencil, and he was engaged in composing a group of extremely roguish-looking and grotesque imps and demons, who were inflicting various ingenious torments upon a perspiring and pot-bellied St.

Anthony, who reclined in the midst of them, apparently in the last stage of drunkenness.[10]

The young artist, however, though incapable of executing, or even of appreciating, anything of true sublimity, had nevertheless discernment enough to prevent his being by any means satisfied with his work; and many were the patient erasures and corrections which the limbs and features of saint and devil underwent, yet all without producing in their new arrangement anything of improvement or increased effect.

The large, old-fashioned room was silent, and, with the exception of himself, quite deserted by its usual inmates. An hour had passed—nearly two—without any improved result. Daylight had already declined, and twilight was fast giving way to the darkness of night. The patience of the young man was exhausted, and he stood before his unfinished production, absorbed in no very pleasing ruminations, one hand buried in the folds of his long dark hair, and the other holding the piece of charcoal which had so ill executed its office, and which he now rubbed, without much regard to the sable[11] streaks which it produced, with irritable pressure upon his ample Flemish inexpressibles.

'Pshaw!' said the young man aloud, 'would that picture, devils, saint, and all, were where they should be—in hell!'

A short, sudden laugh, uttered startlingly close to his ear, instantly responded to the ejaculation.

The artist turned sharply round, and now for the first time became aware that his labours had been overlooked by a stranger.

Within about a yard and a half, and rather behind him, there stood what was, or appeared to be, the figure of an elderly man: he wore a short cloak, and broad-brimmed hat with a conical crown, and in his hand, which was protected with a heavy, gauntlet-shaped glove, he carried a long ebony walking-stick, surmounted with what appeared, as it glittered dimly in the twilight, to be a massive head of gold, and upon his breast, through the folds of the cloak, there shone what appeared to be the links of a rich chain of the same metal.

The room was so obscure that nothing further of the appearance of the figure could be ascertained, and the face was altogether overshadowed by the heavy flap of the beaver which

---

[10] See the Godfried Schalcken paintings "Newly Born" and "Venus" for examples of supernatural beings in his artwork

[11] Dark or black

overhung it, so that not a feature could be discerned. A quantity of dark hair escaped from beneath this sombre hat, a circumstance which, connected with the firm, upright carriage of the intruder, proved that his years could not yet exceed threescore[12] or thereabouts.

There was an air of gravity and importance about the garb of this person, and something indescribably odd, I might say awful, in the perfect, stone-like movelessness of the figure, that effectually checked the testy comment which had at once risen to the lips of the irritated artist. He therefore, as soon as he had sufficiently recovered the surprise, asked the stranger, civilly, to be seated, and desired to know if he had any message to leave for his master.

'Tell Gerard Douw,' said the unknown, without altering his attitude in the smallest degree, 'that Mynher Vanderhauseny of Rotterdam, desires to speak with him to-morrow evening at this hour, and, if he please, in this room, upon matters of weight—that is all. Good-night.'

The stranger, having finished this message, turned abruptly, and, with a quick but silent step, quitted the room, before Schalken had time to say a word in reply.

The young man felt a curiosity to see in what direction the burgher of Rotterdam would turn on quitting the studio, and for that purpose he went directly to the window which commanded the door.

A lobby of considerable extent intervened between the inner door of the painter's room and the street entrance, so that Schalken occupied the post of observation before the old man could possibly have reached the street.

He watched in vain, however. There was no other mode of exit.

Had the old man vanished, or was he lurking about the recesses of the lobby for some bad purpose? This last suggestion filled the mind of Schalken with a vague horror, which was so unaccountably intense as to make him alike afraid to remain in the room alone and reluctant to pass through the lobby.

However, with an effort which appeared very disproportioned to the occasion, he summoned resolution to leave the room, and, having double-locked the door and thrust the key in his pocket, without looking to the right or left, he traversed the passage which had so recently, perhaps still, contained the

---

[12] Sixty years

person of his mysterious visitant, scarcely venturing to breathe till he had arrived in the open street.

'Mynher Vanderhausen,' said Gerard Douw within himself, as the appointed hour approached, 'Mynher Vanderhausen of Rotterdam! I never heard of the man till yesterday. What can he want of me? A portrait, perhaps, to be painted; or a younger son or a poor relation to be apprenticed; or a collection to be valued; or—pshaw! there's no one in Rotterdam to leave me a legacy. Well, whatever the business may be, we shall soon know it all.'

It was now the close of day, and every easel, except that of Schalken, was deserted. Gerard Douw was pacing the apartment with the restless step of impatient expectation, every now and then humming a passage from a piece of music which he was himself composing; for, though no great proficient, he admired the art; sometimes pausing to glance over the work of one of his absent pupils, but more frequently placing himself at the window, from whence he might observe the passengers who threaded the obscure by-street in which his studio was placed.[13]

'Said you not, Godfrey,' exclaimed Douw, after a long and fruitless gaze from his post of observation, and turning to Schalken—'said you not the hour of appointment was at about seven by the clock of the Stadhouse?'

'It had just tolled seven when I first saw him, sir,' answered the student.

'The hour is close at hand, then,' said the master, consulting a horologe[14] as large and as round as a full-grown orange. 'Mynher Vanderhausen, from Rotterdam—is it not so?'

'Such was the name.'

'And an elderly man, richly clad?' continued Douw.

'As well as I might see,' replied his pupil; 'he could not be young, nor yet very old neither, and his dress was rich and grave, as might become a citizen of wealth and consideration.'

At this moment the sonorous boom of the Stadhouse clock tolled, stroke after stroke, the hour of seven; the eyes of both master and student were directed to the door; and it was not until the last peal of the old bell had ceased to vibrate, that Douw exclaimed:

'So, so; we shall have his worship presently—that is, if he means to keep his hour; if not, thou mayst wait for him, Godfrey, if you court the acquaintance of a capricious

---

[13] Gerrit Dou's north-facing studio is best shown in his self portrait painting and the one titled "Young Mother"

[14] Early form of clock that may be small enough to sit on a table

burgomaster.[15] As for me, I think our old Leyden contains a sufficiency of such commodities, without an importation from Rotterdam.'

Schalken laughed, as in duty bound; and after a pause of some minutes, Douw suddenly exclaimed:

'What if it should all prove a jest, a piece of mummery[16] got up by Vankarp, or some such worthy! I wish you had run all risks, and cudgelled[17] the old burgomaster, stadholder,[18] or whatever else he may be, soundly. I would wager a dozen of Rhenish,[19] his worship would have pleaded old acquaintance before the third application.'

'Here he comes, sir,' said Schalken, in a low admonitory tone; and instantly, upon turning towards the door, Gerard Douw observed the same figure which had, on the day before, so unexpectedly greeted the vision of his pupil Schalken.

There was something in the air and mien of the figure which at once satisfied the painter that there was no mummery in the case, and that he really stood in the presence of a man of worship; and so, without hesitation, he doffed his cap, and courteously saluting the stranger, requested him to be seated.

The visitor waved his hand slightly, as, if in acknowledgment of the courtesy, but remained standing.

'I have the honour to see Mynher Vanderhausen, of Rotterdam?' said Gerard Douw.

'The same,' was the laconic reply of his visitant.

'I understand your worship desires to speak with me,' continued Douw, 'and I am here by appointment to wait your commands.'

'Is that a man of trust?' said Vanderhausen, turning towards Schalken, who stood at a little distance behind his master.

'Certainly,' replied Gerard.

'Then let him take this box and get the nearest jeweller or goldsmith to value its contents, and let him return hither with a certificate of the valuation.'

At the same time he placed a small case, about nine inches square, in the hands of Gerard Douw, who was as much amazed

---

[15] Dutch mayor

[16] Performance or charade to fool a person

[17] Beaten

[18] Steward

[19] Rhine River area, but in this case may mean a dozen bottles of wine from this region

at its weight as at the strange abruptness with which it was handed to him.

In accordance with the wishes of the stranger, he delivered it into the hands of Schalken, and repeating his directions, despatched him upon the mission.

Schalken disposed his precious charge securely beneath the folds of his cloak, and rapidly traversing two or three narrow streets, he stopped at a corner house, the lower part of which was then occupied by the shop of a Jewish goldsmith.

Schalken entered the shop, and calling the little Hebrew into the obscurity of its back recesses, he proceeded to lay before him Vanderhausen's packet.

On being examined by the light of a lamp, it appeared entirely cased with lead, the outer surface of which was much scraped and soiled, and nearly white with age. This was with difficulty partially removed, and disclosed beneath a box of some dark and singularly hard wood; this, too, was forced, and after the removal of two or three folds of linen, its contents proved to be a mass of golden ingots, close packed, and, as the Jew declared, of the most perfect quality.

Every ingot underwent the scrutiny of the little Jew, who seemed to feel an epicurean[20] delight in touching and testing these morsels of the glorious metal; and each one of them was replaced in the box with the exclamation:

'*Mein Gott*, how very perfect! not one grain of alloy— beautiful, beautiful!'

The task was at length finished, and the Jew certified under his hand the value of the ingots submitted to his examination to amount to many thousand rix-dollars.

With the desired document in his bosom, and the rich box of gold carefully pressed under his arm, and concealed by his cloak, he retraced his way, and entering the studio, found his master and the stranger in close conference.

Schalken had no sooner left the room, in order to execute the commission he had taken in charge, than Vanderhausen addressed Gerard Douw in the following terms:

'I may not tarry with you to-night more than a few minutes, and so I shall briefly tell you the matter upon which I come. You visited the town of Rotterdam some four months ago, and then I saw in the church of St. Lawrence your niece, Rose Velderkaust. I desire to marry her, and if I satisfy you as to the fact that I am very wealthy—more wealthy than any husband you could dream

[20] Sensual pleasure

of for her—I expect that you will forward my views to the utmost of your authority. If you approve my proposal, you must close with it at once, for I cannot command time enough to wait for calculations and delays.'

Gerard Douw was, perhaps, as much astonished as anyone could be by the very unexpected nature of Mynher Vanderhausen's communication; but he did not give vent to any unseemly expression of surprise, for besides the motives supplied by prudence and politeness, the painter experienced a kind of chill and oppressive sensation, something like that which is supposed to affect a man who is placed unconsciously in immediate contact with something to which he has a natural antipathy—an undefined horror and dread while standing in the presence of the eccentric stranger, which made him very unwilling to say anything which might reasonably prove offensive.

'I have no doubt,' said Gerard, after two or three prefatory hems, 'that the connection which you propose would prove alike advantageous and honourable to my niece; but you must be aware that she has a will of her own, and may not acquiesce in what WE may design for her advantage.'

'Do not seek to deceive me, Sir Painter,' said Vanderhausen; 'you are her guardian—she is your ward. She is mine if YOU like to make her so.'

The man of Rotterdam moved forward a little as he spoke, and Gerard Douw, he scarce knew why, inwardly prayed for the speedy return of Schalken.

'I desire,' said the mysterious gentleman, 'to place in your hands at once an evidence of my wealth, and a security for my liberal dealing with your niece. The lad will return in a minute or two with a sum in value five times the fortune which she has a right to expect from a husband. This shall lie in your hands, together with her dowry, and you may apply the united sum as suits her interest best; it shall be all exclusively hers while she lives. Is that liberal?'

Douw assented, and inwardly thought that fortune had been extraordinarily kind to his niece. The stranger, he thought, must be both wealthy and generous, and such an offer was not to be despised, though made by a humourist, and one of no very prepossessing presence.

Rose had no very high pretensions, for she was almost without dowry;[21] indeed, altogether so, excepting so far as the

---

[21] Assets give by bride or her family to her new husband

deficiency had been supplied by the generosity of her uncle. Neither had she any right to raise any scruples against the match on the score of birth, for her own origin was by no means elevated; and as to other objections, Gerard resolved, and, indeed, by the usages of the time was warranted in resolving, not to listen to them for a moment.

'Sir,' said he, addressing the stranger, 'your offer is most liberal, and whatever hesitation I may feel in closing with it immediately, arises solely from my not having the honour of knowing anything of your family or station. Upon these points you can, of course, satisfy me without difficulty?'

'As to my respectability,' said the stranger, drily, 'you must take that for granted at present; pester me with no inquiries; you can discover nothing more about me than I choose to make known. You shall have sufficient security for my respectability— my word, if you are honourable: if you are sordid, my gold.'

'A testy old gentleman,' thought Douw; 'he must have his own way. But, all things considered, I am justified in giving my niece to him. Were she my own daughter, I would do the like by her. I will not pledge myself unnecessarily, however.'

'You will not pledge yourself unnecessarily,' said Vanderhausen, strangely uttering the very words which had just floated through the mind of his companion; 'but you will do so if it is necessary, I presume; and I will show you that I consider it indispensable. If the gold I mean to leave in your hands satisfy you, and if you desire that my proposal shall not be at once withdrawn, you must, before I leave this room, write your name to this engagement.'

Having thus spoken, he placed a paper in the hands of Gerard, the contents of which expressed an engagement entered into by Gerard Douw, to give to Wilken Vanderhausen, of Rotterdam, in marriage, Rose Velderkaust, and so forth, within one week of the date hereof.

While the painter was employed in reading this covenant, Schalken, as we have stated, entered the studio, and having delivered the box and the valuation of the Jew into the hands of the stranger, he was about to retire, when Vanderhausen called to him to wait; and, presenting the case and the certificate to Gerard Douw, he waited in silence until he had satisfied himself by an inspection of both as to the value of the pledge left in his hands. At length he said:

'Are you content?'

The painter said he would fain have another day to consider.

'Not an hour,' said the suitor, coolly.

'Well, then,' said Douw, 'I am content; it is a bargain.'

'Then sign at once,' said Vanderhausen; 'I am weary.'

At the same time he produced a small case of writing materials, and Gerard signed the important document.

'Let this youth witness the covenant,' said the old man; and Godfrey Schalken unconsciously signed the instrument which bestowed upon another that hand which he had so long regarded as the object and reward of all his labours.

The compact being thus completed, the strange visitor folded up the paper, and stowed it safely in an inner pocket.

'I will visit you to-morrow night, at nine of the clock, at your house, Gerard Douw, and will see the subject of our contract. Farewell.' And so saying, Wilken Vanderhausen moved stiffly, but rapidly out of the room.

Schalken, eager to resolve his doubts, had placed himself by the window in order to watch the street entrance; but the experiment served only to support his suspicions, for the old man did not issue from the door. This was very strange, very odd, very fearful. He and his master returned together, and talked but little on the way, for each had his own subjects of reflection, of anxiety, and of hope.

Schalken, however, did not know the ruin which threatened his cherished schemes.

Gerard Douw knew nothing of the attachment which had sprung up between his pupil and his niece; and even if he had, it is doubtful whether he would have regarded its existence as any serious obstruction to the wishes of Mynher Vanderhausen.

Marriages were then and there matters of traffic and calculation; and it would have appeared as absurd in the eyes of the guardian to make a mutual attachment an essential element in a contract of marriage, as it would have been to draw up his bonds and receipts in the language of chivalrous romance.

The painter, however, did not communicate to his niece the important step which he had taken in her behalf, and his resolution arose not from any anticipation of opposition on her part, but solely from a ludicrous consciousness that if his ward were, as she very naturally might do, to ask him to describe the appearance of the bridegroom whom he destined for her, he would be forced to confess that he had not seen his face, and, if called upon, would find it impossible to identify him.

Upon the next day, Gerard Douw having dined, called his niece to him, and having scanned her person with an air of satisfaction, he took her hand, and looking upon her pretty, innocent face with a smile of kindness, he said:

'Rose, my girl, that face of yours will make your fortune.'

Rose blushed and smiled.

'Such faces and such tempers seldom go together, and, when they do, the compound is a love-potion which few heads or hearts can resist. Trust me, thou wilt soon be a bride, girl. But this is trifling, and I am pressed for time, so make ready the large room by eight o'clock to-night, and give directions for supper at nine. I expect a friend to-night; and observe me, child, do thou trick thyself out handsomely. I would not have him think us poor or sluttish.'

With these words he left the chamber, and took his way to the room to which we have already had occasion to introduce our readers—that in which his pupils worked.

When the evening closed in, Gerard called Schalken, who was about to take his departure to his obscure and comfortless lodgings, and asked him to come home and sup with Rose and Vanderhausen.

The invitation was of course accepted, and Gerard Douw and his pupil soon found themselves in the handsome and somewhat antique-looking room which had been prepared for the reception of the stranger.

A cheerful wood-fire blazed in the capacious hearth; a little at one side an old-fashioned table, with richly-carved legs, was placed—destined, no doubt, to receive the supper, for which preparations were going forward; and ranged with exact regularity, stood the tall-backed chairs, whose ungracefulness was more than counterbalanced by their comfort.

The little party, consisting of Rose, her uncle, and the artist, awaited the arrival of the expected visitor with considerable impatience.

Nine o'clock at length came, and with it a summons at the street-door, which, being speedily answered, was followed by a slow and emphatic tread upon the staircase; the steps moved heavily across the lobby, the door of the room in which the party which we have described were assembled slowly opened, and there entered a figure which startled, almost appalled, the phlegmatic[22] Dutchmen, and nearly made Rose scream with affright; it was the form, and arrayed in the garb, of Mynher Vanderhausen; the air, the gait, the height was the same, but the features had never been seen by any of the party before.

The stranger stopped at the door of the room, and displayed his form and face completely. He wore a dark-coloured cloth

---

[22] Placid

cloak, which was short and full, not falling quite to the knees; his legs were cased in dark purple silk stockings, and his shoes were adorned with roses of the same colour.

The opening of the cloak in front showed the under-suit to consist of some very dark, perhaps sable material, and his hands were enclosed in a pair of heavy leather gloves which ran up considerably above the wrist, in the manner of a gauntlet. In one hand he carried his walking-stick and his hat, which he had removed, and the other hung heavily by his side. A quantity of grizzled hair descended in long tresses from his head, and its folds rested upon the plaits of a stiff ruff, which effectually concealed his neck.

So far all was well; but the face!—all the flesh of the face was coloured with the bluish leaden hue which is sometimes produced by the operation of metallic medicines administered in excessive quantities; the eyes were enormous, and the white appeared both above and below the iris, which gave to them an expression of insanity, which was heightened by their glassy fixedness; the nose was well enough, but the mouth was writhed considerably to one side, where it opened in order to give egress to two long, discoloured fangs, which projected from the upper jaw, far below the lower lip; the hue of the lips themselves bore the usual relation to that of the face, and was consequently nearly black.

The character of the face was malignant, even satanic, to the last degree; and, indeed, such a combination of horror could hardly be accounted for, except by supposing the corpse of some atrocious malefactor, which had long hung blackening upon the gibbet,[23] to have at length become the habitation of a demon— the frightful sport of Satanic possession.

It was remarkable that the worshipful stranger suffered as little as possible of his flesh to appear, and that during his visit he did not once remove his gloves.

Having stood for some moments at the door, Gerard Douw at length found breath and collectedness to bid him welcome, and, with a mute inclination of the head, the stranger stepped forward into the room.

There was something indescribably odd, even horrible, about all his motions, something undefinable, that was unnatural, unhuman—it was as if the limbs were guided and directed by a spirit unused to the management of bodily machinery.

---

[23] Structure where people were hanged by the neck

The stranger said hardly anything during his visit, which did not exceed half an hour; and the host himself could scarcely muster courage enough to utter the few necessary salutations and courtesies: and, indeed, such was the nervous terror which the presence of Vanderhausen inspired, that very little would have made all his entertainers fly bellowing from the room.

They had not so far lost all self-possession, however, as to fail to observe two strange peculiarities of their visitor.

During his stay he did not once suffer his eyelids to close, nor even to move in the slightest degree; and further, there was a death-like stillness in his whole person, owing to the total absence of the heaving motion of the chest, caused by the process of respiration.

These two peculiarities, though when told they may appear trifling, produced a very striking and unpleasant effect when seen and observed. Vanderhausen at length relieved the painter of Leyden of his inauspicious presence; and with no small gratification the little party heard the street-door close after him.

'Dear uncle,' said Rose, 'what a frightful man! I would not see him again for the wealth of the States!'

'Tush, foolish girl!' said Douw, whose sensations were anything but comfortable. 'A man may be as ugly as the devil, and yet if his heart and actions are good, he is worth all the pretty-faced, perfumed puppies that walk the Mall. Rose, my girl, it is very true he has not thy pretty face, but I know him to be wealthy and liberal; and were he ten times more ugly—'

'Which is inconceivable,' observed Rose.

'These two virtues would be sufficient,' continued her uncle, 'to counterbalance all his deformity; and if not of power sufficient actually to alter the shape of the features, at least of efficacy enough to prevent one thinking them amiss.'

'Do you know, uncle,' said Rose, 'when I saw him standing at the door, I could not get it out of my head that I saw the old, painted, wooden figure that used to frighten me so much in the church of St. Laurence of Rotterdam.'

Gerard laughed, though he could not help inwardly acknowledging the justness of the comparison. He was resolved, however, as far as he could, to check his niece's inclination to ridicule the ugliness of her intended bridegroom, although he was not a little pleased to observe that she appeared totally exempt from that mysterious dread of the stranger which, he could not disguise it from himself, considerably affected him, as also his pupil Godfrey Schalken.

Early on the next day there arrived, from various quarters of the town, rich presents of silks, velvets, jewellery, and so forth, for Rose; and also a packet directed to Gerard Douw, which, on being opened, was found to contain a contract of marriage, formally drawn up, between Wilken Vanderhausen of the Boom-quay, in Rotterdam, and Rose Velderkaust of Leyden, niece to Gerard Douw, master in the art of painting, also of the same city; and containing engagements on the part of Vanderhausen to make settlements upon his bride, far more splendid than he had before led her guardian to believe likely, and which were to be secured to her use in the most unexceptionable manner possible—the money being placed in the hands of Gerard Douw himself.

I have no sentimental scenes to describe, no cruelty of guardians, or magnanimity of wards, or agonies of lovers. The record I have to make is one of sordidness, levity, and interest. In less than a week after the first interview which we have just described, the contract of marriage was fulfilled, and Schalken saw the prize which he would have risked anything to secure, carried off triumphantly by his formidable rival.

For two or three days he absented himself from the school; he then returned and worked, if with less cheerfulness, with far more dogged resolution than before; the dream of love had given place to that of ambition.

Months passed away, and, contrary to his expectation, and, indeed, to the direct promise of the parties, Gerard Douw heard nothing of his niece, or her worshipful spouse. The interest of the money, which was to have been demanded in quarterly sums, lay unclaimed in his hands. He began to grow extremely uneasy.

Mynher Vanderhausen's direction in Rotterdam he was fully possessed of. After some irresolution he finally determined to journey thither—a trifling undertaking, and easily accomplished—and thus to satisfy himself of the safety and comfort of his ward, for whom he entertained an honest and strong affection.

His search was in vain, however. No one in Rotterdam had ever heard of Mynher Vanderhausen.

Gerard Douw left not a house in the Boom-quay untried; but all in vain. No one could give him any information whatever touching the object of his inquiry; and he was obliged to return to Leyden, nothing wiser than when he had left it.

On his arrival he hastened to the establishment from which Vanderhausen had hired the lumbering though, considering the times, most luxurious vehicle which the bridal party had employed to convey them to Rotterdam. From the driver of this machine he learned, that having proceeded by slow stages, they had late in the evening approached Rotterdam; but that before they entered the city, and while yet nearly a mile from it, a small party of men, soberly clad, and after the old fashion, with peaked beards and moustaches, standing in the centre of the road, obstructed the further progress of the carriage. The driver reined in his horses, much fearing, from the obscurity of the hour, and the loneliness of the road, that some mischief was intended.

His fears were, however, somewhat allayed by his observing that these strange men carried a large litter,[24] of an antique shape, and which they immediately set down upon the pavement, whereupon the bridegroom, having opened the coach-door from within, descended, and having assisted his bride to do likewise, led her, weeping bitterly and wringing her hands, to the litter, which they both entered. It was then raised by the men who surrounded it, and speedily carried towards the city, and before it had proceeded many yards the darkness concealed it from the view of the Dutch charioteer.

In the inside of the vehicle he found a purse, whose contents more than thrice paid the hire of the carriage and man. He saw and could tell nothing more of Mynher Vanderhausen and his beautiful lady. This mystery was a source of deep anxiety and almost of grief to Gerard Douw.

There was evidently fraud in the dealing of Vanderhausen with him, though for what purpose committed he could not imagine. He greatly doubted how far it was possible for a man possessing in his countenance so strong an evidence of the presence of the most demoniac feelings, to be in reality anything but a villain; and every day that passed without his hearing from or of his niece, instead of inducing him to forget his fears, on the contrary tended more and more to exasperate them.

The loss of his niece's cheerful society tended also to depress his spirits; and in order to dispel this despondency, which often crept upon his mind after his daily employment was over, he was wont frequently to prevail upon Schalken to accompany him home, and by his presence to dispel, in some degree, the gloom of his otherwise solitary supper.

One evening, the painter and his pupil were sitting by the fire, having accomplished a comfortable supper, and had yielded

---

[24] Piece of furniture on which people are carried

to that silent pensiveness sometimes induced by the process of digestion, when their reflections were disturbed by a loud sound at the street-door, as if occasioned by some person rushing forcibly and repeatedly against it. A domestic had run without delay to ascertain the cause of the disturbance, and they heard him twice or thrice interrogate the applicant for admission, but without producing an answer or any cessation of the sounds.

They heard him then open the hall-door, and immediately there followed a light and rapid tread upon the staircase. Schalken laid his hand on his sword, and advanced towards the door. It opened before he reached it, and Rose rushed into the room. She looked wild and haggard, and pale with exhaustion and terror; but her dress surprised them as much even as her unexpected appearance. It consisted of a kind of white woollen wrapper, made close about the neck, and descending to the very ground. It was much deranged and travel-soiled. The poor creature had hardly entered the chamber when she fell senseless on the floor. With some difficulty they succeeded in reviving her, and on recovering her senses she instantly exclaimed, in a tone of eager, terrified impatience:

'Wine, wine, quickly, or I'm lost!'

Much alarmed at the strange agitation in which the call was made, they at once administered to her wishes, and she drank some wine with a haste and eagerness which surprised them. She had hardly swallowed it, when she exclaimed, with the same urgency:

'Food, food, at once, or I perish!'

A considerable fragment of a roast joint was upon the table, and Schalken immediately proceeded to cut some, but he was anticipated; for no sooner had she become aware of its presence than she darted at it with the rapacity of a vulture, and, seizing it in her hands she tore off the flesh with her teeth and swallowed it.

When the paroxysm of hunger had been a little appeased, she appeared suddenly to become aware how strange her conduct had been, or it may have been that other more agitating thoughts recurred to her mind, for she began to weep bitterly and to wring her hands.

'Oh! send for a minister of God,' said she; 'I am not safe till he comes; send for him speedily.'

Gerard Douw despatched a messenger instantly, and prevailed on his niece to allow him to surrender his bedchamber to her use; he also persuaded her to retire to it at once and to rest; her consent was extorted upon the condition that they would not leave her for a moment.

'Oh that the holy man were here!' she said; 'he can deliver me. The dead and the living can never be one—God has forbidden it.'

With these mysterious words she surrendered herself to their guidance, and they proceeded to the chamber which Gerard Douw had assigned to her use.

'Do not—do not leave me for a moment,' said she. 'I am lost for ever if you do.'

Gerard Douw's chamber was approached through a spacious apartment, which they were now about to enter. Gerard Douw and Schalken each carried a wax candle, so that a sufficient degree of light was cast upon all surrounding objects. They were now entering the large chamber, which, as I have said, communicated with Douw's apartment, when Rose suddenly stopped, and, in a whisper which seemed to thrill with horror, she said:

'O God! he is here—he is here! See, see—there he goes!'

She pointed towards the door of the inner room, and Schalken thought he saw a shadowy and ill-defined form gliding into that apartment. He drew his sword, and raising the candle so as to throw its light with increased distinctness upon the objects in the room, he entered the chamber into which the shadow had glided. No figure was there—nothing but the furniture which belonged to the room, and yet he could not be deceived as to the fact that something had moved before them into the chamber.

A sickening dread came upon him, and the cold perspiration broke out in heavy drops upon his forehead; nor was he more composed when he heard the increased urgency, the agony of entreaty, with which Rose implored them not to leave her for a moment.

'I saw him,' said she. 'He's here! I cannot be deceived—I know him. He's by me—he's with me—he's in the room. Then, for God's sake, as you would save, do not stir from beside me!'

They at length prevailed upon her to lie down upon the bed, where she continued to urge them to stay by her. She frequently uttered incoherent sentences, repeating again and again, 'The dead and the living cannot be one—God has forbidden it!' and then again, 'Rest to the wakeful—sleep to the sleep-walkers.'

These and such mysterious and broken sentences she continued to utter until the clergyman arrived.

Gerard Douw began to fear, naturally enough, that the poor girl, owing to terror or ill-treatment, had become deranged; and he half suspected, by the suddenness of her appearance, and the unseasonableness of the hour, and, above all, from the wildness and terror of her manner, that she had made her escape from some place of confinement for lunatics, and was in immediate fear of pursuit.

He resolved to summon medical advice as soon as the mind of his niece had been in some measure set at rest by the offices of the clergyman whose attendance she had so earnestly desired; and until this object had been attained, he did not venture to put any questions to her, which might possibly, by reviving painful or horrible recollections, increase her agitation.

The clergyman soon arrived—a man of ascetic[25] countenance and venerable age—one whom Gerard Douw respected much, forasmuch as he was a veteran polemic,[26] though one, perhaps, more dreaded as a combatant than beloved as a Christian—of pure morality, subtle brain, and frozen heart. He entered the chamber which communicated with that in which Rose reclined, and immediately on his arrival she requested him to pray for her, as for one who lay in the hands of Satan, and who could hope for deliverance—only from heaven.

That our readers may distinctly understand all the circumstances of the event which we are about imperfectly to describe, it is necessary to state the relative position of the parties who were engaged in it. The old clergyman and Schalken were in the anteroom of which we have already spoken; Rose lay in the inner chamber, the door of which was open; and by the side of the bed, at her urgent desire, stood her guardian; a candle burned in the bed-chamber, and three were lighted in the outer apartment.

The old man now cleared his voice, as if about to commence; but before he had time to begin, a sudden gust of air blew out the candle which served to illuminate the room in which the poor girl lay, and she, with hurried alarm, exclaimed:

'Godfrey, bring in another candle; the darkness is unsafe.'

Gerard Douw, forgetting for the moment her repeated injunctions in the immediate impulse, stepped from the bedchamber into the other, in order to supply what she desired.

---

[25] Austere

[26] One who starts controversial arguments

'O God I do not go, dear uncle!' shrieked the unhappy girl; and at the same time she sprang from the bed and darted after him, in order, by her grasp, to detain him.

But the warning came too late, for scarcely had he passed the threshold, and hardly had his niece had time to utter the startling exclamation, when the door which divided the two rooms closed violently after him, as if swung to by a strong blast of wind.

Schalken and he both rushed to the door, but their united and desperate efforts could not avail so much as to shake it.

Shriek after shriek burst from the inner chamber, with all the piercing loudness of despairing terror. Schalken and Douw applied every energy and strained every nerve to force open the door; but all in vain.

There was no sound of struggling from within, but the screams seemed to increase in loudness, and at the same time they heard the bolts of the latticed window withdrawn, and the window itself grated upon the sill as if thrown open.

One last shriek, so long and piercing and agonised as to be scarcely human, swelled from the room, and suddenly there followed a death-like silence.

A light step was heard crossing the floor, as if from the bed to the window; and almost at the same instant the door gave way, and, yielding to the pressure of the external applicants, they were nearly precipitated into the room. It was empty. The window was open, and Schalken sprang to a chair and gazed out upon the street and canal below. He saw no form, but he beheld, or thought he beheld, the waters of the broad canal beneath settling ring after ring in heavy circular ripples, as if a moment before disturbed by the immersion of some large and heavy mass.

No trace of Rose was ever after discovered, nor was anything certain respecting her mysterious wooer detected or even suspected; no clue whereby to trace the intricacies of the labyrinth and to arrive at a distinct conclusion was to be found. But an incident occurred, which, though it will not be received by our rational readers as at all approaching to evidence upon the matter, nevertheless produced a strong and a lasting impression upon the mind of Schalken.

Many years after the events which we have detailed, Schalken, then remotely situated, received an intimation of his father's death, and of his intended burial upon a fixed day in the church of Rotterdam. It was necessary that a very considerable journey should be performed by the funeral procession, which, as it will readily be believed, was not very numerously attended. Schalken with difficulty arrived in Rotterdam late in the day upon which the funeral was appointed to take place. The procession had not then arrived. Evening closed in, and still it did not appear.

Schalken strolled down to the church—he found it open— notice of the arrival of the funeral had been given, and the vault in which the body was to be laid had been opened. The official who corresponds to our sexton,[27] on seeing a well-dressed gentleman, whose object was to attend the expected funeral, pacing the aisle of the church, hospitably invited him to share with him the comforts of a blazing wood fire, which, as was his custom in winter time upon such occasions, he had kindled on the hearth of a chamber which communicated, by a flight of steps, with the vault below.

In this chamber Schalken and his entertainer seated themselves, and the sexton, after some fruitless attempts to engage his guest in conversation, was obliged to apply himself to his tobacco-pipe and can to solace his solitude.

In spite of his grief and cares, the fatigues of a rapid journey of nearly forty hours gradually overcame the mind and body of Godfrey Schalken, and he sank into a deep sleep, from which he was awakened by some one shaking him gently by the shoulder. He first thought that the old sexton had called him, but HE was no longer in the room.

He roused himself, and as soon as he could clearly see what was around him, he perceived a female form, clothed in a kind of light robe of muslin, part of which was so disposed as to act as a veil, and in her hand she carried a lamp.[28] She was moving rather away from him, and towards the flight of steps which conducted towards the vaults.

Schalken felt a vague alarm at the sight of this figure, and at the same time an irresistible impulse to follow its guidance. He followed it towards the vaults, but when it reached the head of the stairs, he paused; the figure paused also, and, turning gently round, displayed, by the light of the lamp it carried, the face and features of his first love, Rose Velderkaust. There was nothing horrible, or even sad, in the countenance. On the contrary, it wore the same arch smile which used to enchant the artist long before in his happy days.

---

[27] Church caretaker

[28] Vision of young woman depicted in the earlier-mentioned painting

A feeling of awe and of interest, too intense to be resisted, prompted him to follow the spectre, if spectre it were. She descended the stairs—he followed; and, turning to the left, through a narrow passage, she led him, to his infinite surprise, into what appeared to be an old-fashioned Dutch apartment, such as the pictures of Gerard Douw have served to immortalise.

Abundance of costly antique furniture was disposed about the room, and in one corner stood a four-post bed, with heavy black-cloth curtains around it; the figure frequently turned towards him with the same arch smile; and when she came to the side of the bed, she drew the curtains, and by the light of the lamp which she held towards its contents, she disclosed to the horror-stricken painter, sitting bolt upright in the bed, the livid and demoniac form of Vanderhausen. Schalken had hardly seen him when he fell senseless upon the floor, where he lay until discovered, on the next morning, by persons employed in closing the passages into the vaults. He was lying in a cell of considerable size, which had not been disturbed for a long time, and he had fallen beside a large coffin which was supported upon small stone pillars, a security against the attacks of vermin.

To his dying day Schalken was satisfied of the reality of the vision which he had witnessed, and he has left behind him a curious evidence of the impression which it wrought upon his fancy, in a painting executed shortly after the event we have narrated, and which is valuable as exhibiting not only the peculiarities which have made Schalken's pictures sought after, but even more so as presenting a portrait, as close and faithful as one taken from memory can be, of his early love, Rose Velderkaust, whose mysterious fate must ever remain matter of speculation.

The picture represents a chamber of antique masonry, such as might be found in most old cathedrals, and is lighted faintly by a lamp carried in the hand of a female figure, such as we have above attempted to describe; and in the background, and to the left of him who examines the painting, there stands the form of a man apparently aroused from sleep, and by his attitude, his hand being laid upon his sword, exhibiting considerable alarm: this last figure is illuminated only by the expiring glare of a wood or charcoal fire.

The whole production exhibits a beautiful specimen of that artful and singular distribution of light and shade which has rendered the name of Schalken immortal among the artists of his country. This tale is traditionary, and the reader will easily perceive, by our studiously omitting to heighten many points of the narrative, when a little additional colouring might have added effect to the recital, that we have desired to lay before him, not a figment of the brain, but a curious tradition connected with, and belonging to, the biography of a famous artist.

Arthur Young
(1741-1820)

Introduction
Pepopukin in Corsica

This unique vampire story was found in Vol. I of the six volume anthology titled *The Stanley Tales*, published from 1826-1827. These original tales were compiled by Ambrose Marten. For this vampire story he only printed the author's initials A.Y., a pseudonym of British author and agriculturalist Arthur Young, best known today for his book *Travels in France During the Years 1787, 1788 and 1789*. France is the country in which "Pepopukin in Corsica" is set. If Arthur Young was the author of this tale, how is it that it was published six years after his death? This is a result of *The Stanley Tales* being published posthumously, after Abrose Marten had died. The odd stories were taken from those he had collected over the years while living in Britain.

This is the third vampire story to originate in the English language, the other two being "The Vampyre" and "The Black Vampyre" of 1819. The vampire of this story derives from Poland and is cursed to haunt the living for ninety years as a sort of penance. He neither lives forever nor can create more vampires. He is a mortal, accursed creature.

Also outside of modern vampire tradition is the vampire who drinks the blood of its victim until they are dead. This concept was first promulgated by Robert Sands in "The Black Vampyre" and was a common perception near the quarter mark of the nineteenth century. Consider these verses from the poetry of "Pepopukin in Corsica":

> But Vampy waits with bloody claws
> To munch and crumble all his bones,
> And with his blood bestrew the stones.

Before you is the first vampire story of a flying vampire with wings and claws. The vampire also chews on human bones.

"Pepopukin in Corsica" was published in 1826 and this is its first republication in nearly 200 years.

𝕻epopukin in Corsica (1826)

All torment, trouble, wonder, and amazement
Inhabits here. Some heavenly power guide us
Out of this fearful country!

The Tempest[1]

SIR GILES DE Montfort was not only superstitious but constitutionally timid. He was one of those men who, during the bloody scenes of the revolution of France,[2] rose himself on the ruins of his betters, and, having acquired immense wealth, considered himself entitled to commit every excess which can be practised by human nature. In the midst of the many extravagant ideas which he had planned for execution, he suddenly took the resolution of visiting the native island of that man who swayed the sceptre not only of France but of the greater part of Europe.[3] He took leave of the capital, after having made the necessary preparation, set out with all the pomp of an eastern monarch, and excited the attention of every town and village through which he travelled.

The principal object which induced him to make this no less sudden than extraordinary visit, was a young. lady, beautiful as Aurora,[4] who had attended her father to Paris to pay his respects to the sovereign of the world, as Bonaparte was styled in Corsica.

Cupid[5] smiled in her looks—her eyes were black—they captivated the knight, who, not doubting that he would be accepted, set forward like a second Don Quixote,[6] and determined never to return without his bride.

---

[1] Play by William Shakespeare (1564-1616)
[2] The first French Revolution lasted from 1789 to 1799
[3] Napoleon Bonaparte (1769-1821) was born in Ajaccio, Corsica
[4] In Roman mythology Aurora was the beautiful goddess of the dawn
[5] God of desire and love in Roman mythology
[6] Main protagonist who quested for a lovely lady he had never met in Miguel de Cervantes Saavedra's (1547-1616) famous comedic novel fully titled *The*

The lady was the youngest sister of three: they were all handsome, but Jane was strikingly so. She alone was as yet unmarried.

In the numerous train of Sir Giles was a young man, who in grace and elegance as far surpassed his master as the Apollo Belvidere[7] surpasses the casts made from it. He was the right hand of the knight, and managed all his affairs with that diligence and honesty which gained him the esteem of all those who knew him.

Several were the ridiculous adventures which befell the knight on his journey, who in bulk equalled Sir John Falstaff;[8] but as we have not time to travel with him from Paris to Marseilles, let it suffice that he arrived in safety at the latter place, whence he embarked for Ajaccio, which he reached in one of those exquisite summer evenings which must ever engage the attention of the most callous. But love—though not that love which filled the bosom of Petrarch,[9] or influenced the heart of the tender Abelard[10]—love alone engrossed his thoughts.

The setting sun cast its departing rays on the rugged rocks that crowned the distant horizon, and yet faintly tinged the receding bay, on the northern side of which is situated the city that gave birth to a man whose talents raised him to the highest pinnacle of glory attainable by human beings; and whose ambition caused that fall which most evidently proved the instability of mortal fabrics.

Sir Giles expected to meet Mademoiselle Jane de Launay on the beach on his landing—why we do not know: in this hope every idea was concentrated. As the tide was ebbing, he was forced to proceed to the town in a boat, and nearly risked falling into the water through his impatience, which was considerably

---

Ingenious Gentleman Don Quixote of La Mancha published in two volumes that spanned a decade: 1605 and 1615

[7] Ancient statue of the god Apollo—sculptor unknown—discovered in the late 1600s and thought to be one of the greatest representations of the male human form

[8] Rotund, boastful knight who is a comedic figure and appears in three of William Shakespeare's plays: "Henry IV," Henry V," and "The Merry Wives of Windsor"

[9] Francesco Petrarca (1304-1374) was an Italian poet and traveling scholar and one of the first proponents of humanism

[10] Peter Abelard (1079-1142) was a French scholar and philosopher who had a widely-known love affair with Heloise d'Argenteuil (1101-1164)

damped by his not finding the lovely Jane, as he had ridiculously expected.

M. Lenoir, anxious that Sir Giles should appear to advantage to the family of Launay, recommended him to send for the necessary persons to set off his figure, before he announced his arrival in the town of Ajaccio. Sir Giles had never learnt to dance. A Frenchman, and not dance! But the chevalier had been born in an obscure village, and his father, the postillion,[11] never entertained the least thought of seeing his son rise on the ruins of his employers; or that he would aspire to the hand of a daughter of the illustrious house of Launay. As he was, however, too far advanced in age to begin to take dancing lessons, he sent for a fencing-master, who immediately made his appearance. This man had formerly instructed one of Jane's brothers-in-law; and the chevalier, hoping to gain some information respecting the family of Launay, asked all that he thought requisite; amongst others, whether the father was rich.

To this the master answered in the affirmative, adding, that he had yet one daughter of exquisite beauty, who was to be married in a few days to an opulent banker of Malta, of the name of Manserol.

"You lie," roared the knight, "for I am come all the way from Paris—and a damned long way it is—to marry this same girl. I will not bear such insults."

"Pray, sir," replied the fencing-master, somewhat startled at this declaration, "will it please you to take a lesson now?"

"Lesson?" exclaimed the knight, "I'll lesson you in a moment! But stop," added he, as the master was leaving the room not a little alarmed, "I think, if you come to-morrow I will take a lesson."

"Very well, sir," said the man; and making a low bow retired, with a determination never to return again.

He was no sooner gone than the knight began to call most vehemently for one of his servants, one of whom immediately appeared, and was thus saluted by his master on entering, whose anger was not readily appeased when once raised: "You villain, why do you keep me so long waiting?"

"I came, sir, as soon as I heard your voice."

"How dare you answer? Take your hat, and go instantaneously to M. de Launay's, and tell him I am coming to see him."

---

[11] Carriage driver

The lacquey delivered the message, and returned with M. de Launay's compliments to Sir Giles, and his desire of seeing him. The invitation was immediately accepted by Sir Giles, who, after having habited himself in a most splendid manner, drove to M. de Launay's, and was by that gentleman received at the door, and conducted to the saloon, where several ladies of Ajaccio were assembled.

The knight cast his eyes around in search of Mademoiselle de Launay, who however entered about half an hour after, with all that grace which had captivated many a heart besides that of the knight; a green handkerchief, embroidered with gold flowers, was negligently thrown over her shoulders.

The knight approached her to pay his respects, and thus addressed the astonished Jane: "I mean," said he, "madam, to marry you, and carry you to the court of France. The empress has promised me to receive you most graciously."

"You are joking with me, sir knight," replied the lady with a smile.

"I will," continued the knight, "entertain a score of cooks, milliners,[12] and shoe-makers, for your exclusive pleasure; besides all the Italian singers in Paris for your diversion."

"One cook, one milliner, or one shoe-maker, will ever be sufficient to please me at any time, and of that I hope M. de Manserol, to whom I am shortly to be married, is well aware."

"M. de Manserol!" roared the knight; "I will sink him in the ocean. You shall be the Lady de Montfort."

"I have no such ambition. Sir, you must excuse me."

"No matter; your fate is fixed," returned the knight, who wished to frighten her, as her father had left the room: "your fate is fixed. I have settled the affair with your father. He agrees to accept my offer."

Sir Giles, who felt he had gone rather too far, as he perceived by the smiles and whisperings of many of the ladies present, made an awkward bow and left the house, highly incensed at the presumption, as he termed it, of Mademoiselle de Launay, in refusing so splendid an offer.

Jane, who had long since given her heart away, but had not as yet obtained the positive consent of her father, who she knew would incline to the greater riches of Sir Giles, trembled for the issue of an affair which had so extraordinary a commencement, and imparted her fears to one of her married sisters, who, after revolving the matter over, proposed to attack Sir Giles on the

---

[12] Maker of women's hats

weak side, having perceived his superstition, and formed a plan for inducing him to believe that a vampire haunted the house.

They had two trusty servants in their family, to whom the secret was confided. The man had studied astrology, and the woman followed his instructions—two fit instruments for their purpose. They were ordered to wait on Sir Giles, and inform him that they were versed in an art he was prone to believe; but above all, they were to acquaint him that vampires were prevalent in Corsica, and very virulent against strangers.

In order to carry their plan into effect, a masquerade was proposed, to which the knight was invited. The company was numerous and brilliant for the place. Sir Giles disguised his face, but he could not disguise his figure, and he was remarked by strangers for his awkward appearance. He sought the fair Jane, but she was not present. He discovered her father, and kept pinioned to his side until the scene of action was to commence. Just as Sir Giles was endeavouring to make a bow to a lady passing by, a voice distinctly pronounced the word "Pepopukin!" in his ear, which caused him to start. The exclamation was followed by these words:—

> While the mood the church-yard lights,
> Or glimmers on the mountain heights,
> The vampire from his earthly den
> Comes forth to haunt the sons of men.

The knight stared in the utmost horror; and imagining the vampire to inhabit the mask, he flung it away, and retreated to another part of the room, apparently exhausted with the agitations of fear. Several gentlemen approached to offer their assistance, when the voice again vibrated on his ear, and thus addressed him:—

> The Turk with his Koran, the Pole with his mail,
> The lord with his musket, the clown with his flail,
> Must yield to the force of the vampire so great,
> For when Vampy is hungry he'll sure find a treat.

The knight could no longer contain his terror, but fled with precipitation, and hurrying along one of the corridors, entered the first door which he found open, which happened to be Madame de Launay's.

He flung himself into one of the aim-chairs, and was not sensible, till somewhat recovered, of the presence of the lovely

Jane. To her he began to relate, with evident signs of the most abject fear, and with great exaggerations, the circumstances which had just transpired; adding, that at a convent near the town of Mersburg, in Poland, he had been attacked by a vampire, which had knocked out his teeth, beat his servants black and blue, stolen his books, his silver lantern, and drank all his wine.

His tormentors, who had closely followed him, renewed the attack, with the exclamation of "Pepopukin, Pepopukin!"

The knight trembled like an aspen leaf, and crept close to Jane, as if for protection. "I have," said he, "a cold shivering; I must retire—the damp air has affected me."

Mademoiselle could scarcely contain herself. Sir Giles had no sooner placed his foot on the threshold than he heard the same voice—

> Stop, stop, Sir Giles,
> You do not know old Vampy's wiles;
> If near that door you dare to go.
> Close to your feet you'll find your foe.

Sir Giles trembled more and more; he seemed rivetted to the spot, unconscious of the approach of Valentine, the man servant, who, pretending to appear concerned, asked what had happened to the noble stranger.

"Oh!" said Sir Giles, "I wish I were but safe back in Paris, away from these vampires—these infernal spirits. Why, ten thousand are now fleeting across the room."

"Where, where?" said Valentine. "I neither see nor hear any one besides your noble self and Mademoiselle, who does not seem frightened, though I believe her nerves are much weaker than yours."

"I tell you," said Sir Giles, "I have seen a vampire."

"A vampire! why what is a vampire?"

"Pepopukin, Pepopukin!" said the voice near Sir Giles.

"That's the vampire!" said the chevalier.

"I do not hear any thing," said Valentine. "It must be some spirit that follows you exclusively. I believe I stated to you that vampires did exist in this island. I have since heard that they attack not only strangers but rich persons."

"Oh that I were but safe back at Paris!" vociferated the knight in an agony of despair. "I shall be robbed, murdered! Oh me, oh me!"

The vampire thus continued—

From my winding-sheet I rise,
And my blood-swol'n body flies
Over rocks and over mountains,
Over rivers, over fountains.
Bones and skeletons I bring,
Which on the castle tops I fling—
Skeletons of warriors old,
Who once did shine in hurnish'd gold.
The Alps beneath my wings I thrust,
And stain with blood the very dust.

The knight could no longer support himself, but fell flat on the floor, and called aloud for assistance.

Mademoiselle de Launay left the room in quest of some of the servants, while Valentine endeavoured to raise him from his disgraceful position, and led him to his carriage, while Jane informed her sisters of the promising success of the plan. Pepopukin, however, was restless in his pursuit of the knight, and even followed him to his chamber, where Sir Giles ordered, or rather begged, his confidant to remain during the night. Exhausted with the exertions he had undergone, the chevalier soon fell asleep; and M. Lenoir, imagining his presence to be no longer necessary, left the room, when Sir Giles was again roused by the tremendous sound of "Pepopukin, Pepopukin!"

He jumped from his couch, and by the help of a rushlight[13] left in the room searched for his sword, but in vain, as it had disappeared from the head of his bed. Imagining that the loss of the sword was a token of the disappearance of the vampire, he cautiously returned to his bed and began to slumber, when he was assailed by the same sounds.

He rose again and seated himself in a chair, unable to grasp the bell to call for assistance, and remained in that position until his courage returned with the light. He soon after received an invitation to breakfast from M. de Launay, who was not aware of the night's occurrences. De Montfort hesitated some time whether he should go or not. How could he make his appearance, after having given such evident marks of his pusillanimity[14] the preceding evening! Yet he thought he must either go or relinquish his pretensions to the lady. This seemed impossible, as no lady in Paris equalled her in beauty.

---

[13] Candle consisting of a rush stalk dipped in tallow
[14] Timidity

Her fortune was great—her family was noble—her accomplishments were exquisite—but how could he meet her? Some little sense of shame dwelt in his mind, but he at last stifled that: he dressed, and with a consummate air of effrontery,[15] which the ignorant alone know how to assume, he entered the breakfast room, where the family was assembled: all the junior parts had by this time been acquainted with the secret. Jane was gay, and received the chevalier so graciously that he began to fancy he had been dreaming about the vampire, and determined not to mention the subject. The breakfast was concluded, and every thing seemed to take its proper course.

M. de Launay, though of considerable property himself, was elated at the hope of his daughter marrying so splendidly, to one who stated himself to be a most intimate friend of the emperor's. Parties of pleasure were proposed and accepted. The knight was in ecstasies: he even ventured so far as to imprint a kiss on the hand of the lady.

Various topics of conversation filled up the morning, and Sir Giles returned to his apartment, buoyed up with the idea that the affair of the preceding evening was a delusion of his brain and unknown to the family. He proposed various rich ornaments for his bride, and again promised her cooks and milliners in abundance, and a coach that should surpass that of the emperor himself, besides a ducal coronet[16] to boot, as he assured them that Napoleon would confer the title upon him whenever he thought proper to ask him.

When returned home, he found a man who, having been sent by Mademoiselle de Launay, offered himself as a *valet de chambre.*[17] Sir Giles, pleased with his appearance, immediately engaged him, and learnt from him, at his toilette, that a vampire was a constant attendant on the family which he (Sir Giles) visited, ever since one of the daughters (now married) had travelled through Poland; that all the learned men of the island had been employed in discovering the reason that this visitor haunted their house in particular; that some believed it to be the ghost of a Vandal,[18] who had inhabited Poland in a remote age; that others imagined it was the spirit of a young Scandinavian gentleman, who had left his native country in the

---

[15] Brashness
[16] Coronation as a duke
[17] Bedroom servant
[18] Germanic tribe that ravaged Rome in 455 A.D.

fifth century; but he affirmed that M. Moreau (Mademoiselle de Launay's brother-in-law) had seen it three evenings before, and heard it say—

> Fi, fa, fum,
> I smell the blood of a Frenchman;
> When, after marriage, he's in bed
> I'll suck his blood until he's dead.

"This is the very vampire," said Sir Giles, "which I met in Poland; but I have got a charm for him—I will drive him away—I will use such spells as will soon banish him hence. I have no fear of vampires or ghosts; but still I wish I never had come to this island, which has already been the tomb of many a Frenchman."

"But," said the valet, "these vampires are most terrific animals; they suck every drop of blood, after innumerable and excruciating torments; and if it does not deprive immediately of life it causes a lingering death in the end, by its repeated attacks."

"Oh," said Sir Giles, "of this I have no fear." But he had no sooner uttered these words than the unwelcome sound of "Pepopukin, Pepopukin!" caused him to tremble in every joint.

"Pray, sir, what is the matter?"

"Oh, oh!" stammered the knight, "it is a fit—of—the ague,[19] to which I have been from my youth subject."

"Pepopukin, Pepopukin!"

"Pray, Francis, did you hear any thing just now?" asked the chevalier.

"I, sir?" answered Francis. "I did not hear the smallest noise."

"Do you think the vampire could follow me?" asked the knight again.

"I am sure I do not know; such a thing might happen?"

"Call M. Lenoir."

M. Lenoir soon made his appearance, and perceiving his master in a most extraordinary posture, requested to know what was the matter.

"Nothing, nothing," said the knight. "However, I wish to know whether such a person as an astrologer could be found here."

---

[19] Recurrent fever that causes shaking

"Oh," said Francis, "I know a person who studies that abstruse science, and will fetch him hither with his companion."

In the course of an hour Francis returned with Valentine and another man, the former of whom Sir Giles did not recollect. They desired to know the object of their visit; and having been obscurely informed of the matter by the knight, they desired him and M. Lenoir, after having stipulated for a considerable payment, to walk into an unfurnished room, and place themselves in the centre, while some magical figures were made round them, and a blue-flame began to rise, in which various figures seemed to float about. The magician commanded silence, and began a chorus.

> Dance, dance; merrily dance.
> That you may be heard from Ajaccio to France.

As the flame advanced in volumes towards Sir Giles he crept behind Lenoir, seized him by the arm, and pinched him, which caused Lenoir to vent his pain in a loud exclamation.

"The charm is dissolved," said a voice of thunder, which caused both Lenoir and his timid master to fall on their faces, when they heard the following words:—

> Old Vampy, like a cunning beast,
> Will, when you expect him least,
> Come bouncing into summer-house,
> And give you there a horrid douce.
> Venetians and Sardinians too
> Have often seen their lights burn blue;
> And ancient Romans, in their pride,
> When homewards they have led their bride.
> Have sometimes seen a horrid ghost
> Come bouncing from infernal coast,
> Which did nuptial feasting curb,
> And hopes of future brides disturb.

It was a long time before either master or man had the courage to raise their heads to see if the coast was clear. Lenoir first demanded if his honour was there.

"Yes," replied the knight; "but I am sure I know not whether I am alive or dead. Are they gone?"

"Yes, sir, the devils seem to have disappeared, but the sulphurous smell is insupportable. They were wizards and witches. I have heard such people are burnt in England."

"I wished," said the knight, "to have my nativity cast by these people."

"You had better resign such projects," said Lenoir, "you have already dearly paid for this fright."

"Why, I wanted to know something of my rival."

"But, sir, is it not better to enjoy the present than look into futurity? If a brilliant future is held out, its effects would be destroyed by anticipation; if a melancholy one, why then our spirits would be depressed, and we should never be happy. Better, sir, support the good and evil of this life as they are awarded by the dispensation of Providence. If Mad. de Launay is destined as your bride Heaven will not withhold her; but if otherwise, you must reconcile yourself to the disappointment."

"Oh, but," said Sir Giles, raising himself entirely from the ground, "that cannot be."

"You, sir, have been, as is too apparent, educated in the school of prosperity, which teaches but little philosophy; but I, on the contrary, have drank deep of the bitter cup of adversity. Let us leave the island, it seems destined to render you miserable."

"What," said Sir Giles, "and leave the lady? No, she shall go too; her father is willing."

"But the lady is not; she has engaged her affections to a Maltese gentleman, as I have been informed, who is very rich."

"But his riches cannot be anything in comparison to mine; you know what I am worth."

"Yes; and I know by observation that riches do not bring happiness, or you have a right to be so in a most pre-eminent degree."

"But, Lenoir," said the knight, "the world will laugh at me."

"It is not the world, sir, that can make you happy, if you cannot make yourself so."

"But the only way to procure happiness is to possess Mademoiselle de Launay; and I will have her, or die in the attempt."

While this conversation was going forward, another scene of disgrace was preparing for the knight. There was a short passage to M. de Launay's house, through a large court-yard, along which Sir Giles was shown. In this yard was an immense heap of straw, from which Valentine determined to assail the knight with the terrific sounds so hateful to his ear. The knight, dressed in his rich attire, was crossing the court-yard with all the expedition his unweildy size could exert, when he was seized and gagged by two men, and placed in the heap of straw, after the forcible application of a huge black mask; and no sooner was he placed there than he was stunned with "Pepopukin, Pepopukin!"

M. de Launay, on passing by, expressed his astonishment at seeing a black mask in the straw. "What can this be?" said he.

"Pepopukin, Pepopukin!"

"Pepopukin?" said M. de Launay, "I will soon discover you," and he began beating the figure most unmercifully, so that the persecuted knight endeavoured, as far as possible, to utter a shriek. "What can this mean?" said M. de Launay again.

"Pepopukin, Pepopukin!"

"I'll Pe-po you," retorted M. de Launay, as he kept exercising his stick; when the chevalier, making a desperate effort, tore off the mask. "Sir Giles de Montfort!" exclaimed de Launay. "Who has dared commit such an outrage?"

"Pepopukin, Pepopukin!" said the walls.

"Oh," said Sir Giles, assuming an air of courage, "it is nothing at all. I fought most valiantly before I would suffer myself to be subdued—I believe I killed twenty of them—they were armed with clubs and staves—I fought like a lion, I can assure you. I should have faced about and overcome them all if they had not been too numerous."

"I will have the perpetrators of this deed brought to justice," said M. de Launay.

"Oh, there is not the least necessity for that, for they will carry the marks with them to the grave."

"Pepopukin, Pepopukin! You lie, sir knight."

M. de Launay begged to escort the chevalier back to his apartment, in order to change his dress; while the ladies, who observed the whole proceeding, were highly amused.

M. de Launay, on returning to his house, commanded the timid Jane to prepare for her wedding with the knight in the course of three days. But marry a man she neither loved nor respected was impossible. All opposition to her father's will was ineffectual—the ornaments were prepared—and the knight was elated beyond all power of description. Jane, however, kept up her spirits: she loved M. de Manserol, who, although rich for the island of Malta, was poor in comparison to the knight.

One of the brothers-in-law resolved, however, to rid her of his intrusion, and proceeded to chastise the knight for his presumption, hoping to force him to withdraw from the island. He was fully persuaded that a challenge from him would produce the desired effect, for he could not bear the idea of seeing his sister-in-law, whom he loved, united to a man every way her inferior except in fortune. Yet he knew not upon what ground exactly to sound his friends, and dreaded infringing the law, as he would be severely punished.

M. Sandino, however, hoping to frighten the knight without having recourse to violence, proceeded to his house, and informed him that he had come to give him his choice of a pair of pistols.

"For what purpose?" asked the knight.

"Why, I intend to blow out your brains."

"Not with gunpowder, I hope," replied the chevalier, "for I dislike the smell of it. I knew by your looks you came with a murderous intent."

"Resign Mademoiselle de Launay, sir, or you are a dead man."

"And you are what shall I call you!—a murderer! I am very nervous."

"Well, one of these pills will be of service to you— they are wonderfully efficacious in nervous disorders."

Madame Sandino then entered, and offered to become the knight's advocate with her husband if he would resign Jane.

"Madame," said he, "behold the great Sir Giles de Montfort at your feet; but he cannot subscribe to your conditions. He must marry your sister—she has been promised by your father."

"Well," said Madame Sandino; "my dear husband, do not torment the poor knight any more; the vampire— (Sir Giles already began to tremble)—the vampire will torment him enough. Have you not heard, sir, that there is one in our family? It will follow my sister wherever she goes."

"Pepopukin, Pepopukin!" resounded through the room.

"Why, knight, how you tremble," resumed the lady. "Here, is there any so volatile?"

"Oh, 'tis only a nervous attack."

"Well, sir, do you intend keeping your resolution?"

"Why, madam, how can I resign the prize," replied de Montfort.

"My father has commanded me to inform you, then, that he would be much honoured by your presence at a masquerade he gives to-night."

"Oh, madam, masquerades have no longer charms for me. I have suffered by the last more than I can express."

"Well, sir, as you please; but I believe my sister expects this of you."

"In that case, madam, you may rely on my presence. But I wish to leave Corsica as soon as possible, and must entreat your good father to expedite this marriage."

"Well, sir, we shall wish you a more agreeable evening."

Madame Sandino and her husband took their leave, and left the knight in no very pleasant mood.

That day M. de Manserol arrived at Ajaccio, in the hope of obtaining the final consent of M. de Launay, when, to his great surprise and grief, he heard Mademoiselle de Launay was to be married, in a very short period, to another. But when informed who and what his rival was, he raised his hopes from the low ebb to which they had sunk, and ventured to seek an interview with Jane, who informed him that, through the intervention of the knight's superstition, he would be ultimately defeated, and that her father would eventually consent to their marriage.

M. de Manserol was diametrically opposite to Sir Giles: he sang, he danced, he played on the lute, with grace; he added to these accomplishments the far more valuable one of a refined mind, and knew how to appreciate the virtues of Jane: he loved her ardently and sincerely.

The masquerade soon began: the knight attended, with terror marked in his face, which was not masked. His ill fate seemed constantly to attend him, for no sooner had he entered, than the sound of *Pepopukin, Pepopukin!* caused him to start from the temporary seat he had selected.

The dance proceeded with seeming regularity until, of a sudden, all the lights were extinguished. The knight was seized by Valentine and his associates, who forced him, much against his inclination, to take an aerial excursion, by raising him above the level of the earth, and treating him, during the operation, with the indelectable sound of *Pepopukin, Pepopukin!*

The knight was too terrified to make the least resistance, and indeed it would have availed little; he was too strongly beset. When he regained possession of his feet, his ear was entertained by several cuffs, and the doleful tune of his tormentor.—

In merry Poland once was I
A fine young man of rank so high;
I drank, I gamed, I tried by play
In sport to pass the hours away;
But death surprised me in my fun,
As once it did the royal Hun.
For ninety years I'm doom'd to roam,
After that high heaven's my home;
And thus I'm spared the jaws of hell.
Which I had once deserved too well.
On sinful bodies now I prey.
Then fling the dripping skin away;
Sometimes on nightmare's backs I ride,
And harlots kill, but spare the bride.
But for de Montfort now I wait.
Though he's elate with pride and state,
Thinks Jane will fall within his jaws.
But Vampy waits with bloody claws
To munch and crumble all his bones,
And with his blood bestrew the stones.

This brought on a more severe shivering fit than the knight
had yet experienced; he fainted from excessive fatigue. Jane and
her sister exulted in their success, feeling confident that he
would never recover the attack in the ball-room. He was carried
home, where Lenoir attended him with his accustomed
assiduity: he, as well as his master, began to wish himself at
Paris. Valentine, by the help of ventriloquism, (which was the
weapon he had hitherto used), continued to pursue the knight,
and frightened him into a nervous fit, as he termed it.

Old Vampy, with his horrid phiz,
Against Sir Giles will sudden whiz.
Assail him with such furious bang.
That he must fall with horrid clang.
When Vampy stalks across the floor.
The foolish knight will stamp and roar;
His wig, his cane, his shoes so black,
Will bounce about with noisy crack.
When Vampy meets him in the wood,
He'll with his teeth, draw his black blood.

All thoughts of Jane were obliterated from the mind of Sir
Giles; he begged M. Lenoir, with a doleful voice, and a more

doleful countenance, to prepare for their departure. M. Lenoir obeyed the orders with the greatest alacrity, for he began to imagine the knight was really deranged, and that nothing could restore his senses but his speedy return to Paris. Taking leave of M. de Launay was impossible; he could not assign any satisfactory reasons for not fulfilling his engagements. What was to be done with the lady?

"Why leave her behind, to be sure," said M. Lenoir.

Many plans were agitated and rejected by the anxious knight. While ruminating on these things a servant informed him that Mademoiselle de Launay had been carried off by a ghost, as it was supposed.

"No, no! it is that horrid vampire—my evil genius—whose rage could only be satisfied by my blood and that of my bride. He has secured her first; and if I don't make haste I shall certainly become his prey. There is no alternative but quitting the island immediately. It cannot be imputed to my charge that the lady has disappeared."

"No," said M. Lenoir; "and the best thing you can possibly do is to return to Paris before the story shall be known. The same ship in which you came hither is prepared to receive you."

"Let us but be sure that the captain is not informed of this extraordinary adventure; and as to the empress, when she inquires for my bride," said the knight "why I can tell her that she was married—or dead—or any thing—before I arrived in Corsica."

Fear became so predominant in the mind of the chevalier that he scarcely stopped to dress; and with his wig on one side, and his hat under his arm, he hurried to the beach, and in his hurry to step into a boat which he found there he lost his balance and fell overboard. Hundreds immediately collected round the spot, and it was with the utmost difficulty that the knight escaped a watery grave.

He was taken out in a miserable plight; and to add to his mortification, he beheld Mademoiselle de Launay, now Madame Manserol, walking down to the beach with her husband, who was the ghost that had carried her off from the masquerade. This was more galling than the voice of the vampire. At this moment Lenoir, who had not been enabled immediately to follow his master, arrived, and ordering the boat to be ready, requested his master to step in, and they were rowed with all expedition to the vessel, which lay off at some distance, while the train and baggage of Sir Giles followed in another boat.

M. de Launay was quietly sitting at his breakfast table when Madame Sandino entered, and, after some preliminary discourse, opened part of the affair, and informed him of the precipitate departure of the knight, without mentioning the marriage of her sister. The gentleman, highly exasperated at what he termed an insult offered to the dignity of his house, went immediately to the beach, and stepping into a boat, followed the knight to the vessel. The latter saw the approaching storm, and exerted his weak brain to evade it, but in vain.

M. de Launay ascended the ship, and addressed him in a manner little calculated to alleviate the fear of the knight. He asked him how he dared to leave the island without fulfilling the engagements he had entered into respecting his daughter; and, in a most peremptory manner, demanded satisfaction for the insult.

"It was contrary to my heart's desire that I was compelled to take this step," replied the trembling knight. "That vampire which attacked me in Poland again tormented me here in so unmerciful a manner that I could no longer support it. The vampire," continued he, "is, I believe, the ghost of some of my ancestors."

M. de Launay, who did not understand a word of this, and who now recollected the vague answers he had received from the knight when he found him in the heap of straw, began to think him really mad; but, notwithstanding, he began to chastise him with a more formidable weapon than his lungs. The latter begged him to desist his anger, and offered even to give half his fortune to Mademoiselle de Launay as a marriage portion, if he might be permitted to depart in-peace.

"I'd rather see her rot on a dunghill," replied the incensed father, "than know she was under an obligation to you, Sir Giles; and if you have any fear of more adequate punishment you will take my advice, and never place your foot on this island again;" and with this he left the vessel, and returned to the town.

The knight blessed his stars that it was no worse, and ordered the commander to set every sail for France.

M. de Launay found his daughter Jane, M. de Manserol, and Monsieur and Madame Sandino, seated under an oak tree at the bottom of his garden. When informed that their union had already taken place, he stretched out his hand in token of forgiveness. The two delinquents threw themselves at his feet, and when they resumed their seats he was further informed of the various tricks which had been practised on the knight, at which he was much amused, but regretted that the rules of hospitality had been transgressed.

Valentine, whose talents and exertions were liberally rewarded, changed his tone, and pronounced the following words to the assembled family, as a farewell in his character of the vampire.

> The snow is deep, the wind is cold,
> Have pity on poor Vampy old,
> For icicles hang on the thorn,
> And poor old Vampy feels forlorn.
> Sir Giles no more doth hear the sound
> Of Pepopukin echoing round.
> Now Vampy walks upon the snow,
> Oh, oh, oh, oh, oh, oh, oh, oh!

Sir Giles soon reached Paris, and resolved never to leave it, at least in pursuit of brides; and all would have passed off to his credit, had not Monsieur and Madame de Manserol been obliged to visit Paris, and hearing how he boasted of the achievements he had performed in the island of Corsica, circulated the tale of his disgrace, and he from thenceforth acquired, and still bears, the surname of Pepopukin.

ROBERT C. SANDS
(1799-1832)

Introduction
The Black Vampyre
A Legend of Saint Domingo

This is the first black vampire short story and only the second vampire story to originate in the English language. It is also the first vampire story written by an American author. Multiple vampires are featured for the first time in an English short story, too. And for these reasons alone it deserves scholarly review.

The tale is the head of all black vampire fiction that has manifested itself over the past two centuries. "The Black Vampyre: A Legend of Saint Domingo" was by far the most difficult to locate of these stories. It is provided here for the first time in its entirety since its original publication in 1819.

Unfortunately it contains extravagant uses of commas, semicolons and exclamation points, jumbled with sweeping use of dramatic phrases. But these contused features are only an annoyance in a groundbreaking vampire tale that deserves our attention and whets our teeth for more.

It is a *long* short story. The author had enough material for a novel and little time to flesh out his ideas to the extremes that they deserved in 1819. Still we are presented with horror, comedic elements, romantic age taboos, and even political satire.

In hindsight, however, he has staked in the ground a very important road marker not only in vampire literature, but perhaps the *first* short story that advocates "emancipation of the Negroes." This was accomplished fourteen years before Lydia Child published *An Appeal in Favor of That Class of Americans Called Africans*, which is widely considered the first anti-slavery non-fiction book. Harriet Beecher Stowe would not publish her first anti-slavery short story until 1853: *Uncle Sam's Emancipation* collection.

But the author did not stop with anti-slavery as the only progressive idea. Mixed marriage was next. "The Black Vampyre" involves the union of a white woman to a black man and ultimately the first mulatto vampire recorded in literature. No wonder "The Black Vampyre" was published under a penname in 1819. Being the first short story in all these important areas, we are compelled to discover the true author who cleverly tried to pin the controversial story (with its shocking and original notions for this time period) on a young seminary student named Richard Varick Day, valedictorian of Columbia College. The following historical records point directly to Robert C. Sands as the author who "wrote on all subjects and for all purposes; and in addition to essays, verses, &c., on topics of his own choice, volunteered to write orations for the commencement displays of young graduates, verses for young lovers, and even sermons for young divines."[1] Robert Sands penned a number of short stories and the evidence will show that he wrote "The Black Vampyre" in 1819, shortly after his graduation from Columbia Law School.

Despite his diverse writing, Robert Sands was a poet at heart and that is how he is remembered today. "The Black Vampyre" has all the trappings of a short story penned by a poet and contains the first poetry in a vampire story originating in the English language. Before the tale is quoted a segment from Lord Byron's "The Giaour: A Fragment of a Turkish Tale." Appended to it was "Vampyrism: A Poem." The extravagant uses of commas, semicolons and exclamation points, jumbled with sweeping usage of dramatic phrases, and short poems or quatrains, point to a poetic creator.

---

[1] *The Writings of Robert C. Sands, Prose and Verse, with a Memoir of the Author*, Vol. I., second edition, 1835, p. 7

Sands's masterpiece poem is undoubtedly "Yamoyden: A Tale of the Wars of King Philip in Six Cantos," which he co-authored with his friend, Rev. James Wallis Eastburn who died the year "The Black Vampyre" was published. "Yamoyden" was composed from November, 1817 to the summer of 1818. "The Black Vampyre" was likely written after "Yamoyden" was finished.

A reviewer[2] likened the horrible and bloody imagery in the poem to that of "The Vampyre" by John Polidori: "We think we see in it proof of an imagination equal to a story of the class of the Vampire,[3] [sic] or the Monk,[4] [sic] which should make those horrible fictions seem almost nursery tales." Sands continued his horror bent as he wrote "The Black Vampyre." In acknowledgment of Polidori's tale, Sands calls out in the Introduction the fresh memory of all who had read "The White Vampyre." [sic] and goes so far as to adopt the ending phraseology: "GLUT THE THIRST OF A VAMPYRE!!!" versus "glutted the thirst of a VAMPYRE!" in Polidori's tale.

The pioneering story includes Latin phrases and references to ancient Greek philosophers and tragedies. Sands was classically trained and began studying Latin at the age of seven.[5] Sands, adhering to the popular style of the day, was concerned with morals in his stories. In his junior year of college at Columbia he started *The Moralist* periodical. "The Black Vampyre" has moralistic undertones without being preachy and includes an afterword simply titled "Moral" that rails on merchant "vampyres." Sands would later write about St. Domingo in his *Historical Notice of Hernan Cortes, Conqueror of Mexico.*

Despite the controversial subject matter of "The Black Vampyre" at the time of its publication, Sands had a more personal reason to send it out into the world anonymously. Two years prior, in 1817, he published one of his earliest poems titled "The Bridal of Vaumond." It was savagely reviewed by New York literary critics.[6] Sands was not about to let this happen to his first short story.

---

[2] *North American Review*, No. XII., p. 466, 1819

[3] "The Vampyre, A Tale.", John Polidori, 1819

[4] *The Monk: A Romance*, Mathew Gregory Lewis, 1796

[5] *The Writings of Robert C. Sands, Prose and Verse, with a Memoir of the Author*, Vol. I., second edition, 1835, p. 3

[6] *The Writings of Robert C. Sands, Prose and Verse, with a Memoir of the Author*, Vol. I., second edition, 1835, p. 8

So he published it under a brilliant pseudonym (Uriah Derick D'Arcy) that was an anagram of Richard Varick Dey, a seminary student and valedictorian of Columbia's bachelor of arts college. The October 19, 1818 issue of *The Academician* recounts the commencement ceremonies. In the afternoon of August 4, 1818 Richard Varick Dey received his bachelor of arts degree and issued his Valedictory address. That same afternoon Robert C. Sands was granted his Master of Arts degree in law from Columbia and heard the address. The anagram is in keeping with the machinations of a literary hoaxster.

"It was his sport to excite public curiosity by giving extracts highly spiced with fashionable allusions and satire, 'from the forth-coming novel;' which novel in truth, was, and is yet to be written; or else to entice some unhappy wight into a literary or historical newspaper discussion, then to combat him anonymously, or under the mask of a brother editor, to overwhelm him with history, facts, quotations, and authorities, all manufactured for the occasion; in short, like Shakespeare's 'merry wanderer of the night,' to lead his unsuspecting victim around 'through bog, through bush, through brier.'"[7] During 1823-4 Sands went so far as to publish the mock *St. Tammany Magazine*.[8]

Yet the most telling piece of evidence that Robert C. Sands was the author of "The Black Vampyre" came twenty-five years after it was published. This is when a friend of the Sands estate came across the story and submitted it to the editor of *The Knickerboker*, which published excerpts of the vampire story and parts of the introduction.[9]

It is clear Robert C. Sands was the anonymous author of "The Black Vampyre." Perhaps he has left us with only "exquisite nonsense" as he stated in the Introduction.

This is debatable. What he has given us, however, is the first black vampire story, the first comedic vampire story, the first story to include a mulatto vampire, the first vampire story by an American author, and perhaps the first anti-slavery short story.

---

[7] Ibid. at 17
[8] Ibid.
[9] *The Knickerboker: or, New-York Monthly Magazine*, Vol. 25, January 1844, p. 73

The Black Vampyre
A Legend of
Saint Domingo
(1819)

But first on earth, as Vampyre sent,
Thy corse shall from its tomb be rent;
Then ghastly haunt the native place,
And suck the blood of all thy race;
There from thy *daughter, sister, wife,*
At midnight drain the stream of life;
Yet loathe the banquet which perforce
Must feed thy livid living corse.

Thy victims, ere they yet expire,
Shall know the demon for their sire;
As cursing thee, thou cursing them,
Thy flowers are withered on the stem.
But one that for *thy crime* must fall,
The youngest, best beloved of all,
Shall bless thee with *A father's* name—
That word shall wrap thy heart in flame!

Yet thou must end thy task and mark
Her cheek's last tinge—her eye's last spark,
And the last glassy glance must view
Which freezes o'er its lifeless blue;
Then with unhallowed hand shall tear
The tresses of her yellow hair,
Of which, in life a lock when shorn
Affection's fondest pledge was worn—
But now is borne away by thee
Memorial of thine agony!

Yet with thine own best blood shall drip;
Thy gnashing tooth, and haggard lip;
Then stalking to thy sullen grave,
Go—and with Gouls and Afrits rave,
Till these in horror shrink away
From spectre more accursed than they.

———

MR. ANTHONY GIBBONS was a gentleman of African extraction. His ancestors emigrated from the eastern coast of Guinea, in a French ship, and were sold in St. Domingo remarkably cheap,[1] as they were reduced to mere skeletons by the yaws[2] on the passage; and all died shortly after their arrival, except one small negro, of a very slender constitution, and fit for no work whatever. The gentleman who purchased *him,* charitably knocked out his brains; and the body was thrown into the ocean. The tide returning in the night, it was washed upon the sands; and the moon then shining bright, the gentleman was taking a walk to enjoy the coolness of the evening; judge of his surprise, when the little corpse got up, and complaining of a pain in its bowels, begged for some bread and butter!

The planter, supposing his business to have been but half done, kicked him back in the water. The element seemed very familiar to him; and he swam back with much grace and agility; parting the sparkling waves with his jet black members, polished like ebony, but reflecting no single beam of light. His complexion was a dead black; his eyes a pure white; the iris was flame color; and the pupils of a clear, moonshiny lustre; but so peculiarly constructed, that, though prominent, they seemed to look into his own head.

His hair was neither curled nor straight; but feathery, like the plumage of a crow. Having paddled again on shore, he came

[1] Now the Republic of Haiti, the former French colony of St. Domingo was a large producer of sugar and coffee beans during the late eighteenth and early nineteenth centuries. Harsh treatment of the slaves led to a bloody revolt in 1791, which finally resulted in the French colony becoming the first black-ruled republic in 1804. See, "A Historical Survey of the French Colony in the Island of St. Domingo," 1797, as reprinted 2010 by Cambridge University Press

[2] Tropical disease that results in high fever and sometimes death. *See* "Manson's Tropical Diseases: A Manual of the Diseases of Warm Climates," Seventh Edition, Sir Patrick Mason, 1921, p. 526

crawling, crab-fashion, to the feet of Mr. PERSONNE. The latter
gentleman, in considerable alarm, (not knowing whether it was
Satan, Obi,[3] or some other worthy, with whom he had to deal,)
mustered up sufficient resolution to tie a large stone round the
boy's middle: then, with a main exertion of strength, he hurled
him into the sparkling ocean. He fell where the reflection of the
moon was brightest, and sunk like lead; but immediately rose
again like cork, perpendicularly, with the stone under his arm;
while the radiant lustre of the planet retreated from his dark
figure, exhibiting in its most striking contrast its utter
blackness!

In this predicament, he came buoyant to land; surrounded,
as he seemed, by a sphere of magic lustre. He now walked up to
the Frenchman, with his arms akimbo, and looking remarkably
fierce. Mr. PERSONNE'S particular hairs stood up on end,

_____Tunc perculit horror
Membra ducis, riguere comæ, grossumque coercens
Languor in extrema tenuit vestigia ripa. LVC.[4]

but being ashamed that a little negro of ten years old should
put him in bodily fear, he knocked him down. The Guineaman
rose again, without bending a joint; as fast as Mr. PERSONNE
could upset him, he recovered his altitude; just like one of those
small toys, fabricated from pith tipped with lead, called witches
and hobgoblins by the rising generation. The planter, in utter
amazement and despair, took hold of the child by both his
extremities, and pressing him to the earth, sat down upon him!
Then, hallooing for his attendants, he ordered a tremendous fire
to be kindled on the sand. This was accordingly done. The Gaul
congratulated himself on his perseverance and sagacity; and as
he had never heard of ignaqueous[5] animals, was confident that
though the water-fiend was so expert in his own element, he
could not stand the fiery ordeal. The boy, meanwhile, lay

---

[3] Obi refers to the god of the West Indie's religious cult named Obeah that
practices witchcraft and sorcery
[4] Translated: Amidst the dusky horrors of the night, A wondrous vision stood
confessed to sight. Quote from a Marcus Annaeus Lucanus "Lucan" (39 A.D.
– 65 A.D.) passage in "Pharsalia" describing the destruction of Pompey. "A
History of Roman Classical Literature," Robert William Browne, 1857, p. 375.
LVC. is the Italian truncation of Lucanus
[5] More commonly igneous, the terms refers to the solidification of molten
magma

perfectly passive, as if he had been a mere log; but presently, when the pile was all in a light blaze, with a sudden expansion, like that of a compressed India-rubber, he popped Mr. PERSONNE up into the air many yards, and he alighted head-foremost into the fire, where he had intended to have dedicated the sable brat, with his nine lives, to Moloch!

Whatever the negro was, it is notorious that Mr. PERSONNE was no salamander. He was rescued from the pyre, which like HERCULES he had (though unwittingly) erected for himself;[6] looking like a squizzed cat, and having apparently no life left in his body. The attention of the domestics was drawn entirely to their master; who soon betrayed signs of animation, though he exhibited a most awful spectacle, being one continual sore and blister. 'His whole body was one wound,' as VIRGIL or some other poet[7] has hyperbolically expressed himself.

Mr. PERSONNE, when he had perfectly recovered his senses, found himself in his own bed, wrapped in greasy sheets, and smarting as if in a Cayenne bath.[8] He called for a glass of brandy, his dear wife EUPMEMIA, and his infant son, who had not yet been christened. His lady, with streaming eyes, presented herself before him; and after tenderly inquiring into the state of his health, told him, (with a voice interrupted with sobs and hiccups,) that when she went in the morning to see her baby, whom she had left in the cradle, there was nothing to be seen, but the *skin, hair,* and *nails!* She declared that there never was such another object; except, indeed, the exsiccation in Scudder's Museum![9]

On the receipt of this horrid intelligence, Mr. PERSONNE was seized with a violent spasmodic affection; and shortly after

---

[6] In Greek mythology Hercules built a huge pyre and burned himself on it, receiving his mortal death

[7] Quote not from Virgil (70 B.C. – 19 B.C), but rather Marcus Annaeus Lucanus "Lucan" (39 A.D. – 65 A.D.) passage in "Pharsalia."

[8] Reference to a bath in the hot pepper cayenne, which is also called the Guinea spice

[9] Reference to John Scudder's American Museum where "the human bodies found in a copperas cave, near the canny branch of the Cumberland River, was very curious. Pieces of cloths which inwrapped [sic] them are now preserved in Mr. Sudder's museum; and an exsiccated foot is also there." *Transaction and Collections of the American Antiquarian Society*, Vol. 1, William Manning, 1820 P. 41. In 1842 Scudder's American Museum was purchased by P.T. Barnum.

expired, muttering something about *sacre,*[10] and the Guinea-negro.

The amiable but unfortunate EUPHEMIA was thrown into several hysterical convulsions; as well she might be, poor woman, when her husband had been made a holocaust, and served up like a broiled and peppered chicken, to feed the grim maw of death; and her interesting infant, the first pledge of her pure and perfect love, had been precociously sucked, like an unripe orange, and nothing left but its beautiful and tender skin. The disconsolate widow caused her husband to be embalmed; and he was buried amid the lamentations and tears of all the funeral; much regretted by all who had the honor of his acquaintance, particularly by his negroes; who could not soon forget him; as he had left too many sincere marks of his regard upon their backs, to be ever obliterated from their recollections.

Time, as all the Greek tragedians, Solomon, and others have remarked, is a benevolent deity. Mrs. PERSONNE'S grief yielded to the soothing hand of the consoling power; and her bloom and spirits returned with more lustre and elasticity than they had before exhibited: as the rose, that had drooped in the fury of the passing storm, erects its blushing honors, and shows more beautiful and vivid tints when the squall is over!

Many years after these occurrences took place, while EUPHEMIA was in second mourning for her third husband, she was indulging in the luxury of solitary grief; and reading Burton's Anatomy of Melancholy,[11] and The Melancholy Poems of Dr. Farmer,[12] in an orangerie.[13] The refreshing breezes from the ocean, which now tempered the sultry heats of the declining day; the soft perfume of the opening blossoms; and the mellow tints of the evening sky, shedding that holy light, so dear to sensitive hearts, diffused a calm over her soul, wrapped in the contemplation of departed days. While lost in this pensive reverie, she perceived two strangers approaching her, in the extremity of the long vista of the grove.

---

[10] Sanctity or holiness

[11] Robert Burton's (1577-1640) *The Anatomy of Melancholy*

[12] Dr. Richard Farmer (1735-1797) *Literary Anecdotes of the Eighteenth Century*, William Bowyer, Vol. II, 1812, p. 618

[13] Building with classical architecture constructed on the property of wealthy private homes in the seventeenth and eighteenth centuries that served as a conservatory.

One of them was a colored gentleman, of remarkable height, and deep jetty blackness; a perfect model of the Congo Apollo.[14] He was dressed in the rich garb of a Moorish Prince; and led by the hand a pale European boy, in an Asiatic dress, whose languid countenance, slender form, and tristful gait were strongly contrasted with the portly appearance and majestic step of his conductor.

They both saluted the lovely widow, and after an interchange of compliments, accepted her polite invitation to sit down, and take tea with her in the bower. She learned from the elder stranger that he had brought out a cargo of slaves, whom his subjects had lately taken prisoners in war; and whom he had resolved to dispose of himself; as he was desirous of seeing the world. His page, he said, was an orphan, left by a slave-merchant in Africa.

The manners and conversation of the PRINCE had an irresistible charm. The regal port was manifest in his gigantic and well-proportioned frame; and majesty was conspicuous on his brow, without its diadem. The turban and crescent had never graced a nobler front; but the winning condescension of his tones and language, while they could not banish the feeling of the presence of royalty, removed every restraint incident to that consciousness. He criticised the works which EUPHEMIA had been perusing, with masterly precision, and displayed more knowledge than even the accomplished ideologist of Lady MORGAN; with infinitely more discretion and good sense.

It is remarked by the Abbe Reynal,[15] that there is a peculiar elegance and beauty in the complexion of the Africans, (when the eyes and nose are accustomed to their hue and odor.) This truth was realized by EUPHEMIA, as she gazed on the open visage of her illustrious guest . She thought surely that in him Nature might stand up and say 'This was a man!' And certainly it is only the weakness and imperfection of our human senses, which, penetrating no farther than the surface is forever deceived by superficial shadows. The empyrean is always blue,[16] whatever vapors may float in our contracted atmosphere. And if we gaze on the rows of skulls which festoon and garnish

---

[14] Mythological Greek and Roman deity of the same name
[15] Abbé Guillaume-Thomas Raynal (1713-1796) who penned L'Histoire philosophique et politique des établissements et du commerce des Européens dans les deux Indes in 1770. This four volume work took an anti-slavery tone.
[16] Highest extent of heavan

Surgeon's Hall,[17] we can apply no standard to determine their relative beauty. They are all equally ugly; and the block of Helen[18] might be mistaken for that of Medusa.[19] Shakespeare, true to nature, has also remarked, 'Black men are pearls in beauteous ladies' eyes.'[20]

The beauty then, the royalty, gentility, and various accomplishments of the BAMBUCK monarch,[21] made captive the too sensible heart of the French widow. She forgot her ogles, graces, and even her loquacity; rooted to her seat, and fixed in immoveable contemplation of the AFRICAN'S face. What peculiar feature or lineament attracted her attention, she knew not: his eyes, though bright, did not sparkle; and the iris, though of a more vivid red than the roseate line in the rainbow,[22] emitted no scintillations. In fact, his whole countenance seemed to look, and to perambulate her own.

The conversation gradually assumed a more empassioned and amorous complexion; and the little page, (who, though meagre and emaciated, evidently showed that he was no gump for his years,) taking certain broad hints, cast a mournful and intelligent look on the widow, said he would fetch a short walk in the plantation, and left the orangerie.

The PRINCE then spreading his glittering sash upon the grass, went down on his knees upon it, and broke out into the

---

[17] Surgeons' Hall Museum of The Royal College of Surgeons of Edinburgh where anatomist John Barclay (1758-1826) donated a collection of over 2500 dead bodies in various states

[18] Daughter of Zeus and Leda in Greek mythology who possessed uncommon beauty

[19] Daughter of Phorcys and Ceto in Greek mythology who was monstrous in appearance

[20] Quote from William Shakespeare's (1564-1616) "The Two Gentlemen of Verona," taken from old proverb: "A black man is a jewel in a fair woman's eyes."

[21] "In the interior parts of Africa, under the twelfth or thirteenth degree of north latitude, there is, says a modern traveller,[sic] a pretty large country, known by the name of Bambuck. It is not subject to a particular king, but governed by village Lords, called Farims. These hereditary and independent chiefs are all obliged to unite for the defence [sic] of the state, when it is either attacked as a community, or only in any one of its members." Abbé Guillaume-Thomas Raynal (1713-1796) who penned *L'Histoire philosophique et politique des établissements et du commerce des Européens dans les deux Indes*, Vol. 3, 1770, p.135

[22] Rose color

most ardent exclamations of love and admiration, and professions of constant attachment. He said that the flat-nosed beauties of Zara;[23] the scarred, squab figures of the golden coast;[24] the well-proportioned Zilias, Calypsos, and Zamas on the banks of the Niger; [25] and even the great Hottentot Venus herself,[26] had never for a moment made the least impression on his heart. His passion was a mystery to himself; its origin secret as the sources of the Nile; but full and impetuous as its ample channel, when replenished from the celestial fountains of Abyssinia;[27] white if Mrs. DUBOIS would shine upon its waves, its enlivened currents would fertilize his vast dominions in the luxuriant realms of central Africa; making them to fructify yet more abundantly, with burning gold and radiant diamonds!

What female heart could resist such pleadings, and the compliment implied in such a preference? When ZEMBO (the page) returned, the parties had agreed to be privately united on the same evening The ceremony was accordingly performed, on the spot, by the family chaplain of Mrs. DUBOIS: not without many remonstrances on his part, as to the impropriety of marrying a negro. The PRINCE did not seem to resent the affront; which, by the by, he had no right to do, as the priest got nothing for the job. ZEMBO too was extremely restless, till Mrs. DUBOIS gave him some sweet-meats, which seemed to quiet his

---

[23] Also called Bobo Jula, reference is to these West African people living predominately in the country of Burkina Faso

[24] Gulf of Guinea, West African colony of the British from 1821-1957, which was occupied by the British at the time "The Black Vampyre" was published

[25] In notes XI to *The African Princess and Other Poems*, Mary Elizabeth Capp, 1813, p. 152 is the following: "On the banks of the Niger, the women are generally handsome, if beauty consists in symmetry of proportion, and not in colour. Modest, affable, and faithful, an air of innocence appears in their looks, and their language is an indication of their bashfulness. The names of Zilia, Calypso, Fanny, Zama, which seem to be the names of pleasure, are pronounced with an inflection of voice, of the softness and sweetness of which our organs are not susceptible." See also, Abbé Guillaume-Thomas Raynal who penned *L'Histoire philosophique et politique des établissements et du commerce des Européens dans les deux Indes*, Vol. 3, 1770, pp. 385 and 387

[26] In 1810 Alexander Dunlop, a British surgeon, brought Saarjite Baartman from Cape Town to London where she was put on display and given the appellation Hottentot Venus, "The Book of Days: A Miscellany of Popular Antiquities," Robert Chambers, Vol. 2, Nov. 26, 1832, p. 621

[27] Ethiopian Empire known for its underground water fountains

conscience; after which he took some stiff punch, and fell asleep!

About midnight, the PRINCE came to him; and shaking him by the ears, bade him rise and follow him. His bride was hanging on his arm, in an enchanting deshabille; and did not seem to be in perfect possession of her right senses. ZEMBO mournfully followed the new married pair.

They went silently out of the back door, with cautious steps, and proceeded through the orangerie. No breath of wind was stirring. The moon was in the zenith, surrounded by a pale halo of ghostly lustre. When they had crossed the plantation, they came to a place of sepulture; where the dark cypresses and lugubrious mahogany admitted but sparse and glimmering streaks of funereal light; which, falling on the rank foliage, the white monuments and broken ground beneath, presented a thousand dusky shapes, flitting in the dim uncertainty, dear to superstition.

Vague terrors seized on the mind of the bride; and she began very naturally to inquire, what was the use of getting out of a comfortable bed, and trailing through the heavy dew, in her undress, to such an unusual spot for midnight recreation.

They now stood near the spot where her three husbands, several children, and the *skin, hair* and *nails* of her first baby, were deposited in a row. At the foot of a tamarind lay her third son, whose Christian name was SPOONER, and who died, according to the tomb-stone, in a fit of intoxication, aged seven years and six months. On him she had bestowed a greater share of tenderness than on any of her other offspring; and his loss had caused her most affliction.[28] The African, making observations on the grave, began to strip himself very expeditiously, assisted by ZEMBO, who seemed to recover from his blues; and by his activity and eagerness, manifested his expectation of soon seeing some fine sport.

Presently the two genii, or gentlemen, or whatever they were, turned towards the East, and performed certain antic prostrations; throwing handfuls of earth three times over their heads. Then returning to the tomb, they tore up the sods with ravenous fury; and soon drew out the last-mentioned son of the

---

[28] Footnote by the author: "This Spooner Dubois having never been heard of since, it is probable that he has been roaming about the world; and it is possible, that he may be the same Lord Ruthven, whose adventures have recently been related." Lord Ruthven is the vampire in John Polidori's "The Vampyre," *New Monthly Magazine*, April 1819

Lady, and threw him on the grass, beside the grave. ZEMBO fell as fiercely upon the corpse, as a hungry dog upon his dinner; but was arrested by the African, who lent him a severe box on the ear, which sent him blubbering to a corner of the cemetery.

What added both to the mother's horrors and admiration, was, that the body of her child was perfectly fresh, and the olfactory nerves experienced no unsavoury sensation from its proximity; while its cheeks were diffused with so deep a tinge of scarlet, that they shone like ruddy fireballs in the darkness of the spot.[29]

Her husband drew a golden goblet from beneath a large stone; then, bending over the corse; he scooped out the heart, with his long and polished nails; and, having pressed the blood into the chalice, mingled with it some dark particles, gathered from the newly turned up earth. From the pure and scanty lymph, which gushed near by and flickered like a streak of quicksilvery-light in the moonbeam, he added a third ingredient of the potion.

Then seizing his passive and trembling spouse by the throat, and presenting the unnatural mixture to her lips; he cried in a hollow voice, whose every inflection thrilled through each fibre of its victim,—"Swear, or if that is against your principles, affirm, by this dirty blood,—and bloody dirt;—by this watery blood,— and bloody water;—by this watery dirt, and dirty water;—that you will never disclose in any manner, aught of what you have seen and shall see this night. Call them all to witness your wish, that in the moment when you even conceive the thought of perjury, your bowels may burst out, and your bones rot! Swear and drink!"[30]

The affrighted woman murmured, (as articulately as the iron gripe of the monster would suffer her,) that she was not thirsty;

---

[29] Footnote by the author: "The universal belief is, that a person sucked by a Vampyre becomes a Vampyre himself, and sucks in his turn. – *Ed. New Mon. Mag.*" Reference to John Polidori's "The Vampyre," *New Monthly Magazine*, April 1819

[30] Footnote by the author: "See Edwards, vol. II. p. 86. Among their other superstitions also, must not be omitted their mode of administering an oath of secrecy or purgation. Human blood, and earth taken from the grave of some near relation, are mixed with water, and given to the party to be sworn, who is compelled to drink the mixture, with an imprecation, that it may cause the belly to burst, and the bones to rot, if the truth be not spoken." This quote is taken from "The History, Civil and Commercial, of the British Colonies in the West Indies; in Two Volumes," Bryan Edwards, Vol. II, 1793, p. 71

and had not breath enough to aspirate such a terrible conjuration.

"No trifling;" roared the fiend, "you have not a moment to deliberate."

But his bellowing and threats were in vain; and he found to his mortification that he had gotten the wrong sow by the ear, or rather by the throat. She stuttered out, in the most accents, which would have softened any heart, (but a Vampyre has none,) that though she was by no means partial to the delectable confectionary of the pharmacopeia, calomel and jalap, ipecacuanha, rhubarb, and tartar-emetic, she would rather take them all, collectively and individually, than the unchristian decoction he held against her teeth.

Foaming with madness, till the white slaver flowed down his sable limbs, the African hurled MRS. PERSONNE, DUBOIS, &c. &c. on the grave of her first husband, and stamping violently on the earth, it seemed to leave as with the throes of an earthquake. Immediately the tumuli yawned! The ponderous stones and slabs were shaken from their ancient sockets; and the ghastly dead, in uncouth attitudes, crawled from their nooks; with their hair curling in tortuous and serpent twinings; and their eyeballs of fire bursting from their heads; while, as they extended their withered arms, and tapering fingers, furnished with blood-hound claws, their gory shrouds fell in wild drapery around them, transiently revealing their forms, bloated as if to bursting, and often incarnadined with clotted blood, yet warm and dripping!!!

The Lady, (as those who have been in similar predicaments may suppose,) soon lost her recollection; not, however, before she had seen Zembo busily employed in tearing up the grave of her first husband; she saw herself surrounded by the specters, and lost all consciousness.

When reason and sense returned, she found herself in the same place; and it was also the midnight hour. She was laying by the grave of MR. PERSONNE, and her breast was stained with blood. A wide wound appeared to have been inflicted there, but was cicatrized. Imagine, if you can, her surprise; when, by a certain carnivorous craving in her maw, and by putting this and that together, she found she was a—vampire!!! and gathered from her indistinct reminiscences, off the preceding night, that she had been their sucked; and that it was now her turn to eject the peaceful tenants of the grave!

With this delightful prospect of immortality before her, she began to examine the graves, for subject to satisfy her furious appetite. When she had selected one to her mind, a new marvel arrested her attention. Her first husband got up out of his coffin, and with all the grace so natural to his countrymen, made her a low bow in the last fashion, and opened his arms to receive her!

What were the emotions of this fond couple, when, after a lingering separation for sixteen years, they again embraced each other, with the ardour of an affection equal to their earliest transports, and which their long divorce served only to increase; tenderly inquiring into the state of each other's health; and the accidents which had befallen them during their disjunction. They forgot even their hunger and thirst; and sitting down on a tombstone, made a thousand inquiries; which, however, as they related to family concerns, might not be as interesting to the reader as they were to the parties concerned.

MR. PERSONNE, however, looked rather glum, when he learned that his Lady had been twice married, since his decease. But she assured him, that she would never more tolerate the addresses of another suitor: and as for the two husbands, they were rotten enough by this time; as she was confident they had not attended the Vampyre Ball, on the preceding night. As for her sable spouse, she trusted that he would never again appear to interrupt their happiness. But while she was expressing his hope, the gentleman in question, (like his relation below, according to the old proverb,) came upon the ground with ZEMBO. MR. PERSONNE, having neither sword nor pistols at hand, armed himself with a gigantic thigh-bone; and warned the Black Prince to stand upon his guard as he meant to punish him severely.

But ZEMBO, rushing between the parties, raised his hands in a supplicating posture; while the generous monarch, making a Salam to his antagonist, begged him to keep himself quiet, and look behind him. They both turned round on this intimation when, to the utter confusion of the Lady, her second and third husbands, MESSIEURS MARQUAND and DUBOIS, arose from their graves, where they had been lovingly deposited by the side of each other. They both advanced to salute their wife; but MR. PERSONNE, brandishing his thigh-bone, warned they to stand off, as he had the first title to the Lady. Much confusion would have ensued, had not the African Prince interfered. He told the gentlemen that so delicate a point could only be settled in an honourable way; and proposed that MR. MARQUAND and MR. DUBOIS should first settle their difference in a personal encounter; after which MR. PERSONNE might give the survivor gentlemanly satisfaction. To this all parties assented.

As they were already stripped, the combatants shook hands, to show their mutual good-will; and proceeded to action, without further ceremony. MR. DUBOIS soon brought claret from MR. MARQUAND; who, in returning the compliment, fibbed MR. DUBOIS so severely in the bowels, that he lost his wind; and gasping for breath, smote the air on all sides, without any of his blows telling. He came to the ground, and his bones rattled as he fell. But soon recovering his breath, he made a desperate attack on MR. MARQUAND'S sconce; and favoured him with so terrible a facer under the gills, that he fell incontinently like a bull smitten in his front; but entangling his own heels with those of MR. DUBOIS, they both came simultaneously to the ground; striking their heads against different tombstones; and knocking out their own brains.

They rose again, refreshed like the giant of old, by their grappling with the earth, and all the better for the loss of their wits, which, indeed, was a mere trifle. But the AFRICAN, who had no time to see more sport, fixed them to the sod by his superior strength; and Zembo dexterously pinned them fast, by driving stakes through their hearts, with a large sledge hammer, (which he carried about his person for such emergencies.) During the operation, their roaring surpassed that which is performed by the Lioness, when bereft of her whelps; but as soon as they were fairly nailed to the counter, they lay motionless and breathless— a horrible pair of spectacles of sin and misery!

The AFRICAN assured the Lady, that she need never fear their second resurrection; and MR. PERSONNE politely offered to settle their controversy, in any mode most agreeable to the Prince:— either to box with him on the spot, or appoint a meeting in future, with pistols, rifles, small or broad sword; or else they might toss up, who should set fire to a barrel of gunpowder. The Prince said that quarrelling was all nonsense, and offered his hand; but MR. PERSONNE refused, saying, "Don't be too familiar, Blackey;" and renewing his threats of cracking him over the noodle with the thigh-bone.

The generous monarch pocketed the affront. "You have been," he said, "sufficiently rewarded, for the cruelties you practiced upon my person, several years ago. I forgive you, my dear sir, what you performed, and intended to perform on me. Here is your son, who has grown considerably, as you may observe; and I assure you that his education has not been neglected. To his exertions last night you are indebted for your revivification. And as, you may remember, you were embalmed, you have kept quite sweet and fresh ever since your interment. Amiable and virtuous VAMPYRES! may you long enjoy that tranquility and contentment, which your merit and accomplishments so eminently deserve! A vessel lies in the port, ready to sail for Europe in an hour. The Island is no longer a place for you. Here is money to pay your passages, and all I have to say, is, that the sooner you're off the better.—Farewell!" So saying he departed, without waiting for the acknowledgements of the party.

MR. PERSONNE and his Lady, whom we shall again call by her first marriage name, did not exactly comprehend what their dingy benefactor meant, by bidding them take French leave of the Island, like pickpockets and outlaws; but, as they were yet wondering at their own existence, like Adam and Eve, the first day of their creation, and as they had reason to believe the Prince a potent magician, who could rouse the dead from their searments, and turn the planets from their courses;—for these reasons, they concluded to follow his bidding, without any impertinent scruples. But as the keen edge of their hunger had been whetted by delay, they would fain have taken supper, and digested a little something wherewithal to strengthen them, before they set out.

ZEMBO, who had filled his own breadbasket very lately, and was in no such urgent necessity, protested with all the vehemence which filial reverence would permit, against the unseasonable gratification of their unnatural craving; and recited, with just emphasis and good discretion, an extract from Counsellor Phillips's harangue, about "the cannibal appetite of his rejected altar;"[31] which his parents did not understand, and of course thought very sublime! But even his master-piece of mystical eloquence would have been delivered in vain; had not the boy given other reasons, of such cogency, that they licked their lips—cast a longing, lingering look at the grave-yard,—and followed him without more opposition.

---

[31] Quote from *The Speeches of Charles Phillips, Esq. Delivered at the Bar and at various public occasions, in Ireland and England*, Charles Phillips, 1817, p. 30, as quoted in "The Edinburgh Review," Vol. 29, 1817, p. 57. In reference to a bigot, "a wretch, whom no philosophy can humanize, no charity soften, no religion reclaim, no miracle convert; a monster, who, red with the fires of hell, and bending under the crimes of earth, erects his murderous divinity upon a throne of skulls, and would gladly feed, even with abro'her's blood, the cannibal appetite of his rejected altar."

They prosecuted their nocturnal march, through closely woven and solemn groves; until they descended into a profound valley, where the light of the pale planet of magic adoration, streamed and quivered on serried files of bright armoury. The leader of the band seemed to have expected their arrival; and mutual tokens of recognition passed between him and ZEMBO. The whole company then set forward their array in silence;—

No cymbal clash'd, no clarion rang,
  Still were the pipe and drum;
Save heady tread, and armour's clang,
  The sullen march was dumb.

By continual descent, they seemed to have penetrated the bowels of a cavern,[32] whose ramifications ran under the sea; as they heard a murmuring roar, as of the ocean, above their heads. The party, by the instructions of ZEMBO, dispersed themselves in different directions; until they had enclosed the interior of the rock, where its largest chamber was, to speak catachrestically, so artfully concealed by nature, that no one, not instructed by an adept in its subterranean topography, could ever have detected the secret of its existence. It had been, in former days, a place of deposit and asylum for the Buccaneers; and its situation had been since known only to the Professors of the OBEAH art, who held here their midnight orgies.

MR. and MRS. PERSONNE, guided by their son, were placed in a situation, where, through the crevices of the inner partition of the rock, they could observe what was passing in the interior.

It seemed, at first view, a vast hall of Arabian romance; supported by immense shafts, and studded with precious stones; so various and beautiful were the hues, which the different spars assumed, in the light of an hundred torches, blazing in every quarter, and illuminating the farthest recesses of the cave. The walls were decorated with other appendages, which added to the mystery, if not to the embellishment of the

---

[32] Footnote from the author: "The ring-leaders held their meetings in certain subterranean passages or caves, in the parish of the La Grande Riviere," &c.— Edwards, Vol. II, p. 52. This quote is taken from "The History, Civil and Commercial, of the British Colonies in the West Indies; in Two Volumes," Bryan Edwards, Vol. I, 1793, p. 51, and should read: "He declares that the ringleaders still maintained the same atrocious project, and held their meetings in certain subterranean passages, or caves, in the parish of La Grande Riviere"

scene; being irregularly stained with blood; decorated with rude tapestry of many coloured plumage;—and stuccoed with the beaks of parrots;—the teeth of dogs, and alligators;—bones of cats;—broken glass and eggshells; plastered with a composition of rum and grave-dirt, the implements of Negro witchcraft![33]

At one extremity of the extensive apartment, on a kind of natural throne, sat several blackamoors in sumptuous Moorish apparel; whom, by their swollen forms, and remarkable eyes, MRS. PERSONNE know to be GOULS; and among whom she recognized her late husband. The whole range of this vast amphitheatre, sweeping from before the throne, was occupied by slaves, rudely attired, and imperfectly armed with clubs and missiles; a decent platoon of black-guards were posted before the Vampyre monarchs; and, in the centre, a band of musicians performed an exquisite symphony. The soft strains of the MERRIWANG;—the lively notes of the DUNDO;—and the martial accompaniment of the GOOMBAY, made, with their united noises, a discordant harmony, [34] whose powers the lyre of Orpheus[35] could not equal; and which would certainly be enough to frighten all the hosts of Pandemonium.[36]

The oratorio being finished, the AFRICAN PRINCE arose, and making an obeisance to the company,—cleared his throat, and began to address them as follows:—"Gentlemen and Vampyres!"—but the Vampyres expressing their resentment against this breach of etiquette, he corrected himself:—

---

[33] Footnote from the author: See, "The History, Civil and Commercial, of the British Colonies in the West Indies; in Two Volumes," Bryan Edwards, Vol. II, 1793, p. 111

[34] See, "The History, Civil and Commercial, of the British Colonies in the West Indies; in Two Volumes," Bryan Edwards, Vol. IV, 1793, p. 102. "In general they prefer a loud and long-continued noise to the finest harmony, and frequently consume the whole night *in beating on a board with a stick.* This is in fact one of their chief musical instruments; besides which, they have the *Banja* or *Merriwang*, the *Dundo* and the *Goombay;* all of African origin. The first is an imperfect kind of violoncello; except that it is played on by the finger like the guitar; producing a dismal monotony of four notes. The Dundo is precisely a tabor; and the Goombay is a rustic drum; being formed of the trunk of a hollow tree, one end of which is covered with a sheep's skin. From such instruments nothing like a regular tune can be expected, nor is it attempted."

[35] The legendary musician of Greek mythology

[36] Word coined by John Milton (1608-1674) in "Paradise Lost" that designates the capitol of Hades

"Vampyres and Gentlemen!"—but the negroes were no more willing to come last, than the Vampyres, and a loud growl, accompanied by a slight hiss, again interrupted the orator. He was not, however, disconcerted, but like Mr. burke, thundered out an iteration of the offensive sentence.

"Yes," said he, "I repeat it, Vampyres and Gentlemen? Shall not the immortal precede the mortal?—Shall not those whose diet surpasses the nectar and ambrosia of celestials, precede the ephemeral race, who fatten on the unclean juice of brutes,—the rank essence of esculent productions,—or the nauseous liquor of the distillery? (*applause—hear! hear! and see-boy! from the Vampyres—groans from the negroes!*)

Gentlemen of colour! I appeal to yourselves; shall not the descendants of the Gods be named before the offspring of the earth-born image, whom Titan impregnated with celestial fire?—For Prometheus was the first Vampyre.[37] You must all know, as you have undoubtedly read Æschylus, that the vulture, who preyed on his liver was neither fish, flesh, nor fowl.[38] He is called a dog, which makes him a quadruped;—he is represented as creeping, which proves him an insect; and is said to have wings, which shows that he was a bird.

Now, from this amphibious monster have descended the Crows,—the Jackalls,—and the Bloodhouds;—the pirate Bat of Madagascar,—and the man-killing Ivunches of Chili;—the Sharks;—the Crocodiles;—the Krakens;—the Horse-leeches;—the Cape-cod Sea Serpents;—the Mermaids;—the Incubi;—and the Succubi!!! (*loud cheering from the Vampyres.*) From Titan himself, descended the Cyclopes, and all other ancient and modern Anthropophagi; and, in lineal descent, the Moco tribe of our own EBOES,[39] to whom I have the honour of being related. Those of you, too, are his posterity, who, after your deaths, return to your native land—the true Elysium; where the balmy bowl of the COCO, the soft bloom of the ANANA, [40] and the coal-

---

[37] Reference to the lost *Prometheia* tragedies *(C5th B.C.)* of *Aeschylus (525 B.C.-456 B.C.); namely, Prometheus Bound, Prometheus Unbound, and Prometheus the Fire-Bringer* where Prometheus stole fire from the gods

[38] Footnote from the author: See Prometheus Vinctus. Ibid

[39] Footnote from the author: See Edwards, Vol. II, p. 90, Abbé Reynal, Vol. III., p. 388.

[40] See anonymous poem "Ode on Seeing a Negro Funeral" published in *The Gentleman's Magazine*, Vol. 79, Part 2, December 1809, p. 1149, which states in part: "To all her children free: For thee, the dulcet reed shall spring, His balmy bowl the Cocoa bring, Th' Anana bloom for thee."

black beauties of the clime of love, shall forever reward your fortitude, and steep in forgetfulness the memory of your wrongs. (*hear! hear! from the negroes.*) but none of these genera or species of our order, must longer engage your dignified and charitable attention. I come to ourselves, full-blooded—unadulterated—immortal bloodsuckers!—To ourselves—whether Gouls, — or Afrits, — or Vampyres; — Vroucolochas,— Vardoulachos, — or Broucolokas;[41] —To ourselves—the terror of the living and of the dead, and the participants of the nature of both;—To ourselves—the emblems at once of corruption and of vitality;—blotted from the records of existence, and replenished to repletion with circulating life;—abandoned by the quick and unrecognized by the dead;—at once relics and relicts;—rocked on the bases of our own eternities;—the chronicles of what was—the solemn and sublime mementoes of what must be!' (*unqualified approbation from both sides of the house.*)

"The estate of Vampyrism is a fee-tail, and may be docked in two different ways. The first mode is the sanguinary practice of perforating the subject with a stake; and this is final. The other is produced by the gentler by the gentler operation of the narcotic portion you behold in this phial; by whose lenient and opiate influence, the individual is restored to the plight, in which he was previous to his death, or his becoming a Vampyre, and belongs to the OBEAH mysteries.[42]

"But to come to the object of our present meeting. Sublime and soul-elevating theme!—The emancipation of the Negroes!—The consecration of the soil of St. Domingo to the manes of murdered patriots in all ages!—No matter whether the bill of sale was scrawled in French or in English;—No matter whether we were taken prisoners, in a battle between the LEOPHARES and

[41] See *The Works of Lord Byron, Notes to the Giaour*, Lord George Gordon N. Byron, 1816, p. 96. "The Vampire superstition is still general in the Levant. Honest Tournefort tells a long story, which Mr. Southey, in the notes on Thalaba, quotes about these 'Vroucolochas' as he calls them. The Romaic term is 'Vardoulacha.' I recollect a whole family being terrified by the scream of a child, which they imagined must proceed from such a visitation. The Greeks never mention the word without horror. I find that 'Broncolokas' is an old legitimate Hellenic appellation—at least is so applied to Arsenius, who, according to the Greeks, was after his death animated by the Devil."
[42] Reference to the voodoo god and the mysterious rituals of voodoo brought from Africa.

the JAKOFFS,[43] or in a skirmish between the SAMBOES and SAWPITS;[44]—No matter whether we were bought for calico and cotton, or for gunpowder or for shot;—No matter whether we were transported in chains or in ropes—in a brig, or a schooner, or a seventy-four—the first moment we come ashore on St. Domingo, our souls shall swell like a sponge in the liquid element;—our bodies shall burst from their fetters, glorious as a curculio from its shell;—our minds shall soar like the car of the æronaut, when its ligaments are cut;[45] in a word, O my bretheren, we shall be free!—Our fetters discandied, and our chains dissolved, we shall stand liberated,—redeemed,— emancipated,— and disenthralled by the irresistible genius of UNIVERSAL EMANCIPATION!!!" (*Unparalleled bursts of unprecedented applause!!!*)[46]

Such was the report of this oration, taken down in short hand by ZEMBO; of whose extraordinary sagacity so many proofs have been exhibited; and who was never unprovided with materials for any emergency. The fiery oratory of the Prince communicated such inspiration to the auditors, that the whole mass of their thick blood leaped up with the quickening pulse of anticipated freedom; they danced and sung, with violent gesticulations, like perfect Corybantes;[47] but unfortunately, their Phyrricks[48] were interrupted by the glittering bayonets of the soldiery; who poured in upon them from every quarter, and hemmed them in, with a bristling *chevaux-de-frise*[49] of steel. The

---

[43] See, "The History, Civil and Commercial, of the British Colonies in the West Indies; in Two Volumes," Bryan Edwards, Vol. II, 1793, p. 111, which states: "The people of Cape Verde," says the writer, "are called *Leophares*, and are counted the goodliest men of all others saving the Congoes, who inhabit this side the Cape de Buena Esperance. These Leophares have wars against the Jaloffs, which are borderers by them. These men "also are more civil than any other, because of their daily trafficke with the Frenchmen, and are of a nature very gentle and loving."

[44] Ibid. at 5

[45] Reference to a hot air balloon and the tethers holding it to earth

[46] This flamboyant oration is perhaps a comedic play on the speeches of Irish attorney Charles Phillips regarding the emancipation of Irish Roman Catholics. See *A Collection of Speeches by Charles Phillips, Esq*, edited by Charles Phillips, 1817, pgs. 8-15 (Speech at the Catholic Aggregate Meeting, Dublin, June 11, 1814)

[47] Accomplished mythical dancers and the sons of Apollo and Thalia

[48] Antiquated term for the part of a throat that vibrates when a person sings

[49] Portable defense instrument from which long spikes protrude.

Vampyres, surprised but undaunted, unsheathed their sabres, and drew up in a gallant style, as if determined to die game; being, indeed, assured, that like so many Phoenixes, they would rise from their own ashes, as often as they might be cut down.

A desperate conflict ensued, during which MRS. PERSONNE observed the phial, mentioned by the Prince, lying on the ground; and very thoughtfully put it in her ridicule. The slaves, seeing how the business was likely to terminate, prudently sneaked off, while the attention of the military was occupied by the Vampyres. The former were violently exasperated to find all their labour so unprofitable; since while they themselves were wounded by every blow of their opponents, the latter, like so many ninepins, were set up, as fast as they were bowled down; bending to the storm, like masts on a tempestuous ocean, and rising again upon the billow in perpendicular triumph.

But, being instructed by ZEMBO, the soldiers pinioned them as fast as they fell; and prevented their rising, by sitting in great numbers on their bodies; though the task was somewhat like that of detaining quicksilver beneath the fingers. The Prince, however, still fought desperately. Brandishing a huge scimitar in either hand, he swayed his arms like the sails of a windmill; while limbs, heads, and bodies flew about him, curvetting and dancing in the air; as when the ingenious MR. MAFFEY pulls to pieces a coach, or an old woman, children, chickens, friars, and petticoats dance about in wild confusion, till the artist's hand again brings order out of chaos:—Or, as when the renowned knight of the BED-CHAMBER, whose name eternal vases shall record, saw the ungenerous caricature on the wall, wielding a ponderous jug, he smote the innocent tables, chairs, and bed-posts, and strode victorious over the gory field: So fought the Prince; till being neatly pricked in the spine, unexpectedly, he soused (as Johannes Porco Latinus[50] remarks) "in principia fundimentalia," and was immediately set upon by a host.

So when a Goetulian lion is pierced by the light bamboo, overpowered by the hunters, he struggles in his thrall like an Enceladus under Aetna,[51] and dies at last with heart-wrung tears of anguish, and reverberating roars of hatred!!!

Stakes were immediately procured, and the whole infernal fraternity securely disposed of; as their compeers, described by Homer,

[50] Juan de Sessa (1518-1597), also known as Johannes Porco Latinus, was one of the first poets to rise out of slavery. His Latin epic on the battle of Lepanto
[51] Mythological Greek giant who was crushed by Athene under Mount Aetna

With burning chains fixed to the brazen floors
And lock'd by hell's inexorable doors.[52]

With their bellowing, the vast chambers of the subterranean rung like the caverns of Delphos,[53] when the inflammable air was fired by the crafty priests. The Inhabitants of the Island started up from their slumbers in shuddering terror, and believed that an earthquake was rumbling beneath their feet.

MR. and MRS. PERSONNE and ZEMBO lost no time in trying the effects of the African's stolen prescription. Being thrown into a tranquil slumber they were conveyed to their plantation; and awoke the next morning, perfectly well, exception slight colds in the head. MR. PERSONNE, having been in *statu quo*, for sixteen years, was now much younger than his lady; a circumstance, for which she was not at all sorry; and which he himself declared by no means displeased him. The remainder of their life was serene as a tropic night;—illumined by the mild effulgence of domestic love;—fanned by the soft aspirations of peaceful bosoms;—and enlivened by the fire-fly scintillations of rapture!!!

ZEMBO, to whose taste and ingenuity they were indebted for their happiness, and who was baptized with the Christian name of BARABBAS, after an uncle of his mother's, recorded what the reader has perused. One only circumstance, like one of those claps of thunder, frequently heard in the unclouded sky, passed over the tranquility of their bosoms. MRS. PERSONNE'S fourth husband's child was a mulatto, and of Vampyrish propensities; of which his mother and MR. PERSONNE were never able entirely to cure him, having used up all the African's preparation.

The intelligent reader, (if any such there be,) will remember that this narrative commenced with the name of MR. ANTHONY GIBBONS, of whom nothing has since been said; and whose adventures (to use a FORUM trope) "must remain buried in the bowels of futurity," until a more convenient opportunity. He is a lineal descendant from the last-mentioned mulatto; and the manuscript, which is now given to the public, was transmitted to him from his ancestors.

He is a resident in Essex county, New-Jersey; and candour requires us to state, that he is no relation to his celebrated

---

[52] Quote from Homer's epic poem "Iliad" 1. VIII. V.13

[53] In legend the caves at Delphos issued strange noises and affected all who came in proximity of it. See *Thaumaturgia, or Elucidations of the Marvellous*, Anonymous, 1835, p. 57

namesake at ELIZABETH-TOWN;[54] as it is notorious to all who have
had the pleasure of witnessing the size of the later gentleman's
waist, that he has too much bowels for so diabolical a
profession; and it is to be hoped in charity, that though he is
such a delicate morsel, when he is laid in the sepulcher of his
fathers, he may not prove a titbit, to GLUT THE THIRST OF A
VAMPYRE!!!

––––––––––––––––––––––––––––

[54] The rotund Thomas Gibbons (1757-1826) was steamboat partner of Aaron
Ogden (1756-1839) and owned a summer home in Elizabethtown, New Jersey.
When Gibbons started his own steamboat company in 1818, Ogden sued,
claiming exclusive steamboat rights between New Jersey and New York. The
case would ultimately be decided by the United State Supreme Court. See,
Gibbons v. Ogden, 22 U.S. 1 (1824)

THEOPHILE GAUTIER
(1811-1872)

Introduction
Clarimonde

"Clarimonde" is a masterpiece in short vampire fiction. The story was first published in the French magazine *La Chronique de Paris* in 1836. The French title, "La Morte Amoureuse," is translated "The Dead Woman in Love." In 1908 it was translated into English by Lafcadio Hearn and titled "Clarimonde" for the first time. A year later, George Burnham Ives also translated it under the title "The Dead Leman" with Leman being an archaic use for the word "lover." The Ives translation does not read as smoothly so the Hearn translation has been republished here.

Like most of the stories in this collection, "Clarimonde" includes a number of firsts for vampire fiction such as the first appearance of a vampire in Venice, Italy, which has now become an all too familiar venue for the undead and their deeds. But most importantly for the genre, "Clarimonde" employs the first use of holy water against a vampire by a priest. Alexander Dumas would later use holy water and other Christian religious symbols in "The Vampire of the Carpathian Mountains."

Clarimonde
(1836)

BROTHER, YOU ASK me if I have ever loved. Yes. My story is a strange and terrible one; and though I am sixty-six years of age, I scarcely dare even now to disturb the ashes of that memory.

From my earliest childhood I had felt a vocation to the priesthood, so that all my studies were directed with that idea in view. Up to the age of twenty-four my life had been only a prolonged novitiate.[1] Having completed my course of theology I successively received all the minor orders, and my superiors judged me worthy, despite my youth, to pass the last awful degree. My ordination was fixed for Easter week.

I had never gone into the world. My world was confined by the walls of the college and the seminary. I knew in a vague sort of a way that there was something called Woman, but I never permitted my thoughts to dwell on such a subject, and I lived in a state of perfect innocence. Twice a year only I saw my infirm and aged mother, and in those visits were comprised my sole relations with the outer world.

I regretted nothing; I felt not the least hesitation at taking the last irrevocable step; I was filled with joy and impatience. Never did a betrothed lover count the slow hours with more feverish ardour; I slept only to dream that I was saying mass; I believed there could be nothing in the world more delightful than to be a priest; I would have refused to be a king or a poet in preference. My ambition could conceive of no loftier aim.

At last the great day came. I walked to the church with a step so light that I fancied myself sustained in air, or that I had wings upon my shoulders. I believed myself an angel, and wondered at the sombre and thoughtful faces of my companions, for there were several of us. I had passed all the night in prayer, and was in a condition wellnigh bordering on ecstasy. The bishop, a venerable old man, seemed to me God the

---

[1] Religious novice

Father leaning over his Eternity, and I beheld Heaven through the vault of the temple.

You well know the details of that ceremony—the benediction,[2] the communion under both forms,[3] the anointing of the palms of the hands with the Oil of Catechumens,[4] and then the holy sacrifice offered in concert with the bishop.

Ah, truly spake Job when he declared that the imprudent man is one who hath not made a covenant with his eyes! I accidentally lifted my head, which until then I had kept down, and beheld before me, so close that it seemed that I could have touched her—although she was actually a considerable distance from me and on the further side of the sanctuary railing—a young woman of extraordinary beauty, and attired with royal magnificence.

It seemed as though scales had suddenly fallen from my eyes. I felt like a blind man who unexpectedly recovers his sight. The bishop, so radiantly glorious but an instant before, suddenly vanished away, the tapers paled upon their golden candlesticks like stars in the dawn, and a vast darkness seemed to fill the whole church. The charming creature appeared in brief relief against the background of that darkness, like some angelic revelation. She seemed herself radiant, and radiating light rather than receiving it.

I lowered my eyelids, firmly resolved not to again open them, that I might not be influenced by external objects, for distraction had gradually taken possession of me until I hardly knew what I was doing.

In another minute, nevertheless, I reopened my eyes, for through my eyelashes I still beheld her, all sparkling with prismatic colours, and surrounded with such a purple penumbra[5] as one beholds in gazing at the sun.

Oh, how beautiful she was! The greatest painters, who followed ideal beauty into heaven itself, and thence brought back to earth the true portrait of the Madonna,[6] never in their delineations even approached that wildly beautiful reality which

---

[2] Roman Catholic service where congregation is blessed by priest
[3] Communion of the Eucharist by taking both wine, which represents the blood of Jesus Christ, and bread, which represents his body at the time of his crucifixion
[4] Christian preparation for confirmation
[5] Glow or radiance
[6] Mary, the mother of Jesus Christ

I saw before me. Neither the verses of the poet nor the palette of the artist could convey any conception of her.

She was rather tall, with a form and bearing of a goddess. Her hair, of a soft blonde hue, was parted in the midst and flowed back over her temples in two rivers of rippling gold; she seemed a diademed queen. Her forehead, bluish-white in its transparency, extended its calm breadth above the arches of her eyebrows, which by a strange singularity were almost black, and admirably relieved the effect of sea-green eyes of unsustainable vivacity and brilliancy. What eyes! With a single flash they could have decided a man's destiny. They had a life, a limpidity, an ardour, a humid light which I have never seen in human eyes; they shot forth rays like arrows, which I could distinctly *see* enter my heart. I know not if the fire which illumined them came from heaven or from hell, but assuredly it came from one or the other. That woman was either an angel or a demon, perhaps both.

Assuredly she never sprang from the flank of Eve,[7] our common mother. Teeth of the most lustrous pearl gleamed in her ruddy smile, and at every inflection of her lips little dimples appeared in the satiny rose of her adorable cheeks. There was a delicacy and pride in the regal outline of her nostrils bespeaking noble blood. Agate gleams played ever the smooth lustrous skin of her half-bare shoulders, and strings of great blonde pearls— almost equal to her neck in beauty of colour—descended upon her bosom.

From time to time she elevated her head with the undulating grace of a startled serpent or peacock, thereby imparting a quivering motion to the high lace ruff which surrounded it like a silver trellis-work. She wore a robe of orange-red velvet, and from her wide ermine-lined[8] sleeves there peeped forth patrician hands[9] of infinite delicacy, and so ideally transparent that, like the fingers of Aurora,[10] they permitted the light to shine through them.

All these details I can recollect at this moment as plainly as though they were of yesterday, for notwithstanding I was greatly troubled at the time, nothing escaped me; the faintest touch of shading, the little dark speck at the point of the chin, the imperceptible down at the corners of the lips, the velvety floss

---

[7] Biblical Eve, the first woman on earth
[8] White fur of the stoat
[9] Hands of refinement or aristocracy
[10] Mythical Roman goddess of the dawn

upon the brow, the quivering shadows of the eyelashes upon the cheeks, I could notice everything with astonishing lucidity of perception.

And gazing I felt opening within me gates that had until then remained closed; vents long obstructed became all clear, permitting glimpses of unfamiliar perspectives within; life suddenly made itself visible to me under a totally novel aspect. I felt as though I had just been born into a new world and a new order of things. A frightful anguish commenced to torture my heart as with red-hot pincers.

Every successive minute seemed to me at once but a second and yet a century. Meanwhile the ceremony was proceeding, and with an effort of will sufficient to have uprooted a mountain, I strove to cry out that I would not be a priest, but I could not speak; my tongue seemed nailed to my palate, and I found it impossible to express my will by the least syllable of negation. Though fully awake, I felt like one under the influence of a nightmare, who vainly strives to shriek out the one word upon which life depends.

She seemed conscious of the martyrdon I was undergoing, and, as though to encourage me, she gave me a look replete with divinest promise. Her eyes were a poem; their every glance was a song.

She said to me:

"If thou wilt be mine, I shall make thee happier than God Himself in His paradise. The angels themselves will be jealous of thee. Tear off that funeral shroud in which thou art about to wrap thyself. I am Beauty, I am Youth, I am Life. Come to me! Together we shall be Love. Can Jehovah[11] offer thee aught in exchange? Our lives will flow on like a dream, in one eternal kiss.

"Fling forth the wine of that chalice, and thou art free. I will conduct thee to the Unknown Isles. Thou shalt sleep in my bosom upon a bed of massy gold under a silver pavilion, for I love thee and would take thee away from thy God, before whom so many noble hearts pour forth floods of love which never reach even the steps of His throne!"

These words seemed to float to my ears in a rhythm of infinite sweetness, for her look was actually sonorous, and the utterances of her eyes were re-echoed in the depths of my heart as though living lips had breathed them into my life. I felt myself willing to renounce God, and yet my tongue mechanically

---

[11] God

fulfilled all the formalities of the ceremony. The fair one gave me another look, so beseeching, so despairing that keen blades seemed to pierce my heart, and I felt my bosom transfixed by more swords than those of Our Lady of Sorrows.[12]

All was consummated; I had become a priest.

Never was deeper anguish painted on human face than upon hers. The maiden who beholds her affianced lover suddenly fall dead at her side, the mother bending over the empty cradle of her child, Eve seated at the threshold of the gate of Paradise, the miser who finds a stone substituted for his stolen treasure, the poet who accidentally permits the only manuscript of his finest work to fall into the fire, could not wear a look so despairing, so inconsolable.

All the blood had abandoned her charming face, leaving it whiter than marble; her beautiful arms hung lifelessly on either side of her body as though their muscles had suddenly relaxed, and she sought the support of a pillar, for her yielding limbs almost betrayed her. As for myself, I staggered toward the door of the church, livid as death, my forehead bathed with a sweat bloodier than that of Calvary;[13] I felt as though I were being strangled; the vault seemed to have flattened down upon my shoulders, and it seemed to me that my head alone sustained the whole weight of the dome.

As I was about to cross the threshold a hand suddenly caught mine—a woman's hand! I had never till then touched the hand of any woman. It was cold as a serpent's skin, and yet its impress remained upon my wrist, burnt there as though branded by a glowing iron. It was she.

"Unhappy man! Unhappy man! What hast thou done?" she exclaimed in a low voice, and immediately disappeared in the crowd.

The aged bishop passed by. He cast a severe and scrutinizing look upon me. My face presented the wildest aspect imaginable; I blushed and turned pale alternately; dazzling lights flashed before my eyes. A companion took pity on me. He seized my arm and led me out. I could not possibly have found my way back to the seminary unassisted. At the corner of a street, while the young priest's attention was momentarily turned in another direction, a negro page, fantastically garbed, approached me, and without pausing on his way slipped into my

---

[12] Reference to Mary, the mother of Jesus Christ, and the sorrow in her life

[13] The forehead of Jesus Christ was bloodied during his crucifixion by a crown of thorns placed on his head

hand a little pocket-book with gold-embroidered corners, at the same time giving me a sign to hide it. I concealed it in my sleeve, and there kept it until I found myself alone in my cell.

Then I opened the clasp. There were only two leaves within, bearing the words, "Clarimonde. At the Concini Palace."

So little acquainted was I at that time with the things of this world that I had never heard of Clarimonde, celebrated as she was, and I had no idea as to where the Concini Palace was situated. I hazarded a thousand conjectures, each more extravagant than the last; but, in truth, I cared little whether she were a great lady or a courtesan, so that I could but see her once more.

My love, although the growth of a single hour, had taken imperishable root. I gave myself up to a thousand extravagancies. I kissed the place upon my hand which she had touched, and I repeated her name over and over again for hours in succession. I only needed to close my eyes in order to see her distinctly as though she were actually present; and I reiterated to myself the words she had uttered in my ear at the church porch: "Unhappy man! Unhappy man! What hast thou done?"

I comprehended at last the full horror of my situation, and the funereal and awful restraints of the state into which I had just entered became clearly revealed to me. To be a priest!—that is, to be chaste, to never love, to observe no distinction of sex or age, to turn from the sight of all beauty, to put out one's own eyes, to hide forever crouching in the chill shadows of some church or cloister, to visit none but the dying, to watch by unknown corpses, and ever bear about with one the black soutane[14] as a garb of mourning for one's self, so that your very dress might serve as a pall for your coffin.

What could I do in order to see Clarimonde once more? I had no pretext to offer for desiring to leave the seminary, not knowing any person in the city. I would not even be able to remain there but a short time, and was only waiting my assignment to the curacy[15] which I must thereafter occupy. I tried to remove the bars of the window; but it was at a fearful height from the ground, and I found that as I had no ladder it would be useless to think of escaping thus. And, furthermore, I could descend thence only by night in any event, and afterward how should I be able to find my way through the inextricable labyrinth of streets? All these difficulties, which to many would

[14] Cassock is a robe worn by priests that extends to the shoes
[15] Cleric for a parish who must tend to the souls of the congregation

have appeared altogether insignificant, were gigantic to me, a poor seminarist who had fallen in love only the day before for the first time, without experience, without money, without attire.

"Ah!" cried I to myself in my blindness, "were I not a priest I could have seen her every day; I might have been her lover, her spouse. Instead of being wrapped in this dismal shroud of mine I would have had garments of silk and velvet, golden chains, a sword, and fair plumes like other handsome young cavaliers. My hair, instead of being dishonoured by the tonsure, would flow down upon my neck in waving curls; I would have a fine waxed moustache; I would be a gallant."[16] But one hour passed before an altar, a few hastily articulated words, had forever cut me off from the number of the living, and I had myself sealed down the stone of my own tomb; I had with my own hand bolted the gate of my prison!

I went to the window. The sky was beautifully blue; the trees had donned their spring robes; nature seemed to be making parade of an ironical joy. The place was filled with people, some going, others coming; young *b'aux* and young beauties were sauntering in couples toward the groves and gardens; merry youths passed by, cheerily trolling refrains of drinking songs—it was all a picture of vivacity, life, animation, gaiety, which formed a bitter contrast with my mourning and my solitude.

On the steps of the gate sat a young mother playing with her child. She kissed its little rosy mouth still impearled with drops of milk, and performed, in order to amuse it, a thousand divine little puerilities such as only mothers know how to invent. The father standing at a little distance smiled gently upon the charming group, and with folded arms seemed to hug his joy to his heart. I could not endure that spectacle. I closed the window with violence, and flung myself on my bed, my heart filled with frightful hate and jealousy, and gnawed my fingers and my bed covers like a tiger that has passed ten days without food.

I know not how long I remained in this condition, but at last, while writhing on the bed in a fit of spasmodic fury, I suddenly perceived the Abbe Serapion, who was standing erect in the centre of the room, watching me attentively. Filled with shame of myself, I let my head fall upon my breast and covered my face with my hands.

"Romuald, my friend, something very extraordinary is transpiring within you," observed Serapion, after a few

---

[16] A dashing man who favors the company of women

moments' silence; "your conduct is altogether inexplicable. You—always so quiet, so pious, so gentle—you to rage in your cell like a wild beast! Take heed, brother—do not listen to the suggestions of the devil. Fear not. Never allow yourself to become discouraged. The most watchful and steadfast souls are at moments liable to such temptation. Pray, fast, meditate, and the Evil Spirit will depart from you."

The words of the Abbe Serapion restored me to myself, and I became a little more calm.

"I came," he continued, "to tell you that you have been appointed to the curacy of C. The priest who had charge of it has just died, and Monseigneur the Bishop has ordered me to have you installed there at once. Be ready, therefore, to start tomorrow."

To leave tomorrow without having been able to see her again, to add yet another barrier to the many already interposed between us, to lose forever all hope of being able to meet her, except, indeed, through a miracle! Even to write her, alas! would be impossible, for by whom could I despatch my letter? With my sacred character of priest, to whom could I dare unbosom myself, in whom could I confide? I became a prey to the bitterest anxiety.

Next morning Serapion came to take me away. Two mules freighted with our miserable valises awaited us at the gate. He mounted one, and I the other as well as I knew how.

As we passed along the streets of the city, I gazed attentively at all the windows and balconies in the hope of seeing Clarimonde, but it was yet early in the morning, and the city had hardly opened its eyes. Mine sought to penetrate the blinds and window-curtains of all the palaces before which we were passing. Serapion doubtless attributed this curiosity to my admiration of the architecture, for he slackened the pace of his animal in order to give me time to look around me.

At last we passed the city gates and commenced to mount the hill beyond. When we arrived at its summit I turned to take a last look at the place where Clarimonde dwelt. The shadow of a great cloud hung over all the city; the contrasting colours of its blue and red roofs were lost in the uniform half-tint, through which here and there floated upward, like white flakes of foam, the smoke of freshly kindled fires. By a singular optical effect one edifice, which surpassed in height all the neighbouring buildings that were still dimly veiled by the vapours, towered up, fair and lustrous with the gilding of a solitary beam of sunlight—although actually more than a league away it seemed quite near. The smallest details of its architecture were plainly distinguishable—the turrets, the platform, the window-casements and even the swallow tailed weather vanes.

"What is that place I see over there, all lighted up by the sun?" I asked Serapion.

He shaded his eyes with his hand, and having looked in the direction indicated, replied: "It is the ancient palace which the Prince Concini has given to the courtesan Clarimonde. Awful things are done there!"

At that instant, I know not yet whether it was a reality or an illusion, I fancied I saw gliding along the terrace a shapely white figure, which gleamed for a moment in passing and as quickly vanished. It was Clarimonde.

Oh, did she know that at that very hour, all feverish and restless—from the height of the rugged road which separated me from her and which, alas! I could never more descend—I was directing my eyes upon the palace where she dwelt, and which a mocking beam of sunlight seemed to bring nigh to me, as though inviting me to enter therein as its lord? Undoubtedly she must have known it, for her soul was too sympathetically united with mine not to have felt its least emotional thrill, and that subtle sympathy it must have been which prompted her to climb—although clad only in her night-dress—to the summit of the terrace, amid the icy dews of the morning.

The shadow gained the palace, and the scene became to the eye only a motionless ocean of roofs and gables, amid which one mountainous undulation was distinctly visible. Serapion urged his mule forward, my own at once followed at the same gait, and a sharp angle in the road at last hid the city of S forever from my eyes, as I was destined never to return thither.

At the close of a weary three-days' journey through dismal country fields, we caught sight of the cock upon the steeple of the church which I was to take charge of, peeping above the trees, and after having followed some winding roads fringed with thatched cottages and little gardens, we found ourselves in front of the façade, which certainly possessed few features of magnificence. A porch ornamented with some mouldings, and two or three pillars rudely hewn from sandstone; a tiled roof with counterforts[17] of the same sandstone as the pillars, that was all.

To the left lay the cemetery, overgrown with high weeds, and having a great iron cross rising up in its centre; to the right

---

[17] Buttress for strengthening a wall

stood the presbytery,[18] under the shadow of the church. It was a house of the most extreme simplicity and frigid cleanliness. We entered the enclosure. A few chickens were picking up some oats scattered upon the ground; accustomed, seemingly, to the black habit of ecclesiastics,[19] they showed no fear of our presence and scarcely troubled themselves to get out of our way. A hoarse, wheezy barking fell upon our ears, and we saw an aged dog running toward us.

It was my predecessor's dog. He had dull bleared eyes, grizzled hair, and every mark of the greatest age to which a dog can possibly attain. I patted him gently, and he proceeded at once to march along beside me with an air of satisfaction unspeakable. A very old woman, who had been the housekeeper of the former cure, also came to meet us, and after having invited me into a little back parlour, asked whether I intended to retain her. I replied that I would take care of her, and the dog, and the chickens, and all the furniture her master had bequeathed her at his death. At this she became fairly transported with joy, and the Abbe Serapion at once paid her the price which she asked for her little property.

For a whole year I fulfilled all the duties of my calling with the most scrupulous exactitude, praying and fasting, exhorting and lending ghostly aid to the sick, and bestowing alms even to the extent of frequently depriving myself of the very necessaries of life. But I felt a great aridness within me, and the sources of grace seemed closed against me. I never found that happiness which should spring from the fulfillment of a holy mission; my thoughts were far away, and the words of Clarimonde were ever upon my lips like an involuntary refrain. Oh, brother, meditate well on this! Through having but once lifted my eyes to look upon a woman, through one fault apparently so venial,[20] I have for years remained a victim to the most miserable agonies, and the happiness of my life has been destroyed forever.

I will not longer dwell upon those defeats, or on those inward victories invariably followed by yet more terrible falls, but will at once proceed to the facts of my story. One night my door-bell was long and violently rung. The aged housekeeper arose and opened to the stranger, and the figure of a man, whose complexion was deeply bronzed, and who was richly clad in a

---

[18] Structure of church used by the clergy
[19] Counsel of the clergy
[20] Small or slight

foreign costume, with a poniard[21] at his girdle, appeared under the rays of Barbara's lantern.

Her first impulse was one of terror, but the stranger reassured her, and stated that he desired to see me at once on matters relating to my holy calling. Barbara invited him upstairs, where I was on the point of retiring. The stranger told me that his mistress, a very noble lady, was lying at the point of death, and desired to see a priest. I replied that I was prepared to follow him, took with me the sacred articles necessary for extreme unction,[22] and descended in all haste.

Two horses, black as the night itself, stood without the gate, pawing the ground with impatience, and veiling their chests with long streams of smoky vapour exhaled from their nostrils. He held the stirrup and aided me to mount upon one; then, merely laying his hand upon the pummel of the saddle, he vaulted on the other, pressed the animal's sides with his knees, and loosened rein. The horse bounded forward with the velocity of an arrow. Mine, of which the stranger held the bridle, also started off at a swift gallop, keeping up with his companion.

We devoured the road. The ground flowed backward beneath us in a long streaked line of pale grey, and the black silhouettes of the trees seemed fleeing by us on either side like an army in rout. We passed through a forest so profoundly gloomy that I felt my flesh creep in the chill darkness with superstitious fear. The showers of bright sparks which flew from the stony road under the ironshod feet of our horses, remained glowing in our wake like a fiery trail; and had any one at that hour of the night beheld us both—my guide and myself—he must have taken us for two spectres riding upon nightmares.

Witch-fires ever and anon flitted across the road before us, and the night-birds shrieked fearsomely in the depth of the woods beyond, where we beheld at intervals glow the phosphorescent eyes of wildcats. The manes of the horses became more and more disheveled, the sweat streamed over their flanks, and their breath came through their nostrils hard and fast. But when he found them slacking pace, the guide reanimated them by uttering a strange, guttural, unearthly cry, and the gallop recommenced with fury. At last the whirlwind race ceased; a huge black mass, pierced through with many bright points of light, suddenly rose before us, the hoofs of our horses echoed louder upon a strong wooden drawbridge, and we

---

[21] Slim dagger
[22] Anointment of oil during last rites

rode under a great vaulted archway which darkly yawned between two enormous towers.

Some great excitement evidently reigned in the castle. Servants with torches were crossing the courtyard in every direction, and above lights were ascending and descending from landing to landing. I obtained a confused glimpse of vast masses of architecture—columns, arcades, flights of steps, stairways—a royal voluptuousness and elfin magnificence of construction worthy of fairyland. A negro page—the same who had before brought me the tablet from Clarimonde, and whom I instantly recognized—approached to aid me in dismounting, and the major-domo,[23] attired in black velvet with a gold chain about his neck, advanced to meet me, supporting himself upon an ivory cane. Large tears were falling from his eyes and streaming over his cheeks and white beard.

"Too late!" he cried, sorrowfully shaking his venerable head. "Too late, sir priest! But if you have not been able to save the soul, come at least to watch by the poor body."

He took my arm and conducted me to the death chamber. I wept not less bitterly than he, for I had learned that the dead one was none other than that Clarimonde whom I had so deeply and so wildly loved. A *prie-dieu*[24] stood at the foot of the bed; a bluish flame flickering in a bronze patera filled all the room with a wan, deceptive light, here and there bringing out in the darkness at intervals some projection of furniture or cornice.

In a chiseled urn upon the table there was a faded white rose, whose leaves—excepting one that still held—had all fallen, like odorous tears, to the foot of the vase. A broken black mask, a fan, and disguises of every variety, which were lying on the arm-chairs, bore witness that death had entered suddenly and unannounced into that sumptuous dwelling. Without daring to cast my eyes upon the bed, I knelt down and commenced to repeat the Psalms for the Dead,[25] with exceeding fervour, thanking God that He had placed the tomb between me and the memory of this woman, so that I might thereafter be able to utter her name in my prayers as a name forever sanctified by death.

But my fervour gradually weakened, and I fell insensibly into a reverie. That chamber bore no semblance to a chamber of death. In lieu of the foetid and cadaverous odours which I had

---

[23] Chief steward

[24] Desk-like piece of furniture used to kneel on during prayer

[25] Verses from the book of Psalms prayed for the dead

been accustomed to breathe during such funereal vigils, a languorous vapour of Oriental perfume—I know not what amorous odour of woman— softly floated through the tepid air. That pale light seemed rather a twilight gloom contrived for voluptuous pleasure, than a substitute for the yellow-flickering watch-tapers which shine by the side of corpses. I thought upon the strange destiny which enabled me to meet Clarimonde again at the very moment when she was lost to me forever, and a sigh of regretful anguish escaped from my breast.

Then it seemed to me that some one behind me had also sighed, and I turned round to look. It was only an echo. But in that moment my eyes fell upon the bed of death which they had till then avoided. The red damask[26] curtains, decorated with large flowers worked in embroidery, and looped up with gold bullion, permitted me to behold the fair dead, lying at full length, with hands joined upon her bosom.

She was covered with a linen wrapping of dazzling whiteness, which formed a strong contrast with the gloomy purple of the hangings, and was of so fine a texture that it concealed nothing of her body's charming form, and allowed the eye to follow those beautiful outlines— undulating like the neck of a swan—which even death had not robbed of their supple grace. She seemed an alabaster statue executed by some skilful sculptor to place upon the tomb of a queen, or rather, perhaps, like a slumbering maiden over whom the silent snow had woven a spotless veil.

I could no longer maintain my constrained attitude of prayer. The air of the alcove intoxicated me, that febrile perfume of half-faded roses penetrated my very brain, and I commenced to pace restlessly up and down the chamber, pausing at each turn before the bier to contemplate the graceful corpse lying beneath the transparency of its shroud. Wild fancies came thronging to my brain. I thought to myself that she might not, perhaps, be really dead; that she might only have feigned death for the purpose of bringing me to her castle, and then declaring her love. At one time I even thought I saw her foot move under the whiteness of the coverings, and slightly disarrange the long, straight folds of the winding sheet.

And then I asked myself: "Is this indeed Clarimonde? What proof have I that it is she? Might not that black page have passed into the service of some other lady? Surely, I must be

---

[26] Stiff and luxurious fabric

going mad to torture and afflict myself thus!" But my heart answered with a fierce throbbing: "It is she; it is she indeed!"

I approached the bed again, and fixed my eyes with redoubled attention upon the object of my incertitude. Ah, must I confess it? That exquisite perfection of bodily form, although purified and made sacred by the shadow of death, affected me more voluptuously than it should have done, and that repose so closely resembled slumber that one might well have mistaken it for such. I forgot that I had come there to perform a funeral ceremony; I fancied myself a young bridegroom entering the chamber of the bride, who all modestly hides her fair face, and through coyness seeks to keep herself wholly veiled.

Heartbroken with grief, yet wild with hope, shuddering at once with fear and pleasure, I bent over her and grasped the corner of the sheet. I lifted it back, holding my breath all the while through fear of waking her. My arteries throbbed with such violence that I felt them hiss through my temples, and the sweat poured from my forehead in streams, as though I had lifted a mighty slab of marble. There, indeed, lay Clarimonde, even as I had seen her at the church on the day of my ordination. She was not less charming than then. With her, death seemed but a last coquetry.[27]

The pallor of her cheeks, the less brilliant carnation of her lips, her long eyelashes lowered and relieving their dark fringe against that white skin, lent her an unspeakably seductive aspect of melancholy chastity and mental suffering; her long loose hair, still intertwined with some little blue flowers, made a shining pillow for her head, and veiled the nudity of her shoulders with its thick ringlets; her beautiful hands, purer, more diaphanous than the Host, were crossed on her bosom in an attitude of pious rest and silent prayer, which served to counteract all that might have proven otherwise too alluring— even after death—in the exquisite roundness and ivory polish of her bare arms from which the pearl bracelets had not yet been removed.

I remained long in mute contemplation, and the more I gazed, the less could I persuade myself that life had really abandoned that beautiful body forever. I do not know whether it was an illusion or a reflection of the lamplight, but it seemed to me that the blood was again commencing to circulate under that lifeless pallor, although she remained all motionless. I laid my hand lightly on her arm; it was cold, but not colder than her

---

[27] Flirtation

hand on the day when it touched mine at the portals of the church. I resumed my position, bending my face above her, and bathing her cheeks with the warm dew of my tears. Ah, what bitter feelings of despair and helplessness, what agonies unutterable did I endure in that long watch! Vainly did I wish that I could have gathered all my life into one mass that I might give it all to her, and breathe into her chill remains the flame which devoured me.

The night advanced, and feeling the moment of eternal separation approach, I could not deny myself the last sad sweet pleasure of imprinting a kiss upon the dead lips of her who had been my only love. . . . Oh, miracle! A faint breath mingled itself with my breath, and the mouth of Clarimonde responded to the passionate pressure of mine. Her eyes unclosed, and lighted up with something of their former brilliancy; she uttered a long sigh, and uncrossing her arms, passed them around my neck with a look of ineffable delight.

"Ah, it is thou, Romuald;" she murmured in a voice languishingly sweet as the last vibrations of a harp. "What ailed thee, dearest? I waited so long for thee that I am dead; but we are now betrothed; I can see thee and visit thee. *Adieu*, Romuald, *adieu!* I love thee. That is all I wished to tell thee, and I give thee back the life which thy kiss for a moment recalled. We shall soon meet again."

Her head fell back, but her arms yet encircled me, as though to retain me still. A furious whirlwind suddenly burst in that window, and entered the chamber. The last remaining leaf of the white rose for a moment palpitated at the extremity of the stalk like a butterfly's wing, then it detached itself and flew forth through the open casement, bearing with it the soul of Clarimonde. The lamp was extinguished, and I fell insensible upon the bosom of the beautiful dead.

When I came to myself again I was lying on the bed in my little room at the presbytery, and the old dog of the former cure was licking my hand which had been hanging down outside of the covers. Afterward I learned that I had lain thus for three days, giving no evidence of life beyond the faintest respiration. Barbara told me that the same coppery-complexioned man who came to seek me on the night of my departure from the presbytery, had brought me back the next morning in a close litter, and departed immediately afterward; but none knew of any castle in the neighbourhood answering to the description of that in which I had again found Clarimonde.

One morning I found the Abbe Serapion in my room. While he inquired after my health in hypocritically honeyed accents, he constantly kept his two great yellow lion-eyes fixed upon me, and plunged his look into my soul like a sounding lead. Suddenly he said, in a clear vibrant voice, which rang in my ears like the trumpets of the Last Judgment:

"The great courtesan Clarimonde died a few days ago, at the close of an orgie which lasted eight days and eight nights. It was something infernally splendid. The abominations of the banquets of Belshazzar[28] and Cleopatra[29] were re-enacted there. Good God, what age are we living in? The guests were served by swarthy slaves who spoke an unknown tongue, and who seemed to me to be veritable demons. The livery of the very least among them would have served for the gala-dress of an emperor. There have always been very strange stories told of this Clarimonde, and all her lovers came to a violent or miserable end. They used to say that she was a ghoul, a female vampire; but I believe she was none other than Beelzebub[30] himself."

He ceased to speak and commenced to regard me more attentively than ever, as though to observe the effect of his words on me. I could not refrain from starting when I heard him utter the name of Clarimonde, and this news of her death, in addition to the pain it caused me by reason of its coincidence with the nocturnal scenes I had witnessed, filled me with an agony and terror which my face betrayed, despite my utmost endeavours to appear composed.

Serapion fixed an anxious and severe look upon me, and then observed: "My son, I must warn you that you are standing with foot raised upon the brink of an abyss; take heed lest you fall therein. Satan's claws are long, and tombs are not always true to their trust. The tombstone of Clarimonde should be sealed down with a triple seal, for, if report be true, it is not the first time she has died. May God watch over you, Romuald!"

And with these words the Abbe walked slowly to the door. I did not see him again at that time, for he left for S almost immediately.

I became completely restored to health and resumed my accustomed duties. The memory of Clarimonde and the words of the old Abbe were constantly in my mind; nevertheless no extraordinary event had occurred to verify the funereal

---

[28] Prince of Babylon in the 6th century B.C.
[29] Cleopatra VII, queen of Egypt and last pharaoh
[30] Satan

predictions of Serapion, and I had commenced to believe that his fears and my own terrors were over exaggerated, when one night I had a strange dream.

I had hardly fallen asleep when I heard my bed-curtains drawn apart, as their rings slided back upon the curtain rod with a sharp sound. I rose up quickly upon my elbow, and beheld the shadow of a woman standing erect before me. I recognized Clarimonde immediately. She bore in her hand a little lamp, shaped like those which are placed in tombs, and its light lent her fingers a rosy transparency, which extended itself by lessening degrees even to the opaque and milky whiteness of her bare arm.

Her only garment was the linen winding-sheet which had shrouded her when lying upon the bed of death. She sought to gather its folds over her bosom as though ashamed of being so scantily clad, but her little hand was not equal to the task. She was so white that the colour of the drapery blended with that of her flesh under the pallid rays of the lamp.

Enveloped with this subtle tissue which betrayed all the contour of her body, she seemed rather the marble statue of some fair antique bather than a woman endowed with life. But dead or living, statue or woman, shadow or body, her beauty was still the same, only that the green light of her eyes was less brilliant, and her mouth, once so warmly crimson, was only tinted with a faint tender rosiness, like that of her cheeks. The little blue flowers which I had noticed entwined in her hair were withered and dry, and had lost nearly all their leaves, but this did not prevent her from being charming—so charming that notwithstanding the strange character of the adventure, and the unexplainable manner in which she had entered my room, I felt not even for a moment the least fear.

She placed the lamp on the table and seated herself at the foot of my bed; then bending toward me, she said, in that voice at once silvery clear and yet velvety in its sweet softness, such as I never heard from any lips save hers:

"I have kept thee long in waiting, dear Romuald, and it must have seemed to thee that I had forgotten thee. But I come from afar off, very far off, and from a land whence no other has ever yet returned. There is neither sun nor moon in that land whence I come: all is but space and shadow; there is neither road nor pathway: no earth for the foot, no air for the wing; and nevertheless behold me here, for Love is stronger than Death and must conquer him in the end. Oh what sad faces and fearful things I have seen on my way hither! What difficulty my soul, returned to earth through the power of will alone, has had in finding its body and reinstating itself therein! What terrible efforts I had to make ere I could lift the ponderous slab with which they had covered me! See, the palms of my poor hands are all bruised! Kiss them, sweet love, that they may be healed!"

She laid the cold palms of her hands upon my mouth, one after the other. I kissed them, indeed, many times, and she the while watched me with a smile of ineffable affection.

I confess to my shame that I had entirely forgotten the advice of the Abbe Serapion and the sacred office wherewith I had been invested. I had fallen without resistance, and at the first assault. I had not even made the least effort to repel the tempter. The fresh coolness of Clarimonde's skin penetrated my own, and I felt voluptuous tremors pass over my whole body. Poor child! in spite of all I saw afterward, I can hardly yet believe she was a demon; at least she had no appearance of being such, and never did Satan so skilfully conceal his claws and horns.

She had drawn her feet up beneath her, and squatted down on the edge of the couch in an attitude full of negligent coquetry. From time to time she passed her little hand through my hair and twisted it into curls, as though trying how a new style of wearing it would become my face. I abandoned myself to her hands with the most guilty pleasure, while she accompanied her gentle play with the prettiest prattle. The most remarkable fact was that I felt no astonishment whatever at so extraordinary an adventure, and as in dreams one finds no difficulty in accepting the most fantastic events as simple facts, so all these circumstances seemed to me perfectly natural in themselves.

"I loved thee long ere I saw thee, dear Romuald, and sought thee everywhere. Thou wast my dream, and I first saw thee in the church at the fatal moment. I said at once, 'It is he!'

"I gave thee a look into which I threw all the love I ever had, all the love I now have, all the love I shall ever have for thee—a look that would have damned a cardinal or brought a king to his knees at my feet in view of all his court. Thou remainedst unmoved, preferring thy God to me!

"Ah, how jealous I am of that God whom thou didst love and still lovest more than me!

"Woe is me, unhappy one that I am! I can never have thy heart all to myself, I whom thou didst recall to life with a kiss—dead Clarimonde, who for thy sake bursts asunder the gates of the tomb, and comes to consecrate to thee a life which she has resumed only to make thee happy!"

All her words were accompanied with the most impassioned caresses, which bewildered my sense and my reason to such an extent, that I did not fear to utter a frightful blasphemy for the sake of consoling her, and to declare that I loved her as much as God.

Her eyes rekindled and shone like chrysoprases.[31] "In truth?—in very truth? as much as God!" she cried, flinging her beautiful arms around me. "Since it is so, thou wilt come with me; thou wilt follow me whithersoever I desire. Thou wilt cast away thy ugly black habit. Thou shalt be the proudest and most envied of cavaliers; thou shalt be my lover! To be the acknowledged lover of Clarimonde, who has refused even a Pope, that will be something to feel proud of! Ah, the fair, unspeakably happy existence, the beautiful golden life we shall live together! And when shall we depart, my fair sir?"

"Tomorrow! Tomorrow!" I cried in my delirium.

"Tomorrow, then, so let it be!" she answered. "In the meanwhile I shall have opportunity to change my toilet, for this is a little too light and in nowise suited for a voyage. I must also forthwith notify all my friends who believe me dead, and mourn for me as deeply as they are capable of doing. The money, the dresses, the carriages—all will be ready. I shall call for thee at this same hour. *Adieu*, dear heart!"

And she lightly touched my forehead with her lips. The lamp went out, the curtains closed again, and all became dark; a leaden, dreamless sleep fell on me and held me unconscious until the morning following.

I awoke later than usual, and the recollection of this singular adventure troubled me during the whole day. I finally persuaded myself that it was a mere vapour of my heated imagination. Nevertheless its sensations had been so vivid that it was difficult to persuade myself that they were not real, and it was not without some presentiment of what was going to happen that I got into bed at last, after having prayed God to drive far from me all thoughts of evil, and to protect the chastity of my slumber.

I soon fell into a deep sleep, and my dream was continued. The curtains again parted, and I beheld Clarimonde, not as on the former occasion, pale in her pale winding-sheet, with the violets of death upon her cheeks but gay, sprightly, jaunty, in a superb travelling dress of green velvet, trimmed with gold lace, and looped up on either side to allow a glimpse of satin

---

[31] Green gemstone

petticoat. Her blond hair escaped in thick ringlets from beneath a broad black felt hat, decorated with white feathers whimsically twisted into various shapes. In one hand she held a little riding whip terminated by a golden whistle. She tapped me lightly with it, and exclaimed: "Well, my fine sleeper, is this the way you make your preparations? I thought I would find you up and dressed. Arise quickly, we have no time to lose."

I leaped out of bed at once.

"Come, dress yourself, and let us go," she continued, pointing to a little package she had brought with her. "The horses are becoming impatient of delay and champing their bits at the door. We ought to have been by this time at least ten leagues distant from here."

I dressed myself hurriedly, and she handed me the articles of apparel herself one by one, bursting into laughter from time to time at my awkwardness, as she explained to me the use of a garment when I had made a mistake. She hurriedly arranged my hair, and this done, held up before me a little pocket mirror of Venetian crystal,[32] rimmed with silver filigree-work, and playfully asked: "How dost find thyself now? Wilt engage me for thy *valet de chambre*?"

I was no longer the same person, and I could not even recognize myself. I resembled my former self no more than a finished statue resembles a block of stone. My old face seemed but a coarse daub of the one reflected in the mirror. I was handsome, and my vanity was sensibly tickled by the metamorphosis. That elegant apparel, that richly embroidered vest had made of me a totally different personage, and I marvelled at the power of transformation owned by a few yards of cloth cut after a certain pattern. The spirit of my costume penetrated my very skin, and within ten minutes more I had become something of a coxcomb.[33]

In order to feel more at ease in my new attire, I took several turns up and down the room. Clarimonde watched me with an air of maternal pleasure, and appeared well satisfied with her work.

"Come, enough of this child's-play! Let us start, Romuald, dear. We have far to go, and we may not get there in time." She took my hand and led me forth. All the doors opened before her at a touch, and we passed by the dog without awaking him.

[32] Venice, Italy became the world's foremost crystal producer in the 13th century
[33] Man who enjoys dressing lavishly

At the gate we found Margheritone waiting, the same swarthy groom who had once before been my escort. He held the bridles of three horses, all black like those which bore us to the castle—one for me, one for him, one for Clarimonde. Those horses must have been Spanish genets born of mares fecundated[34] by a zephyr,[35] for they were fleet as the wind itself, and the moon, which had just risen at our departure to light us on our way, rolled over the sky like a wheel detached from her own chariot.

We beheld her on the right leaping from tree to tree, and putting herself out of breath in the effort to keep up with us. Soon we came upon a level plain where, hard by a clump of trees, a carriage with four vigorous horses awaited us. We entered it, and the postilions[36] urged their animals into a mad gallop.

I had one arm around Clarimonde's waist, and one of her hands clasped in mine; her head leaned upon my shoulder, and I felt her bosom, half bare, lightly pressing against my arm. I had never known such intense happiness. In that hour I had forgotten everything, and I no more remembered having ever been a priest than I remembered what I had been doing in my mother's womb, so great was the fascination which the evil spirit exerted upon me. From that night my nature seemed in some sort to have become halved, and there were two men within me, neither of whom knew the other.

At one moment I believed myself a priest who dreamed nightly that he was a gentleman, at another that I was a gentleman who dreamed he was a priest. I could no longer distinguish the dream from the reality, nor could I discover where the reality began or where ended the dream. The exquisite young lord and libertine railed at the priest, the priest loathed the dissolute habits of the young lord. I always retained with extreme vividness all the perceptions of my two lives.

Only there was one absurd fact which I could not explain to myself—namely, that the consciousness of the same individuality existed in two men so opposite in character. It was an anomaly for which I could not account—whether I believed myself to be the cure of the little village of C, or II Signor Romualdo, the titled lover of Clarimonde.

---

[34] Impregnated
[35] Sudden gust of wind
[36] Carriage driver

Be that as it may, I lived, at least I believed that I lived, in Venice. I have never been able to discover rightly how much of illusion and how much of reality there was in this fantastic adventure. We dwelt in a great palace on the Canaleio,[37] filled with frescoes and statues, and containing two Titians in the noblest style of the great master,[38] which were hung in Clarimonde's chamber.

It was a palace well worthy of a king. We had each our gondola, our *barcarolli*[39] in family livery, our music hall, and our special poet. Clarimonde always lived upon a magnificent scale; there was something of Cleopatra in her nature. As for me, I had the retinue of a prince's son, and I was regarded with as much reverential respect as though I had been of the family of one of the twelve Apostles[40] or the four Evangelists[41] of the Most Serene Republic.[42] I would not have turned aside to allow even the Doge[43] to pass, and I do not believe that since Satan fell from heaven, any creature was ever prouder or more insolent than I. I went to the Ridotto,[44] and played with a luck which seemed absolutely infernal. I received the best of all society—the sons of ruined families, women of the theatre, shrewd knaves, parasites, hectoring swashbucklers. But notwithstanding the dissipation of such a life, I always remained faithful to Clarimonde.

I loved her wildly. She would have excited satiety itself, and chained inconstancy. To have Clarimonde was to have twenty mistresses; aye, to possess all women: so mobile, so varied of aspect, so fresh in new charms was she all in herself—a very chameleon of a woman, in sooth. She made you commit with her the infidelity you would have committed with another, by donning to perfection the character, the attraction, the style of beauty of the woman who appeared to please you. She returned my love a hundred-fold, and it was in vain that the young

---

[37] Grand canal that is carved through Venice
[38] Tiziano Vecelli (1488-1576), or "Titian," was a famous Venetian painter
[39] Singing gondolier
[40] Twelve apostles of Jesus Christ
[41] Mathew, Mark, Luke and John who penned the first four books of the New Testament
[42] Ancient name for Venice
[43] Duke of Venice
[44] Large wing of the San Moise Palace in Venice that was made into a government-sanctioned gambling area

patricians and even the Ancients of the Council of Ten[45] made her the most magnificent proposals.

A Foscari[46] even went so far as to offer to espouse her. She rejected all his overtures. Of gold she had enough. She wished no longer for anything but love—a love youthful, pure, evoked by herself, and which should be a first and last passion. I would have been perfectly happy but for a cursed nightmare which recurred every night, and in which I believed myself to be a poor village cure, practising mortification and penance for my excesses during the day.

Reassured by my constant association with her, I never thought further of the strange manner in which I had become acquainted with Clarimonde. But the words of the Abbe Serapion concerning her recurred often to my memory, and never ceased to cause me uneasiness.

For some time the health of Clarimonde had not been so good as usual; her complexion grew paler day by day. The physicians who were summoned could not comprehend the nature of her malady and knew not how to treat it. They all prescribed some insignificant remedies, and never called a second time. Her paleness, nevertheless, visibly increased, and she became colder and colder, until she seemed almost as white and dead as upon that memorable night in the unknown castle. I grieved with anguish unspeakable to behold her thus slowly perishing; and she, touched by my agony, smiled upon me sweetly and sadly with the fateful smile of those who feel that they must die.

One morning I was seated at her bedside, after breakfasting from a little table placed close at hand, so that I might not be obliged to leave her for a single instant. In the act of cutting some fruit I accidentally inflicted rather a deep gash on my finger.

The blood immediately gushed forth in a little purple jet, and a few drops spurted upon Clarimonde. Her eyes flashed, her face suddenly assumed an expression of savage and ferocious joy such as I had never before observed in her. She leaped out of her bed with animal agility—the agility, as it were, of an ape or a cat—and sprang upon my wound, which she commenced to suck with an air of unutterable pleasure. She swallowed the

---

[45] A secretive governing body of Venice from 1310-1797

[46] A doge of Venice; Francesco Foscari (1373-1457) was a doge of Venice for nearly 25 years

blood in little mouthfuls, slowly and carefully, like a connoisseur tasting a wine from Xeres[47] or Syracuse.[48]

Gradually her eyelids half closed, and the pupils of her green eyes became oblong instead of round. From time to time she paused in order to kiss my hand, then she would recommence to press her lips to the lips of the wound in order to coax forth a few more ruddy drops. When she found that the blood would no longer come, she arose with eyes liquid and brilliant, rosier than a May dawn; her face full and fresh, her hand warm and moist—in fine, more beautiful than ever, and in the most perfect health.

"I shall not die! I shall not die!" she cried, clinging to my neck, half mad with joy. "I can love thee yet for a long time. My life is thine, and all that is of me comes from thee. A few drops of thy rich and noble blood, more precious and more potent than all the elixirs of the earth, have given me back life."

This scene long haunted my memory, and inspired me with strange doubts in regard to Clarimonde; and the same evening, when slumber had transported me to my presbytery, I beheld the Abbe Serapion, graver and more anxious of aspect than ever.

He gazed attentively at me, and sorrowfully exclaimed: "Not content with losing your soul, you now desire also to lose your body. Wretched young man, into how terrible a plight have you fallen!"

The tone in which he uttered these words powerfully affected me, but in spite of its vividness even that impression was soon dissipated, and a thousand other cares erased it from my mind. At last one evening, while looking into a mirror whose traitorous position she had not taken into account, I saw Clarimonde in the act of emptying a powder into the cup of spiced wine which she had long been in the habit of preparing after our repasts. I took the cup, feigned to carry it to my lips, and then placed it on the nearest article of furniture as though intending to finish it at my leisure.

Taking advantage of a moment when the fair one's back was turned, I threw the contents under the table, after which I retired to my chamber and went to bed, fully resolved not to sleep, but to watch and discover what should come of all this mystery. I did not have to wait long.

Clarimonde entered in her night-dress, and having removed her apparel, crept into bed and lay down beside me. When she

---

[47] Wine region of Spain famous for sherry
[48] Wine region in Syracuse, Italy

felt assured that I was asleep, she bared my arm, and drawing a gold pin from her hair, commenced to murmur in a low voice:

"One drop, only one drop! One ruby at the end of my needle. . . . Since thou lovest me yet, I must not die! . . . Ah, poor love! His beautiful blood, so brightly purple, I must drink it. Sleep, my only treasure! Sleep, my god, my child! I will do thee no harm; I will only take of thy life what I must to keep my own from being forever extinguished. But that I love thee so much, I could well resolve to have other lovers whose veins I could drain; but since I have known thee all other men have become hateful to me. . . . Ah, the beautiful arm! How round it is! How white it is! How shall I ever dare to prick this pretty blue vein!"

And while thus murmuring to herself she wept, and I felt her tears raining on my arm as she clasped it with her hands. At last she took the resolve, slightly punctured me with her pin, and commenced to suck up the blood which oozed from the place. Although she swallowed only a few drops, the fear of weakening me soon seized her, and she carefully tied a little band around my arm, afterward rubbing the wound with an unguent which immediately cicatrized[49] it.

Further doubts were impossible. The Abbe Serapion was right. Notwithstanding this positive knowledge, however, I could not cease to love Clarimonde, and I would gladly of my own accord have given her all the blood she required to sustain her factitious life. Moreover, I felt but little fear of her. The woman seemed to plead with me for the vampire, and what I had already heard and seen sufficed to reassure me completely. In those days I had plenteous veins, which would not have been so easily exhausted as at present; and I would not have thought of bargaining for my blood, drop by drop. I would rather have opened myself the veins of my arm and said to her: "Drink, and may my love infiltrate itself throughout thy body together with my blood!" I carefully avoided ever making the least reference to the narcotic drink she had prepared for me, or to the incident of the pin, and we lived in the most perfect harmony.

Yet my priestly scruples commenced to torment me more than ever, and I was at a loss to imagine what new penance I could invent in order to mortify and subdue my flesh. Although these visions were involuntary, and though I did not actually participate in anything relating to them, I could not dare to touch the body of Christ with hands so impure and a mind defiled by such debauches whether real or imaginary.

---

[49] Stopped the bleeding

In the effort to avoid falling under the influence of these wearisome hallucinations, I strove to prevent myself from being overcome by sleep. I held my eyelids open with my fingers, and stood for hours together leaning upright against the wall, fighting sleep with all my might; but the dust of drowsiness invariably gathered upon my eyes at last, and finding all resistance useless, I would have to let my arms fall in the extremity of despairing weariness, and the current of slumber would again bear me away to the perfidious shores.

Serapion addressed me with the most vehement exhortations, severely reproaching me for my softness and want of fervour. Finally, one day when I was more wretched than usual, he said to me:

"There is but one way by which you can obtain relief from this continual torment, and though it is an extreme measure it must be made use of; violent diseases require violent remedies. I know where Clarimonde is buried. It is necessary that we shall disinter her remains, and that you shall behold in how pitiable a state the object of your love is. Then you will no longer be tempted to lose your soul for the sake of an unclean corpse devoured by worms, and ready to crumble into dust. That will assuredly restore you to yourself."

For my part, I was so tired of this double life that I at once consented, desiring to ascertain beyond a doubt whether a priest or a gentleman had been the victim of delusion. I had become fully resolved either to kill one of the two men within me for the benefit of the other, or else to kill both, for so terrible an existence could not last long and be endured. The Abbe Serapion provided himself with a mattock,[50] a lever, and a lantern, and at midnight we wended our way to the cemetery of the location and place of which were perfectly familiar to him.

After having directed the rays of the dark lantern upon the inscriptions of several tombs, we came at last upon a great slab, half concealed by huge weeds and devoured by mosses and parasitic plants, whereupon we deciphered the opening lines of the epitaph:

Here lies Clarimonde
Who was famed in her life-time
As the fairest of women.

---

[50] A digging tool shaped like a pickaxe

lei git Clarimonde
Qui fut di: son vivant
La plus belle du monde.

The broken beauty of the lines is unavoidably lost in the translation.

"It is here without a doubt," muttered Serapion, and placing his lantern on the ground, he forced the point of the lever under the edge of the stone and commenced to raise it. The stone yielded, and he proceeded to work with the mattock. Darker and more silent than the night itself, I stood by and watched him do it, while he, bending over his dismal toil, streamed with sweat, panted, and his hard-coming breath seemed to have the harsh tone of a death rattle.

It was a weird scene, and had any persons from without beheld us, they would assuredly have taken us rather for profane wretches and shroud-stealers than for priests of God. There was something grim and fierce in Serapion's zeal which lent him the air of a demon rather than of an apostle or an angel, and his great aquiline face,[51] with all its stern features brought out in strong relief by the lantern-light, had something fearsome in it which enhanced the unpleasant fancy.

I felt an icy sweat come out upon my forehead in huge beads, and my hair stood up with a hideous fear. Within the depths of my own heart I felt that the act of the austere Serapion was an abominable sacrilege; and I could have prayed that a triangle of fire would issue from the entrails of the dark clouds, heavily rolling above us, to reduce him to cinders.

The owls which had been nestling in the cypress-trees, startled by the gleam of the lantern, flew against it from time to time, striking their dusty wings against its panes, and uttering plaintive cries of lamentation; wild foxes yelped in the far darkness, and a thousand sinister noises detached themselves from the silence. At last Serapion's mattock struck the coffin itself, making its planks re-echo with a deep sonorous sound, with that terrible sound nothingness utters when stricken.

He wrenched apart and tore up the lid, and I beheld Clarimonde, pallid as a figure of marble, with hands joined; her white winding-sheet made but one fold from her head to her feet. A little crimson drop sparkled like a speck of dew at one corner of her colourless mouth.

---

[51] Face like an eagle's

Serapion, at this spectacle, burst into fury: "Ah, thou art here, demon! Impure courtesan! Drinker of blood and gold!" And he flung holy water upon the corpse and the coffin, over which he traced the sign of the cross with his sprinkler.

Poor Clarimonde had no sooner been touched by the blessed spray than her beautiful body crumbled into dust, and became only a shapeless and frightful mass of cinders and half-calcined bones.

"Behold your mistress, my Lord Romuald!" cried the inexorable priest, as he pointed to these sad remains. "Will you be easily tempted after this to promenade on the Lido or at Fusina with your beauty?"

I covered my face with my hands, a vast ruin had taken place within me. I returned to my presbytery, and the noble Lord Romuald, the lover of Clarimonde, separated himself from the poor priest with whom he had kept such strange company so long.

But once only, the following night, I saw Clarimonde. She said to me, as she had said the first time at the portals of the church:

"Unhappy man! Unhappy man! What hast thou done? Wherefore have hearkened to that imbecile priest? Wert thou not happy? And what harm had I ever done thee that thou shouldst violate my poor tomb, and lay bare the miseries of my nothingness? All communication between our souls and our bodies is henceforth forever broken. *Adieu!* Thou will yet regret me!"

She vanished in air as smoke, and I never saw her more.

Alas! she spoke truly indeed. I have regretted her more than once, and I regret her still. My soul's peace has been very dearly bought. The love of God was not too much to replace such a love as hers. And this, brother, is the story of my youth. Never gaze upon a woman, and walk abroad only with eyes ever fixed upon the ground; for however chaste and watchful one may be, the error of a single moment is enough.

Short Stories Considered

Anonymous
    The Curse

Lord Byron
    1816 The End of My Journey (fragment)

Alexandre Dumas
    1848 The Vampire of the Carpathian Mountains

Joseph Sheridan le Fanu
    1839 Strange Event in the Life of Schalken the Painter

Théophile Gautier
    1836 Clarimonde

Mrs. Gore (Catherine Grace Frances)
    1829 The Elizabethines

MacDavus
    1847 Truths Contained in Popular Superstitions

Dr. Herbert Mayo
    1849 [The Vampire Arnod]

Charles Pigault-Lebrun
    1825 The Unholy Compact Abjured

John Polidori
    1819 The Vampyre

Ernst Raupach
    1823 Wake Not The Dead

Robert C. Sands
    1819 The Black Vampyre, a Legend of Saint Domingo

Ludwig Tieck
    1823 The Sorcerers

Arthur Young
    1826 Pepopukin in Corsica

Index of Real Names

About Andrew Barger

Andrew Barger's most recent work is *The Divine Dantes* trilogy that follows the characters of *The Divine Comedy* through modern times. He is the award winning author of *Coffee with Poe: A Novel of Edgar Allan Poe's Life*, and *6a66le: The Best Horror Short Stories 1800-1849: A Classic Horror Anthology*. His first short story collection, *Mailboxes – Mansions – Memphistopheles: A Collection of Dark Tales*, was a finalist in the International Book Awards short story collection category.

He is the editor of a number of other acclaimed books, including *Edgar Allan Poe Annotated Entire Stories and Poems* and the award-winning *BlooDeath: The Best Vampire Stories 1800-1849*. Andrew is recognized for his scholarly and creative writing. He is a leading voice in the Gothic literature space.

Connect with Andrew Online:

WEBSITE:
AndrewBarger.com

BLOG:
AndrewBarger.blogspot.com

Amazon
Amazon.com/author/andrewbarger

FACEBOOK:
facebook.com/Andrew-Bargers-Official-Facebook-Page

GOODREADS:
Goodreads.com/author/show/1362598.Andrew_Barger

TWITTER:
twitter.com/andrewbarger

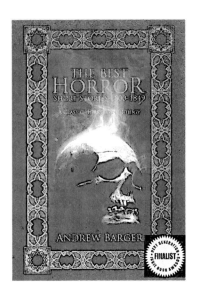

6a66le
The Best Horror Short Stories 1800-1849

Thanks to Edgar Allan Poe, Honoré de Balzac, Nathaniel Hawthorne and others, the first half of the 19th century is the cradle of all modern horror short stories. Andrew Barger read over 300 horror stories to find the dozen best from such leading periodicals of the day such as *Blackwood's* and *Atkinson's Casket.*

Phantasmal
The Best Ghost Stories 1800-1849

Ghost stories became very popular in the first half of the nineteenth century and this collection by Andrew Barger contains the very scariest of them all, some of which have not been published for over 150 years.

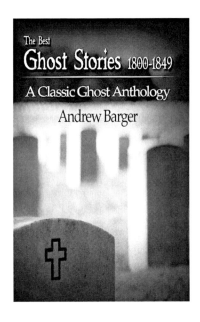

DH

808.
838
738
083
75
BES

500168046X

Lightning Source UK Ltd.
Milton Keynes UK
UKOW05f0322111013

218861UK00001B/111/P